For Jake

My greatest blessing calls me Mum

The Meeting Place

Copyright © 2023 by Tina L Angell

Cover design Copyright © Tina L Angell

All rights reserved.

No part of this book may be reproduced or used in any manner without the prior written permission of the copyright owner, except for the use of brief quotations in a book review.

Disclaimer: This is a work of fiction. Names, characters, businesses, places, events, and incidents are either the products of the author's imagination or used in a fictitious manner. Any resemblance to actual persons, living or dead, or actual events is purely coincidental.

www.tina-angell.co.uk

The Meeting Place

A debut novel by
Tina L Angell

Chapter 1

Isabelle

So, here we are, just coming out of the other side of a global pandemic. The world stopped, the country was put into lockdown and thousands of lives lost. It has been a dark two years, but we are finally getting back to normality. Like so many others, the loneliness I experienced sometimes was unbearable. Not being able to see family and friends for fear of putting them at risk and breaking rules that were put in place by the government was incredibly difficult. I was fortunate compared to some and I am so grateful for that. Technology got us through. Zoom calls and quizzes became the new norm for a long time; we even held a birthday party for my friend Jess via video, each of us in our own lounges, prosecco in hand, arrayed in varying fancy dress costumes that we'd managed to put together using what we had in our closets. It was fun but not the same. It's hard to believe we have lived through something that will forever be remembered. Our children and their children will learn about the Covid-19 pandemic for years to come. It felt almost surreal at times. At first it felt like a bit of a novelty, having to stay home, only being allowed to leave our homes for essential reasons. I enjoyed the peace and quiet of no traffic on the roads or planes in the sky, just the sound of nature. The weather was glorious during the first 3-month lockdown which made life a lot more bearable. Being able to walk out in the sunshine was blissful when you couldn't see loved ones outside of a phone or computer screen. Of course, the novelty soon wore off and it became incredibly tedious, but we got through it.

Despite the loneliness that I've dipped in and out of over the last two years, I feel incredibly blessed with my life. I own a gorgeous apartment in a beautiful small town in Wiltshire, I'm a florist with my own store 'The Watering Can', and I am surrounded with amazing people.

My grandmother left the The Watering Can to me when she passed away four years ago. I will be forever thankful to her for giving me the opportunity to do what I love. I used to spend hours as a child helping her put together bouquets for special occasions and I loved every minute of it. Sitting on the glass topped counter helping her choose ribbon colours, her hands wrapped around mine as she showed me how to tie them into beautiful bows so they looked perfect against the chosen cellophane. My favourite day was always Valentine's Day. I loved seeing all the roses, beautifully wrapped, cards attached with words of everlasting love and adoration being put into the delivery van knowing they were going to make somebody feel special and loved. I was such an old romantic, even at 10 years old. Now, I'm more of a realist when it comes to love, romance and matters of the heart.

My grandmother, Ruth, taught me everything I know now about floristry, how to mix lilies with carnations and chrysanthemums, and how to add roses for a more dramatic effect, how tulips can look so elegant without an accompanying bloom just by using the right vase. She used to call me her little fledgling. I wonder if it was her plan all along to train me up and leave me the business. My heart broke the day she died. It was unexpected but peaceful, and I was with her at the end. Knowing I'm continuing to keep her business alive fills me with joy. I know she would be so proud of what I've achieved with the little store.

I haven't had a date in over 18 months. I'm blaming the pandemic but, in all honesty, it's been a relief to have an excuse to take a break from finding 'the one' because let me tell you, it's exhausting. You meet, go on a few dates, begin a relationship, plan your future together, then boom! Just like that, it's over. There are many reasons this happens. You naturally grow apart, you want different things, or he just turns out to be a cheat. Anyway, moving on… The last few days, I have been thinking about online dating. I tried it a few years ago and it was disastrous, an absolute train wreck.

Let me tell you about Craig. I'd been chatting to him for a couple of weeks when we arranged a date, a lovely Italian restaurant for lunch. I always prefer lunch or coffee for a first date. Evening dinners can go on forever, and if you're not really feeling it, it can be very tricky to escape. Of course you can have the good old back up plan of an 'emergency' phone call but that's been done before, far too obvious for the poor soul sitting opposite you who has to put on a brave face. 'Of course I understand, she's your friend, it's an emergency, she needs you…'

Anyway, back to Craig and lunch. I arrived at the restaurant to find him waiting outside. He looked great, though not my usual type. I like them classically tall, dark and handsome. Craig was fair and only an inch or so taller than me, dressed in smart jeans and a shirt casually open at the neck. Now at this point on a first date, you are usually met with a kiss on the cheek, an awkward hug, or even a handshake. Craig's idea of greeting me for the first time was a slap on my backside followed by words every girl wants to hear when she meets a potential boyfriend for the first time: "Alright Sweetheart, why don't we just sack off lunch and head back to your place? It's where we'll end up anyway!" This was followed up with a very cringey attempt at a 'sexy' wink, at least, I think that's what he was trying to achieve. I kid you not, that was exactly what happened, right there in broad daylight outside the restaurant where diners were enjoying their lunch Al fresco in the glorious spring sunshine. Needless to say, he was sent packing with words to some effect of us clearly looking for very different things. I enjoyed a very pleasant lunch of pizza quattro formaggio and a large Sauvignon Blanc on my own in the sunshine.

Then there's Jonathan. He's a regular at The Watering Can; every Friday just before we close, he comes in to buy flowers for his wife. He gushes about how amazing she is, looking after the kids and keeping the house together whilst he works away. I make sure there's a bouquet of her favourite white tulips, beautifully wrapped, ready for when he stops in on his way home from work. Jonathan, who I then saw on the dating app, his bio clearly stating that he is just looking for 'discreet fun'. He still comes in every Friday to buy the flowers for his poor unknowing wife. The price of his bouquet has now nearly doubled. Sorry Jonathan, that's inflation for you!

Anyone who has tried online dating knows it's a minefield. One false move, one wrong step and your confidence and faith in love and happy endings are destroyed. They crumble right before you, and boy, does it take time to recover from that crap.

Luckily, I have an incredible group of friends. We're a small team but with their help, I pick myself up and dust myself off every time another possible 'one' comes along and breaks my heart. Ok, maybe breaks my heart is a little dramatic. I've only actually had my heart broken once. I was 11 and Matthew Bond danced with Sarah Jefferies at the end of year school disco. He asked her right in front of me. I was devastated and swore I'd never love again. What I wouldn't give to have that simple innocence back.

This is a new chapter. This time I have a little more hope: one of my closest friends Rebecca met her now fiancé Isaac online. He is an absolute gem. If I could have picked out any man for her, it would have been Isaac. They are blissfully happy; in just a few weeks they become husband and wife and I could not be happier for them. They've restored my faith in love and that it can possibly be found in a little app sitting in my phone.

So here I go, the dreaded bio. Always over thought and often great works of fiction that would give JK Rowling a run for her money. I should know myself better than anyone but trying to choose words to describe myself to attract a mate, a companion, (or just a mating companion in some cases) is ridiculously hard.

I settle down in the reclining chair on my balcony overlooking the town. This became my sanctuary when we were put into lockdown and unable to leave our homes. Along with the recliner, it has a little bistro table and chairs, fairy lights hang across the top, and lanterns are nestled in the corner, giving it a cosy feel. The town looks beautiful in the evening sunshine. I can see the church and a little of the river; there are a few people paddle boarding and people are sitting on the grass watching with picnics. I can hear laughter and music, and the faint smell of a BBQ is lingering. I can't help but smile. It's true what they say: the sunshine really does make you feel happier. I take out my phone and open the dating app. It's been so long it takes a few attempts to remember my password, Wateringcan123, of course.

I begin to type.

'Isabelle, Age 30'

'A florist from Wiltshire.'

How do you do this without sounding generic?

'Loves fluffy kittens and my friends blah blah blah…' (Actually, I prefer dogs.)

'Just a girl who loves a good time'.

Uh, no, scrap that one.

I think about calling Eve, another of my closest friends. We've known each other since Matthew Bond broke my heart at the school disco. She's a ball busting defence lawyer. I've seen her in action in the courtroom and she can be terrifying. I've seen grown men literally quiver in front of her. Not only is she taller than most of them, even without her killer heels, her words would have them feeling like little boys getting a telling off from the school headmistress. I'm so glad I'm her friend. I'd hate to be her enemy! She'd know what to say in my bio, but then again, she has no interest in finding love. She's a career girl all the way; she has a few 'friends with benefits' and it seems to suit her. It would take one hell of a guy to get her to settle down and I fear for any man who has the balls to try. She comes from a line of very strong Caribbean women. I've met both her mum and her nani as we call her; the three of them together are a real force.

No, I can do this, just don't overthink it.

How do you sell yourself without sounding too brash or overconfident?

Take two.

'Isabelle, Age 30'

'A florist from Wiltshire'

'Just your average dog loving, pizza eating (3 slice max, a 4th and I'm always regretful), girl next door'

'You'll never have to buy me flowers; a beer and cheesy pizza on the other hand....'

I very nearly put 'I'm easily pleased' at the end of that sentence but I've walked this road before and that is just asking for trouble.

There, it's simple and not too much info.

Save.

Ok, now for the pictures. I start flicking through the photo album on my phone. So many memories of times with the girls, brunches that started at 11am and finished at 2am with somebody missing a shoe (usually Jess), festivals where it mostly rained but we never let that dampen our spirits, the day we tried stand up paddle boarding. I swallowed so much river water I thought I would end up with some life-threatening disease. I think the amount of prosecco and grossly coloured shots that followed would have killed anything off, so I was actually quite safe.

I decide on one from a festival we attended, pre-pandemic, flowers in my hair, a genuine happy smile on my face. My fair hair is naturally highlighted from the sun, its natural wave falling over my shoulders. The sunlight gives my face a beautiful, tanned glow, if I do say so myself.

For the second, I opt for one of me crossing the finishing line of a charity 5km run. I'm no runner so this was quite an achievement for me, but it was for charity, and it made me get off my backside to go for a run regularly for the two months beforehand. I look red and sweaty but happy, arms in the air like I've just completed a marathon. Like I said, I'm a realist, I can't have all of them with me looking made up and glam.

No filters here, the poor guy needs to see what he's really letting himself in for.

And save.

There, it's done.

I sit on my balcony for a little while longer and finish my wine, taking in the summer evening atmosphere and contemplating what I might find in my inbox tomorrow. I flick my notifications off. It's so easy to get obsessed with checking for 'matches'. I've made that mistake before; I got distracted at work, I was always on my phone when I was with friends, it started to take over, so now I'm taking a more casual approach. This way I can put time aside each day to look rather than wait for that anticipated ping.

Wish me luck!

Chapter 2

James

"And you're certain he'll be ok now? He doesn't need to stay another night just to be sure?" she asks, her concern clearly etched on her face.

"I promise you, Mrs Richards, if I thought it was necessary, I would be keeping Dougie in, but he's had his IV antibiotics and fluids, and his appetite is back. Just keep an eye on him when you're out walking. I think he ate something he shouldn't have. Erica is on call tonight and over the weekend so if you have any concerns at all just give her a call," I say as I touch her shoulder gently, trying to reassure her.

"Thank you, Doctor James, you know how I'd be lost if anything happened to him."

I do know. Dougie has been her only companion since her husband died 18 months ago; they had been married for nearly 40 years. She brings Dougie into the surgery almost weekly, fearful that something awful is happening to him, that he's going to be the next loss she has to mourn. I can't even begin to imagine how she'll cope when the little terrier goes. We've tried everything to keep her trips to us to a minimum, even offering to make quick home visits twice a month on our way home, free of charge, but she declined. We know she can't afford to keep up the visits, especially as Dougie isn't insured, so Erica and I have agreed that we won't charge anything if we're just putting her mind at ease and no major treatment is needed. She lost her only child, Charlotte, serving for our country in Iraq, so I feel it's the least we can do. That little dog is all she has left, and I'm determined to help keep him with her for as long as possible. Sometimes I wonder if she just comes in for the company, for somebody to talk to. Our receptionist Rachael is brilliant with her. She makes her a cup of tea and sits and chats to her; she even keeps stock of her favourite biscuits behind the desk.

"A weekend off then, Doctor James, have you got yourself a date lined up? It's about time you found a nice lady to settle down with," she says with a wink. Her concerns about Dougie have clearly eased.

"You know me, Mrs Richards, I'm married to the job. This surgery is my second home and looking after little ones like your Dougie is my focus," I reply as I give the dog a tummy rub. He is a cute little thing, but at 11 years old, I'm not sure how much longer he'll be her faithful companion. "Now, get him home and settled, and remember, call Erica if you have any concerns."

I watch as she leaves, putting Dougie ever so carefully into her car like she's handling the crown jewels. I lock up and head outside into the sunshine. It's a lovely, balmy evening. The sky is a hue of pinks and oranges; it frames the fields and crops that surround the clinic beautifully. I stand for a minute and just take it all in. There's a slight breeze that sends gentle waves through the corn that's growing magnificently in the field to the right of me. It must be at least 6 feet tall.

Cedar Lodge Veterinary Hospital is a beautiful old manor house set in the Wiltshire countryside. It was left to an animal charity by Dr Phillip Simmonds, an incredible veterinary surgeon who dedicated his life to the welfare of animals. His innovative ideas saved so many lives; the man was a genius. He was also a workaholic with no family or close friends to leave his riches to, so for the last twelve years, the old manor has played host to animals of every kind in need. Despite being an old building, it's been transformed into one of the most prestigious veterinary hospitals in the southwest and possibly all of the UK. It's quite a sight: benches line the driveway that lead up to the impressive entrance, there are two of the most beautiful cedar trees on either side of the stunning frontage, and it has a vast garden surrounding it that is flourished in greenery. I can't imagine working anywhere else.

I work alongside Erica who is one of the finest vets I've ever worked with. We've worked together for 5 years. She's not only my colleague, she's also one of my closest friends. She's the most genuine person you will ever meet, down to earth, compassionate, kind and she has the patience of a saint. She's married to Fiona, Fi as she likes to be called, a brilliant artist. She's bold, brash and incredibly self-assured, everything I imagine an artist to be. She owns a little gallery in town where she often holds events. I attend as many as I can, but I'm nearly always introduced to a 'very nice' lady and I guess there has been some attempt at matchmaking involved. I say attempt because as much as they are 'nice ladies,' I am yet to meet one I would like to see again. I know Erica and Fi have been trying to conceive with the help of a donor for over two years; the plan is for Fi to be the one to carry the child. I have to be honest, I was incredibly relieved to hear that. I don't know what I'd do if Erica went on maternity leave. Selfish, I know. It breaks my heart every time I see that look on her face that tells me the treatment has failed again.

We also have three veterinary nurses, Tim, Emily and Sarah. It's them and Rachael that keep this place going. I don't know what we'd do without any of them.

On the drive home, I think about the evening ahead and it's a lonely one. Like most of the country, I have found the last two years difficult; my parents live in the south of France and are enjoying retirement to the fullest. My brother is in the forces based in Germany with his family, his wife Julia and my 4-year-old niece Ella. Unfortunately, I haven't been able to see them with the travel restrictions that have been in place. I feel like I've missed out on so much with Ella. She is the most wonderful little girl, the perfect mix of cheekiness and kindness; she just melts my heart.

I am so grateful that I am in a job where I was able to continue working, albeit under very different circumstances. Social distancing ourselves from owners, heart breaking situations where people weren't able to be with their beloved pets during their final minutes. The crestfallen owners weren't the only ones who shed tears during those moments. Coming into Cedar Lodge and seeing the team was my saviour, but I still missed company. I still miss it, the companionship that comes with a relationship, somebody to come home to, cook dinner together, share a bottle of wine; it's what I crave. I don't want to end up like Dr Simmonds. It's that thought that makes the decision for me: I'm going to try online dating again.

I must be mad after my previous experiences with it. Let me share a few, just to give you an idea…

Imogen. Lovely, sweet and normal, or so I thought. We spent a lot of time talking on the phone before meeting, hours in fact, sharing stories about our day. She was a primary school teacher, so she was never short of tales to tell. On paper we were the perfect match, a vet and a teacher, both caring professions. I honestly thought I'd found someone special. I invited her on a picnic in the park for our first date. I know, romantic, right? I have my moments.

I arrived early. I'd laid out a blanket, bottle of wine in a cooler, food fit for royalty (thanks to Waitrose). When Imogen arrived, she was carrying books, a lot of books, reels of paper, pens of every colour in a pencil case adorned with unicorns…. I was baffled; she looked like she was on her way to an art class. It turns out she has a hobby. Astrology, and she's very serious about it. She sat there for the whole date and mapped out our zodiac charts, when we should conceive our children so they could be born under the best star signs. She worked on our love compatibility calculator. I don't even know what that means, but what I do know is that I don't need a chart to tell me if I'm compatible with somebody and we most definitely were not.

The final nail in the coffin for me, the one date that had me vowing never to use a dating app again, was Gemma. Beautiful, and as it turned out, filtered beyond recognition Gemma. Why? I just don't understand why you would use so many filters that your date doesn't recognise you when you meet. Yep, true story. I had no idea who she was when she approached our table that day for lunch. Not only did she look nothing like her photos, she had company on our date; she brought along her toy poodle Trixie. Now, I love dogs, of course I do, I'm a vet, but I found this very odd. Gemma was obsessed with Trixie, and I mean OBSESSED. She barely looked at me for the whole painful 90 minutes; she insisted the chef make a special chicken and rice dish for the spoilt pooch and hand fed her every last bit at the table.

So, you can see why I'm hesitant at diving into this pool of unpredictability again, but it does seem the way forward. Gone are the days of boy meets girl in a bar and they live happily ever after. I tried it that way too. I met Amy in a bar five years ago. I'd just moved to the area from North London to start my job at Cedar Lodge. We dated for 8 months before moving in together. I thought I had found the one: she was smart, beautiful and funny; everybody loved her. Unfortunately, the pressures of me starting a new job and working long, on-call hours took its toll. She worked a 9-5, no weekends job in admin so anything outside of those hours were alien to her. The constant cancelling of plans, being called out in the middle of the night and working weekends became too much and she started to resent me, which resulted in me returning the feeling. We decided to call it quits after two years and she moved out. We're still Facebook friends but that's as far as it goes. She is now married with her first child on the way, and I am genuinely happy for her.

I get home, shower, order pizza and open a beer.

I really dislike this part, writing about myself to make it look like I am at least a potential date.

'James Age 32'

'A vet from Wiltshire'

'Hi, I'm James. I'm 32 and a Taurus (zodiac signs are very important to some people apparently). Keen runner but not a gym fan, give me the great outdoors, even in the rain, over a sweaty gym any day of the week.

Now that normality is resuming, I thought I'd get myself back out there and give this another try.

Wish me luck, or better still, let's 'Match' and see where it takes us'

I pick out a few pictures from my social media pages.

Obligatory wearing a suit at a wedding holding a glass of champagne picture – check.

Crossing the line at a 10km charity run, sporty and charitable – check.

Laughing uncontrollably at I have no idea what, but it makes it look like I hang out with great company – check.

There's the doorbell and the pizza delivery guy.

I hit save.

Chapter 3

Isabelle

I wake up to the sound of my alarm at 6 am. It's a Saturday, so for most people this should be unheard of, but it's always our busiest day of the week. I have to be there early to take delivery of all the beautiful fresh flowers and get them into the coolers. The sun is shining through the bedroom blinds. I love feeling the warmth from it on my face. The early starts are so much easier during the summer months. When that alarm goes off during winter when it's cold and dark outside, I just want to stay in the comfort and warmth of my bed.

I walk to work every day via a little Italian deli. 'Bella Vita Deli' is run by Luca, the sweetest man you'll ever meet. He has the most wonderful smile; he's always there in his striped apron, in the colours of the Italian flag of course. "Ciao Bella," he says as he hands me my coffee, no order needed; he knows.

"Ciao Luca, how are you today?" I ask, taking the cup from him. I'm craving the bitterness of the caffeine, black, no sugar. We exchange a few words about how glorious the weather is going to be and bid each other a good day. We both know there's a very good chance I'll be back again later in the day for lunch. His savoury pastries are to die for.

As I turn the corner, I can see the delivery truck is there outside the store, and Mitch the driver is already unloading. He's been delivering to us for years. My grandmother was very fond of him; she'd bake him a lemon drizzle cake every week to take home to his wife and children. I think he misses her almost as much as I do. I attempted to bake one for him once, to see if I could keep up the tradition. I think it's safe to say that, although I have been blessed with my grandmother's floristry skills, I do not, however, share her baking talents.

"Hi, Mitch," I say as I approach the truck. "How is everyone?" I ask, referring to his family.

"Just grand love, just grand," he says as he continues to lift the buckets of flowers carefully into the store, wiping the sweat that's forming on his forehead with the back of his hand. I get him a cold glass of water and he fills me in briefly on how his children are doing at school and in their extracurricular activities before he leaves for his next delivery stop.

Once all the flowers are unloaded and we've said our goodbyes, I stand by the coolers for a minute. It's my favourite time of day, first thing in the morning before Gina, one of my assistants arrives, when it's just me and the incredible smell of the mixed flowers. I stay here for a few minutes just taking it all in, the colours and textures of the tulips, sunflowers, peonies, lilies. I silently thank my grandmother as I do every morning in this exact spot and head to the front of the store. Gina arrives not long after, the same smile on her face that she greets me with every morning. Gina has been my saviour since my grandmother died; she's become a surrogate in some ways. She has the kindest eyes and a heart of pure gold. I know she's close to retirement. I don't know what I'll do without her.

The morning goes quickly. We have so many orders to get out before lunch. Along with Gina, I have Dom who helps part-time. The man is a godsend. He really knows his stuff when it comes to flowers, and Kate, his wife makes up the team. They work alternate hours to allow for childcare. It suits everyone. I know it's a cliché, but we really are like a little family here and I wouldn't have it any other way.

It's almost 2 pm before I get to pop out for lunch. I head to Luca's, grab a sandwich for myself and a few extra treats to take back to the store. I find a bench by the river. I sit here for a while, eating my sandwich and watching the world go by. Children are squealing with excitement as they watch the baby ducks paddle by, closely watched by their parents, phones in hand to capture the memories. I spot a couple sitting next to each other on a bench. Her legs are folded over his as she's leaning into his chest, and he's stroking her hair. They're almost completely shielded by a big willow tree, but I can see that they look blissfully happy, and I feel a pang of loneliness. It's only then that I remember what I'd done the night before and pull my phone out from my jeans pocket with more than a little apprehension.

There's a text from Jess asking if I remember we have dinner plans that evening. Jess is the fourth member of our friendship group. She's happily married to her childhood sweetheart Adrian. They have Grace who is

5 and twin two-year-old boys named Jack and Ethan. They are sickeningly happy. I don't know how she does it. She is your typical mother earth: she bakes, does endless crafts with the children, her home is beautiful, and her cooking is out of this world. Oh, and she always looks impeccable. If she wasn't my friend, I would dislike her a lot. I fire a quick reply telling her I haven't forgotten and confirming our plans to meet at 7 pm for cocktails first.

I take a breath and switch on my notifications. Suddenly it's like the 4th of July celebrations have taken over the screen in front of me. There are lights and noises, some of which I wasn't even aware my phone made, notifications from the dating app and emails notifying me of messages on the app, I'd forgotten it did that; that needs rectifying before my phone gives me epilepsy.

I scroll through my inbox and start with message one.

'Hi Isabelle, well arnt u just a pic of cutenes, lets meet, Jeff xx'

Delete. I'm sorry but that 'grammar' is a big no no for me, and cuteness (assuming that's what he means) ummmmm no. Let's meet? We haven't even exchanged messages! Jeff, I wish you well, but you are not for me. I delete the message without replying.

Message two.

'Hello, my name is Rick, I'm 31 and an accountant, please don't let that put you off, yes, it is as dull as it sounds but hopefully, I am not.

Your pictures look lovely, it's so nice to see a genuine smile on here, most photos are filtered and fake, unfortunately there's a lot of that in the world of online dating.

I also love dogs, I have 2 border collies, maybe we could meet for a walk with them? I hope to hear from you soon,

Rick'

He is correct, his job does sound dull but that doesn't mean he has to be. I open his profile. He has only one picture; should I be worried? I've always been wary of profiles with only one picture. It makes me feel like they have something to hide. If it is him in the photo then he looks pleasant enough, not obviously good looking, but he has an honest look about him and I like that. I mentally put Rick in the 'keep' file and open the next message.

Message three.

Not even repeatable. Just no. What is wrong with some of these guys?

Delete.

The following 18 messages are all pretty generic, most of which I delete but I do reply to Rick, Jason a landscape gardener (yes, I'm thinking about a tanned toned body, don't judge) and Ben, a computer game designer who seems fun and is HOT.

I realise I have been sitting here a lot longer than planned and quickly head back to the store to finish the day with a little spring in my step.

I arrive 10 minutes late to meet Jess. She's sat sipping a margarita on the terrace of our favourite wine bar. As usual, she looks gorgeous; her long dark hair has a slight wave giving it a summery look and she's wearing a floral maxi dress, showing off her slim, tanned figure. She swears she stays in shape by running around after the kids all day. I think she's hiding a secret personal trainer from us, but really, who am I kidding? She's as honest as they come. It's one of the many reasons I love her.

"I'm sorry, I'm sorry," I say as I kiss her on the cheek. "I got stuck at the store."

"You're here now," she says as she slips her sunglasses onto her head. "I'm just enjoying the peace and quiet of no children running around. Adrian will be tearing his hair out with bath and bedtime right now," she says with a wicked grin, "I'll show him my gratitude when I get home," she adds, winking at me.

"More than I need to know thank you," I say as I get the waiter's attention to order a passion fruit martini.

"When did you turn into a prude? You need to get laid, my friend. How long has it been now?"

"Too bloody long! Talking of which, I signed up for online dating again last night…" I don't even realise I'm holding my breath in anticipation of her response until I see her smile, and I let out a long exhale.

"I'm so glad you aren't put off after the last few dates. That was a long time ago. The world has changed a lot since then, and hopefully some men have too." I love her optimism.

I open my phone to show her my messages so far to find all three have replied.

'Isabelle, thank you so much for replying, it was lovely to hear from you, and thank you for not assuming I'm dull and boring as my job title would suggest. I've had both dogs, Libby and Jazz, for a little over 6 years, they were both from a rescue centre, left on a farm when the owners moved away, how anybody could do that is beyond me, I haven't looked back since bringing them home.

I hope you don't find this too forward but are you free to meet on Sunday? We could walk the dogs and stop for coffee, there's a lovely café along the canal path,

Looking forward to hearing from you

Rick'

"Boring!" says Jess, already on her third cocktail, "Next."

"Give the guy a chance," I say in Rick's defence, "It's only his second message!"

"Is he floating your boat? Do you think he's the one to make your toes curl in the bedroom?" she asks, looking at me quizzically. "You need to feel something instantly, none of this 'he's a nice guy, maybe it will come with time', if it's not there now it never will be."

Ok, I see her point. He doesn't really float my paddle, let alone my boat.

The next message is from Ben.

"Holy cow! Why the hell is he on a dating website?" Jess is clearly taken with Ben. "Now he looks like he could throw you around and show you a good time," she says, raising an eyebrow in my direction.

I'm not sure if I should be offended that she didn't ask why I need to be on a dating website, but I'll let it slide.

She has a point; he's even hotter than I remember from this morning. He has those 'come to bed' eyes. As Eve would say, "Eyes that would make you drop your knickers in a heartbeat!"

'Your reply made my day, Thank you for taking an interest in my job, computer games are not something most women are interested in. They rarely ask about it and assume it's just cartoons. I actually have two degrees, one in animation and the other in graphic design. It's taken a lot of hard work to get where I am and I'm very proud of what I have achieved. I'd love to hear how you got into floristry; did you always want to do it? Was it your dream as a child or something you just fell into? Maybe we can discuss our chosen careers and other subjects over a beer and pizza?

Ben x'

"Ok, he has my attention," says Jess as she takes my phone to get a better look, "even more than he had it before."

"Christ, down girl! Maybe I should be asking you how long it's been since you last got laid," I say, giving her a wink.

"Two days," she replies, flicking her hair dramatically for effect.

We finish our drinks and start the short walk to the restaurant from the cocktail bar. I make a mental note to ask for extra water on the table. Having small children means Jess doesn't drink much; she'll be feeling this in the morning.

We sit down and order our tapas. I decide on a beer this time; tomorrow is my day off and I don't want to spend it in bed hungover.

While we wait for our food, I read the message from Jason aloud so Jess can hear. I'm not entirely sure she'd even be able to focus on it if I handed her the phone.

'Hi Isabelle, I loved hearing about how you acquired your store, it sounds delightful, you must be very proud to be able to carry on your grandmother's work. I must run to catch a train as I'm working in London for the next few days so I have to keep it brief, I've attached my number if you would prefer and feel comfortable enough to chat over the phone,

Have a lovely weekend

Jason'

"Well," says Jess, "two out of three ain't bad!"

There were other messages from new guys, but I'm here to enjoy my evening with Jess. I pop my phone into my bag and that's where it stays until I text Adrian to say I've put her into a taxi and she is safely on her way home.

Chapter 4

James

I wake up to the sound of my phone ringing. The sunlight is piercing through the blinds. I have no idea what time it is. I reach across to the bedside table and see it's just before 8 am. Daniel's name flashes on my phone.

"Morning," I answer sleepily.

"Ah, man, did I wake you? I just wanted to remind you that we're painting the bar today, remember?" He doesn't give me a chance to answer. "I'm on my way to pick up supplies, but I'll meet you there in an hour."

That wasn't a question, clearly more of an instruction.

We say our goodbyes. I get up, put on a T-shirt over my boxers and head to the kitchen for coffee. I love this apartment, but I can't help feeling it's missing something. It is very much your average bachelor pad. I've tried to make it homey with family photos, cushions and a throw over the back of the corner sofa, but it's definitely missing a woman's touch.

I had totally forgotten I had agreed to this today. Daniel owns a bar in our local small town, and I've agreed to help him with some touch-up work, although the way he said 'painting the bar' makes me feel like I've signed up for more than a little touch-up job.

Daniel is my oldest and best friend. He moved from London to join me here 6 months after I arrived. We've known each other since we were in pre-school. He took a very different path than me when we left school. I went off to uni and at first, he seemed to be on the right track. He isn't studious, so further education wasn't for him, but he is a people person. He can talk to anyone, and he has a face that ladies, young and old, love. He has this knack of just being able to converse with anyone, any gender, any age, it doesn't matter. He put those skills to good use and started working with young people and he loved it. These were troubled teens who had nobody else. Their parents didn't care where they were, or who they were with. They'd been in trouble with the law. Dan was usually the one phone call they got when they ended up in the cells for the night. They felt like the world had disowned them, but he knew how to get through to them. He had this ability to make them see things from a different perspective, to see that regardless of their past, they could have a future, and before long he was the manager for a charity for underprivileged young people, and in his spare time, he volunteered at a youth centre. I was so incredibly proud of him; he had found his purpose.

I don't really know how it happened, how it all went so horribly wrong, but he got in with the wrong crowd. It sounds silly saying that about a grown man. He wasn't a teenager being led down the wrong path by a group of unscrupulous friends; he was a man with a brilliant future ahead of him, but that is exactly what happened. I'm not even sure how he met them, he's always been vague on the details. Looking back now, I think it's just simply that he can't remember, because he spent the next few years permanently high.

He got addicted to drugs. It started off with a bit of weed and it escalated quickly into cocaine and God only knows what else. He was destroying his life right in front of me and no matter how hard I tried, I could do nothing to help. It's true what they say, you can't help somebody unless they want to be helped. I was in constant contact with his parents who were distraught. Between us, we tried everything, but it seemed to push him further away. He didn't even look like the man I'd grown up with. I honestly thought we would lose him to an overdose. We tried constantly to talk him into going into rehab, but it was all to no avail.

A year before I moved here, a tragedy happened, one that I feel was inevitable. Daniel had a girlfriend, 'Raz', who was also an addict. Unlike Daniel, she had no family or friends to try and help her. I don't know her background or where she came from, but I do know that she did not deserve to die in a stinking drug den after overdosing on what the police said was a very bad batch of heroin. Daniel woke next to her to find her gone, needle still in the vein in her foot. I am thankful every day that it wasn't Daniel. Don't get me wrong, it was awful, nobody deserves that. If she had just had the right help, a family that cared, then maybe she would have had a chance. We spent the next few weeks taking turns to watch his every move, terrified he would take his own life, and we eventually talked him into going into rehab. His parents had the means to pay for it privately. I know it wiped out everything they had, but it was worth it because it worked. He spent six months in a facility getting help. We couldn't see him for the first 12 weeks, and I swear that was the hardest 12 weeks of my life, not knowing if he was ok, if he was coping with the detox programme. I met with his parents every week during that time. We supported each other through it and I'm still close to them now.

When I told him I was moving for this incredible position I'd been offered, he said he wanted to join me, that he wanted a fresh start. We agreed he'd take some time to think about it while I got settled, and the rest, as they say, is history.

You can see why we were all surprised and more than a little concerned when he said he was opening a bar. We tried to talk him out of it, but he secured a loan and proved us wrong. He's made it a huge success. 'The Meeting Place' is the place to be. The food is amazing, they have regular live music events, and he managed to survive through lockdown. He's turned things around. He's been clean and sober since the day he left rehab. He holds meetings every Tuesday night for recovering addicts (hence the bar name) and is back volunteering at a youth club, and although there will always be that little fear inside me that his demons will return and take over, I am incredibly proud of him. That fear gets weaker and smaller every day.

Sitting with my coffee at the kitchen table, I open the dating app to check my messages and I'm informed that I have 7 new ones. Given that women don't like to message first on these things, I'll take that as a compliment.

'Hi James, I just love a man who looks after himself and you certainly look like you do that!

I'm Katja and I'm looking for a man who can treat me the way I deserve and keep me in a lifestyle of luxury........'

I've read enough of that one. Delete.

'Hi James, how are you today? I really like your profile. I work at a rescue centre for cats and dogs, my role is to try and match them with their perfect human companions, so I feel we have a lot in common, apart from the running part, I walk the dogs on my days off so that's enough exercise for me!

I'd love to know more about you, if you'd like that, you know where to find me

Lizzie xx'

Well, she seems nice, and her pictures are cute.

'Good morning Lizzie,

Thank you so much for your message, that's a tough job, I'm full of admiration! It must be so hard seeing the things you do at work, and I can sympathise. How did you get into working with animals? Between that and spending your days off walking the dogs do you ever have any free time?? You have some serious job dedication. I was going to ask what you like to do in your spare time but I'm not sure you get any!

Have a great day,

James'

I read a few more but nothing really jumps out at me, so I get ready and head off to meet Daniel.

I find him already covered in paint, standing and admiring the tiny strip of wall he's painted like he's Da Vinci admiring the Mona Lisa.

"Wow. You should frame it," I say as I stand next to him, taking in the colour he's chosen.

"Funny guy," he replies sarcastically, "Do you like it?" He asks picking up the tin. "It's called Loch Blue."

"I'll tell you when it's finished," I say as I pick up a spare brush and get started. "So, I put myself back out there last night," I say nonchalantly.

"Oh yeah? Get lucky, did you? Hot piece turn up with a poorly pup and you heroically saved its life?"

"Dickhead. No, and don't be so crude." For somebody who is so good with people, he has a way with words around his mates. "I set myself back up on the dating app," I say as I stroke the 'Loch blue' against the wall.

"Oh," he says, a little too dramatically than is necessary, "Was the first time not enough to feed your curiosity?"

"It's alright for you, Dan, you have company every night in this place," I say, waving my free hand around, gesturing to the bar, "and you're never short of female attention. I'm in a good place and I want to meet someone to share my life with, and I'm not getting any younger," I say as I layer the paint on the wall, "And before you say it, I know we're not old, but you know I want a family one day. I'm not saying I'll meet 'the one' but there's no harm in going on a few dates, and you just never know."

"Yeah, we can't all be as lucky as Justin," Dan replies, sweeping his brush harshly against the wall. He's referring to our friend, Justin Locke. His story is the good old-fashioned boy meets girl, they fall in love and are married within a year. He and his wife Steph are blissfully happy with baby number two on the way.

"Come on, let's get this finished so you can open for the lunchtime rush."

"About that..." Dan starts to say, and I know what's coming, "any chance you could help out for an hour or so when we open? Jake will be late; his mum has been taken ill so he's at the hospital with her," he says as he flutters his eyelashes at me in a dramatic fashion.

"It's not like I have anything better to do," I reply, rolling my eyes, but sadly it's true. I really don't have anywhere else to be or anyone else to be with. I lay my brush down and sit on one of the bar stools to take a drink of the cold water Dan has put in front of me and I can't help wondering if this is it for me, spending my weekends off helping my mate out with his bar. I let out a deep exhale and get back to painting.

"Whilst we're on the subject of you helping me out, I want to run an idea by you," he says sheepishly. "Let me present my case before you give me that look," he says, not giving me a chance to respond. He puts down his brush and comes to sit on the floor next to where I'm still painting. "There is this young guy at the youth centre that I'm really struggling to get through to. I don't know what it is. He sees everything as a negative," he says, running a hand through his hair, "It's like he can't see any joy in any aspect of his life. I get it; he's had a really shitty upbringing. I can usually find a way through but I am really struggling here. He's so angry at the world and everyone in it."

I can hear the frustration in his voice, and I really feel for him. I'm yet to find out where I come in.

"So," he continues, "I was wondering how you'd feel about letting him spend a day with you at the surgery?"

"I'm not really sure how that will help," I reply, "I know how much helping these kids mean to you, but we see a lot of sad cases. It could make his vision of the world worse, not better," I say as I stop painting and sit next to him on the floor.

"I know, I was thinking more of that puppy clinic thing you do. I know it won't change his life, but it might give him a little bit of joy, even if it's only for one day," he says, and I can hear the hopeful tone in his voice.

I pause to think about it for a minute. "Let me speak to Erica. I'd have to check where we stand with our insurance and things like that, so I'm making no promises," I say, giving him a stern look.

"Absolutely! Thanks, man, I really appreciate it!" he says, nudging me with his shoulder. I can tell his mood has instantly lifted.

"No promises, remember!" I remind him, but I think it's fallen on deaf ears.

Chapter 5

Isabelle

It's now a week after I started messaging with Jason and I'm doing something I've never done before. Let me fill you in before you judge me.

We have spent a lot of time on the phone over the past seven days, and I mean a lot! We've facetimed every evening for the last four nights and spent at least half an hour talking every time. He makes me laugh and is easy to talk to, so when he told me his work visit to London had been extended and asked if I would like to go and spend the day with him there, after some careful deliberation, I said yes. This is not something I would usually do. It's madness really, but why not? He has sent me pictures and videos from the gorgeous gardens he is working on so I have forwarded all of them to Eve, not that I think for one minute I'll come to any harm, but I would be stupid not to pass on all the information I have on him. I've also promised her I'll check in every hour. It may seem extreme but a girl can't be too careful, and I'm quite sure that if she hasn't already, she will be conducting her own research on the poor guy. I haven't told the others yet. It's not that I think they wouldn't approve; I just don't think they'd be as 'open' to the idea as Eve, and Rebecca is getting married in a few weeks, so she has enough going on.

So here I am, on the train heading for London. The sun is shining, and I can't help but feel positive about today. I spent forever choosing an outfit. He told me has lots planned but it's all a surprise, so I've opted for cropped fitted white jeans, a loose, light blue blouse, and I've enhanced the waves in my hair, casual but girly. I ring Eve to pass the time and help settle the butterflies currently throwing a dance party in my stomach.

"Hi," she says, "how's the tummy?" She knows me so well.

"Ugh, can you send in the fun police to stop the party?" I say, feeling physically sick. "Seriously, Eve, what am I doing? What if he's a weirdo? Or a serial killer? Or worse, a nerd?"

Eve lets out a chuckle. "Or what if he's perfectly normal and charming and you have a lovely day? But just to be clear, if he's any of those other things, I'll be straight in the car to get you. Just relax and enjoy it. If nothing comes of it, then you've had a day out in London. What have you got to lose?"

"My self-esteem, my dignity, my pride, my life…"

"Alright, alright, drama queen," she says, interrupting me. "I'm hanging up now. Remember to check in, love you," and with that, she's gone.

I spend the rest of the journey trying to get lost in music on Spotify, but that only seems to encourage the party.

I arrive at London Waterloo station at 10.55. I think I'm going to throw up. I'm not normally this nervous on dates, but this is a whole day and I'm a long way from home and the comfort blanket that are my friends.

As I step off the train, the warmth of the day hits me. It's going to be a hot one. I begin to think I should have worn something cooler. Then I spot him. He's leaning against a pillar checking his phone. His jet-black hair is gelled to within an inch of its life, and he's dressed casually in khaki cargo shorts and a white short sleeved shirt. He clearly has great taste in clothes. At that moment, he looks up, sees me and starts smiling, well, grinning like a Cheshire cat, and right then I feel like I have made a terrible mistake. I can't explain it. Gut feeling, maybe, but something tells me I should not be here.

"Izzy," he says as he wraps his arms around me. I mean really around me. I feel like I'm suffocating. "You look so beautiful!"

Firstly, Izzy? When did he ever ask if I liked to be called Izzy?? He didn't. Surely it's polite to ask somebody if they like their name shortened? My friends call me Izzy, or Iz, but we have only just met. I wriggle with some force from his grip and step back a little, hoping that he'll notice he's made me feel uncomfortable.

"Hi Jason," I say awkwardly. "We picked a lovely day."

"I just need to stand and look at you for a moment," he says, stepping closer, tilting his head and speaking far too loudly for my liking.

Where did that accent come from? It's like he's trying to sound 'Posh'; that's the only way I can describe it. That definitely wasn't there before.

"So, where are we heading?" I ask, trying to change the subject and hurry the date along so I can get hell out of there.

"I have everything planned, Darling, let's just enjoy saying hello properly," he says as he puts his arm around my waist to pull me closer to him.

I resist the urge to turn around and run, mainly because I wouldn't know where to go. Maybe I'm overreacting, maybe it's the nerves, maybe he's just really, really nervous and this is how he acts when he's feeling like that. I decide to ride it out for a little longer and see what happens.

"First, let's get you a ticket for the tube," he says, letting his arm fall from my waist and gripping my hand. I think I can feel palpitations starting.

I pull my hand away and reach for my phone. "I just need to let my friend know I arrived safely," I say, glad of an excuse to have my hand back.

He gives me a wave as if to say it's fine, or is he dismissing me? Giving me non-verbal permission to do so?

I text Eve.

'What have I done? Don't panic, I'm fine, just in need of a very large drink and a quick escape route!'

Her response was immediate.

'On my way, where can I meet you?'

'No, it's ok, I'm going to ride this one out, I'll check in later x'

'Call me IMMEDIATELY if you change your mind or anything happens x'

He starts walking ahead of me which I find a little rude. He knows I don't know London or the tube system, but I follow him anyway as I have no idea where I'm going.

"Here, I've set it up for you to buy a day pass, you just need to pay," he says stepping aside, gesturing to the machine.

I pull my bank card out of my purse and touch it to the screen.

"We're heading for Greenwich. I have such a wonderful day planned, Izzy, you're going to love it."

I don't bother correcting him on my name because it really doesn't matter. I can categorically tell you now that I will never be seeing this man again.

I have no idea which tube leads where. I have only ever visited London as a tourist, and it was all mapped out for me, but he navigates it with ease. We get on a train and just about manage to find a seat; sardines springs to mind. He's sitting a little too close for my liking but it's busy and there isn't really the space to put any distance between us. I'm about to ask him how he knows London so well when he turns his face towards mine.

"Your hair is so beautiful, Izzy, I just want to stroke it," he says and then literally starts to run his hands over my hair. What is happening right now? I met the guy ten minutes ago. His voice is so loud and brash that a few people actually turn to look at us. Ground, open up now and just swallow me. This is mortifying. And I swear that accent is getting stronger.

"Did I tell you I was a TV presenter before becoming a landscape gardener?" he says, his hand still stroking the hair around my face.

That might explain the loud, overconfident voice. People look again as if they hope to recognise him. "Um no, you didn't," I reply, "How long until our stop?"

"I'll show you my reel tape if you like," he says, completely ignoring my question.

No, I would not like. "Sure," is all I can muster.

Whilst he's wittering on about his 'TV career,' I try really hard to look enthused but all I can think about is how I can get away early and it dawns on me that I have made a very big mistake, apart from the obvious one of actually being here that is: I haven't booked an open return on the train. I am stuck here until the 18.05 train home. I don't know whether to laugh or cry. He's still going on about his TV career, waving his hands around (which is clearly not going down well with the people pushed up against us). I just sit and nod in all the right places. After what feels like a lifetime, we arrive at our stop and head for Greenwich Park. I wonder if they have a bar.

As we walk through the park, he again attempts to take my hand, but I pull it away and push a non-existent hair behind my ear. I'm not sure if he notices this is a deliberate move to avoid physical contact with him. If he does, he doesn't show it. It's lovely here; the sun is shining, the park is full of children playing, families having picnics, couples are sitting close to each other sharing secret words, and I feel that pang again. We make small talk, but he has no interest in me. It's all about him and his career. He stops at a bench and sits down, tapping his hand on the space next to him, clearly expecting me to follow suit. I sit at the opposite end, but he moves closer and starts to stroke my hair. What is it with him and my hair? Is it some weird fetish? I casually brush his hand away.

"You said something about a showreel?" I ask, getting the focus back on him and away from my hair.

He pulls his phone out and starts scrolling. He stops at a video and presses play. I wouldn't really describe what I'm seeing as 'TV presenting'. It's a shopping channel, one I have never heard of, not that I ever watch these channels, but I would recognise one or two names.

Ok, now I see where the loud voice comes from. He's very confident but honestly, bloody terrible. I sit through several of these clips, all very similar, him standing in a bland looking studio trying to sell kitchenware. I add the occasional polite "That's good," and "Oh, you're great, what a shame it didn't work out for you," whilst trying very hard not to laugh, because it is laughable. Not only his 'presenting', but the whole situation I have found myself in.

"It just wasn't for me," he says when he finally puts his phone away, "I didn't like being cooped up in a studio all day, so I quit."

I'm not entirely sure this is true. I think he just wasn't good enough but, of course, I don't say that. He shows those videos far too proudly for it to be something he chose to walk away from.

"How about some lunch?"

"Great idea," I reply enthusiastically. A restaurant with a bar is just what I need.

We start walking and he casually puts his arm around my shoulders. He's still telling me about his presenting days, how he could have been a star but fate had other ideas for him. People are looking at us, turning to see where this loud voice is coming from. It's getting unbearable. I try my best to switch off and enjoy the beautiful park but it's futile.

We eventually stop outside what looks like a Deli; it's quaint but not a patch on Bella Vita.

"Here we are, they do great paninis here," he says as he steps inside leaving me to follow. "You should try the pesto chicken one, it's great. I'll order for you," and before I have a chance to reply or ask for something else, he's at the till ordering. Good job I'm not vegetarian or vegan.

"I'm sorry, Sir, but your card has been declined," I hear the girl behind the till say. I don't even need to look over. I know she's talking to Jason. I continue to casually browse the contents of the drinks fridge, not wanting to look over and add to any embarrassment that he might already be feeling.

"Try again," he says arrogantly.

I continue to browse.

The girl tries his card again. "I'm sorry. Do you have another card I could try?" she asks as she smiles at him delicately.

This is painful. I quickly step in and hand her my card. "Lunch is on me," I say, smiling, or grimacing. I'm not sure which. Don't get me wrong, I'm happy to pay my way but this is just turning out to be a comedy sketch.

We stand in a very awkward silence as we wait for our food. Finally, after what feels like an eternity, our lunch is ready, and we head outside to find a bench.

"I'm sorry, Izzy, I'll find a cashpoint. Must be my card playing up." He doesn't sound sorry at all.

"It's fine," I say, "It happens, technology eh!" I exclaim as I take a bite of my food.

We sit and eat in a long uncomfortable silence. I'll give him credit here though, it's a damn good panini. I may suggest this one to Luca.

"Ready for the first surprise of the day?" he asks excitedly once we've finished eating.

First surprise? I'm on about surprise number 7, and none of them have been good ones.

"OK," I say, trying to sound at least a little enthusiastic but I just can't seem to match his excitement. "Where are we going?"

"You'll see," he says as we stand, and he tries to take my hand again.

I pull my phone from my bag. "Sorry, I just need to check in with my friend, so she knows I'm safe." I'm running out of reasons to avoid holding his hand.

'Have you set me up? Am I on one of those candid camera shows?'

'That bad???'

'Yes, Jesus, this is one to tell over several glasses of wine, it's that hilarious I'm not sure anyone will believe me. I'll check in again later'

'You're ok though? You don't feel unsafe?'

'No, just mortified that I've allowed myself to be in this situation.'

We start walking through the park and I see signs for The Royal Observatory. Ok, he has planned something, and this could be interesting. I've never been before but I have heard of it; it has the meridian line going through it, the line is used by astronomers as a zero-reference line to help build a map of the sky. It has a planetarium and it's also the reference point for Greenwich Mean Time. I think. It sounds quite fascinating. At least I might learn something today, so all is not lost.

As we walk towards the information desk, I start to relax a little. If we're busy doing things, the day will pass quickly and I'm genuinely interested in the Observatory.

"Two adults please," he says, not even looking at the friendly face behind the glass.

We haven't stopped at a cashpoint so I can only assume I'm paying for this too.

"I'm sorry but it's advance booking only," replies the cashier.

"Well, do you have any availability today?" asks Jason, sounding more than a little irritated.

"We're fully booked today, I'm afraid. I can look to see if we have any availability for tomorrow," the man behind the desk says, trying to be helpful.

"We wanted today," replies Jason, frowning.

"I'm very sorry, it does say on our website that it's advance booking only."

Great planning, Jason.

"It's ok," I say to the man who is looking a little exasperated. "We should have checked, thank you for your time," I say with a smile as I walk away to let other people through.

"Well, they've ruined my plans," says Jason, sounding annoyed as he follows me.

I resist the urge to point out that 'they' haven't ruined anything.

I suggest we still take a look at the Meridian line. I noticed that we don't need tickets for that, and it might just ease his irritation.

"You stand on it and I'll take a photo of you," he says, pulling out his phone.

"Oh, I really don't like having my photo taken," I reply. If he saw the photo album on my phone, he would know this was a blatant lie. I don't dislike it, but just thinking of him having a picture of me on his phone from today makes me feel very uncomfortable.

I start to worry about how we're going to spend the rest of the afternoon. If that was his plan for the day then we're screwed. I'm not sure how much more I can take of that voice and his ego; this was a huge mistake. How did I not see this side of him? I guess people only show us what they think we want to see. As if he can read my mind, he tells me there is something else planned and we can head there now. I don't bother asking what it is as I know I'll only be told it's a surprise, so we head for the tube again. I'm starting to feel a little nauseous at the thought of being in such an enclosed space with him and his touchy-feely hands.

The tube is busy so I can't put some much-needed distance between us, and again his hand reaches for my hair.

"I really can't help myself, it's so beautiful and soft, my darling Izzy." People turn to the sound of his voice. Why wouldn't they? You can hardly miss it.

He spends the rest of the journey telling me again about his TV career. I've heard the same stories over and over again. I think I yawn about six times; I don't even try to hide it and I don't think he even notices. After a few changes, we get off near the O2. "How are you with heights, my love?" he asks as we walk along. The word love from his lips makes me squirm.

"Fine," I say, "Why do you ask?"

"Because this is your next surprise," he says, pointing up towards some cable carts.

"Oh, wow." I don't really know what else to say.

"They go over the Thames River and you get a beautiful view of the city," he says enthusiastically.

Any other time, I would love this. I love to do 'touristy' things, but the thought of being up there with him in that small space doesn't exactly fill me with joy.

"How long does it take?" I ask tensely. I can feel a knot forming in my stomach.

"Only about ten minutes. Are you afraid of heights?" he asks, coming close to put his arms around me. "Don't worry, darling Izzy, I'll keep you safe."

The only thing I'm afraid of is being able to resist the urge to push him out of it.

"No not at all, I'm perfectly fine with heights," I say with the biggest fake smile I can manage as I again wriggle from his grasp.

We walk across to the ticket desk, and I can't help noticing how quiet it is. There's nobody around. This must be one of the city's biggest attractions yet it's like there's been an apocalypse.

And that explains why. There is a big sign on the window.

'Attraction closed today for safety checks. Sorry for any inconvenience caused.'

Seriously. Where are those candid cameras? This has to be some kind of joke.

"Excuse me," I hear Jason say as he walks towards a man in a high-vis jacket holding a clipboard.

"Yes, Sir, can I help?" he replies, smiling.

"Is this closed for the whole day?" Jason asks.

"I'm afraid so. We have to do regular safety checks, can't take any chances with these things," he says chirpily.

"So, you just close it for the day without warning?"

"Oh gosh no, Sir, we always put our safety check dates on our website to avoid disappointment," he replies.

In my peripheral vision, I spot some outdoor food stalls. They look like street food vendors, and a bar! Thank God.

"Thank you for your help," I say with a smile, stepping in to avoid any further questions from Jason. "Why don't we get a drink over there?" I say, gesturing towards the stalls, and start heading off before he has a chance to answer.

I stop at the first one that says 'licensed'.

"Sauvignon Blanc, please," I say to the barman, "a large one."

Jason joins me at the bar, looking rather annoyed.

"What would you like?" I ask him. I get out my bank card. I know I'm paying but I'm past caring now.

"Just a coke, please, I don't really drink."

We stand at a high table that looks like it's made of old beer barrels. He's got his phone out and seems engrossed in something, so I text Eve.

'Found a bar! Very large wine in hand'

'I really can't wait to hear about this. Are you sure you're ok? Are you safe?'

'Honestly, I'm ok, just 4 hours to go……. This is one date I will never forget, and for all the wrong reasons'

The rest of the day can only be described as torturous. We went on so many tubes I lost count and wandered the streets like lost tourists. He did take me to a sports bar in Leicester Square because he remembered me saying that I like football and rugby. Yes, I paid. His irritation swiftly lifted, and he became overly happy, constantly telling me how he was having the most amazing day. I honestly don't know if he meant that or if he knew it was a train wreck and was trying to convince himself otherwise. He continued to talk in a loud, overconfident brash way and his weird obsession with my hair did not stop. I have been called darling, love and baby more times today than I have in my entire life, but the time has finally come for me to leave, and I could not be happier.

As we head for the station, I'm trying to plan how to get away without any awkward goodbyes, or the dreaded 'When can I see you again?' question, but it's too late, the words are coming out of his mouth before I can think of anything.

"I'm very busy with the store," I say feebly, "why don't we just play it by ear?" I can see the station just up ahead and all I want to do is run but that wouldn't be fair. "Thank you for today." It's the politest thing I can think of saying.

He takes my hand in his and holds onto it tightly. "It's been my absolute pleasure, Izzy. I've had the most wonderful day with you." And then it happens. He leans in to kiss me, and he's not aiming for my cheek. Before I can dodge his open lips, they're on mine. I'm not sure what he's trying to do with his tongue; it's like he's trying to clean the inside of my cheek! I pull away quickly.

"I should go before I miss my train." I know I have plenty of time, but I need to get away, and fast. As I walk away he calls after me, telling me to let him know when I'm home safely. I don't look back or respond. I breathe a sigh of relief and practically run for the safety of my platform.

Chapter 6

James

I'm getting ready for my first date with Lizzie. We've been chatting for just over a week and the time has come to finally meet. Man, am I nervous. We've had a busy week at the surgery. One of the local farms has had an E-coli outbreak between its dairy cows and we have been there almost daily to administer antibiotics and give advice on how to reduce the risk of it spreading. I haven't had time to dwell on today's date which is a good thing, or I may have backed out. Lizzie seems genuinely lovely. We have chatted on the phone almost daily. She's been understanding of me having to cancel once already due to work and doesn't complain when I have to cut our calls short because my work phone is ringing. She laughs at my jokes and makes some pretty good ones of her own. We've decided to spend the afternoon together at a local Country Park and Manor house, something nice and casual, and if it does go well, we could stretch it out to dinner, but we'll see. I don't want to let myself get carried away this early. I've been here before, and as we know, it didn't end well. Looking through my wardrobe, I'm stuck on what to wear. I don't mind admitting I have a lot of clothes. When I moved into this apartment, I had to have an extra wardrobe built to accommodate them all. It's my only vice, and one I share with my father.

It's a beautiful day so I decide on some long shorts that would come under the smart/casual category, and a white linen shirt. I roll up the sleeves and leave it open at the neck for a more casual look. I did offer to pick her up, but she said she would prefer it if we met somewhere else. I totally get it; she doesn't want me knowing where she lives. Women (and men) have to be careful. It's a big risk meeting someone for the first time when you've only spoken on the phone. I could be the next Ted Bundy for all she knows. So, we've arranged to meet by the car park in town at 2 pm. She'll leave her car there and we'll take mine. I hear my phone beep to let me know there's a text.

'Good luck my friend, why don't you bring her by the bar later so I can meet her? Providing it goes well of course, Justin is stopping by around 6 if you want to scare her off'

Dan is joking about Justin. He's a great guy, as solid as they come.

'Cheers Bud, I'm a little out of practice so I may not need any help scaring her off! Will keep you posted.'

I put my phone in my pocket and check the time. Ok, let's do this.

I arrive at the car park five minutes early but she's already there. I recognise her straight away from her photos and that is a relief in itself. She's stood casually leaning against a wall looking at her phone; she hasn't noticed me yet. What should I do? Do I pull up in front of her? Do I park up and walk over to say hello? I decide on the latter; pulling up for her to get in on our first date seems a little 'seedy'. I park up my white Audi and try to look casual as I walk over to her.

"Lizzie? Hi."

"James, hello." She leans towards me, and we give each other a polite kiss on the cheek. She's a good 5 inches shorter than me so I have to bend down a little.

"I hope I haven't kept you waiting," I say apologetically, even though I'm not late.

"No, not at all," she replies, smiling. "I have this weird thing about being late. I'm always early." I notice that she has a lovely smile.

"Noted for future reference," I say, and she laughs. She looks pretty in a long summer dress, her blonde hair pulled into a loose bun on the top of her head, but I feel it's far too early into the date to tell her this. Or maybe I should? See, I'm totally out of practice, not a clue what I should or shouldn't be doing.

"Shall we?" I say gesturing to where my car is parked. We head across the car park, and I open the passenger door for her.

"A gentleman, thank you," she says, sounding impressed as she gets in. I walk around to the driver's side and we head off. We make small talk along the way; the conversation flows easily so the thirty-minute journey passes quickly.

I park in the expansive car park and walk around to open the door for her. My father was an old school gentleman; he taught me how to be one from a very young age, open doors, always walk on the outside of the pavement so the lady is on the inside, and those things have always stayed with me. We walk across to the entrance, and I head for the ticket office. I was also taught paying for the first date is the gentlemanly thing to do.

"I'm just going to freshen up. I won't be a sec."

"I'll meet you outside by the coffee shop, would you like something to drink for the walk around?"

"Just a water please," she says as she disappears off in the direction of the ladies' room.

I pay for our tickets and walk outside into the sunshine. The gardens here are beautiful and the manor is quite a building. It was owned by a landscape designer in 1899 who completely reformed the gardens. With its ancient statues and terraces, it's quite breathtaking. I have no idea if she is interested in the history, but I can at least tell her what I know, should an awkward silence present itself. When I return from the coffee shop with two bottles of water, Lizzie is waiting for me and I can tell from the look on her face that she is impressed.

"It's just stunning," she says as she glances around, shielding her eyes from the sun, "I've never been here before."

"It really is beautiful; my parents live in France and every time they come to visit, they insist I bring them here."

"They're French?" she asks, sounding genuinely interested.

"They would love to be, but no, they retired to the south of France. My father was a vet so I followed in his footsteps. My mother was a teaching assistant; she worked part time so she could divide her time between work and home." I had a very privileged upbringing. I come from a very loving and supportive family. It's something I never take for granted.

"Do you have any siblings?"

"I have a brother, two years older. He didn't follow the lead from my father; he joined the forces and is now living in Germany. He's married, and I have a niece who I adore but I don't see anywhere near as often as I'd like."

We start walking through the gardens towards the country park.

"What about you?" I ask, "Are you close to your family?"

"Ah, well, my upbringing was as far from yours as it could possibly be," she says, looking pensive. "I was raised by a single mum. I never knew my dad; he upped and left the day she found out she was pregnant with me. She later found out he was married and already had his own family, so it was doomed from the start. She struggled when I was born, but I know she tried her best. She worked two jobs, sometimes three. Our neighbour Jenny would look after me so she could work. I grew up with very little, but I was never resentful. I knew she was doing the best she could. I was more fortunate than some."

I can see the emotion on her face, and I try to think of a way to turn the conversation onto something lighter.

"Enough of that, tell me about your practice," she says as if she's read my mind. We spend the rest of the walk to the park chatting about my job and how Cedar Lodge came about.

"Will you excuse me," she says as she heads off to the ladies' room.

I take the opportunity to take in the beautiful views. I can see the house from here; it looks like something out of a period drama with Virginia creeper climbing the walls, framing the windows and doors. I look down to where the deer are and decide that's where we should go next. You can buy little cups of food to hand feed them, so I'll ask if she'd like to do that. Not everyone is comfortable putting their hands near a wild animal. When she returns, I put my idea to her and she says she'd love to, so we walk off in the direction of the food hut. She's incredibly chatty and seems to have relaxed a little; maybe talking about her childhood has brought a little relief for her.

"Here let me show you," I say as I lay her hand flat to feed the deer, "If you cup your hand they can't really get to it and may nibble a finger by mistake." She looks alarmed but laughs. "If you do it like this, you'll be ok," I say, laughing with her, "and if they do mistake your finger for food, they'll realise very quickly and let go. It won't hurt."

I can't help but notice her face is looking a little flushed. Would it be rude to mention it? It's a very sunny day; it must be in the mid 20s and I'm worried she may be getting sunburnt. She's a grown woman, so if I do say something, she may get offended or even embarrassed and I would hate to make her feel like that so I decide on a different approach.

"I'm so glad I put suncream on today," I say as I wipe my brow for effect with the back of my hand, "The forecast said it would be warm, but they have been known to get it very wrong."

She tilts her head and looks at me intently. "You aren't burning but I have sun cream in my bag if you feel like you need more."

That answers that question. She wouldn't have it in her bag and not have any on. "Great thanks, I'll let you know if I need any."

We finish feeding the deer and start walking through the rest of the park. "Tell me about your job. It sounds tough, all those strays you have to deal with day in, day out. I'd be wanting to take them all home with me."

"It can be heartbreaking at times. We see some really awful things, a bit like your job I'm sure. But we also see the good. I can't tell you how amazing it is to see an animal walk off to their forever home with people you just know are going to love them unconditionally."

She looks genuinely happy when she's talking about her work.

"It's not what I always wanted to do. I've always loved animals but if you'd asked a 12-year-old me what I wanted to do, the answer would have been air hostess. Well that's what they were called back then. I believe cabin crew is the correct term now. They always looked so glamorous when I saw them on TV, glamorous and travelling the world. And here I am working in a tiny office in a rescue centre helping animals find their perfect homes. How different can it get?"

"Any regrets?" I ask.

"Oh no, definitely not, it may not be glamorous, but I love what I do. I feel like I make a difference…"

Mid-sentence she loses her footing on the path and stumbles almost to the ground. I manage to hold her arm to stop her from hitting the floor.

"Oh gosh, I'm so sorry. I don't know what happened there," she says, looking to the ground to see what she could have tripped on.

"Are you ok? Did you hurt yourself?" I ask, concerned.

"No, I'm ok," she says, rubbing her ankle.

I guide her by her elbow to a nearby bench. "Here, take a seat for a minute."

"I'm so embarrassed," she says as she sits down. "Tripping over my own feet, what a wally."

I chuckle at her use of the word 'wally'. "You aren't a wally, the path is a little uneven. I'm glad I wore trainers."

She looks down at my feet and my glistening white shoes. "They're pretty nice looking trainers," she says, looking at her own feet. "Maybe sandals weren't my wisest outfit choice," she says with a laugh.

"If it's any consolation, they look great." We both laugh and I help her to her feet. Once we're confident there's no injury and she can walk with no problems, we continue on our way.

"There's a coffee hut just up ahead, shall we stop for a drink?" I ask, and she nods in agreement.

I take her order of a cappuccino and go to buy the drinks while she finds a table. When I return, she excuses herself again and I wonder if her ankle is actually hurting more than she wants to admit. She might be applying a cold compress, which is not a bad idea. Maybe I should have suggested that. I see her walking back to the table and she appears to be, I don't know, limping maybe? She then pulls her chair from the other side of the table and puts it right next to mine.

"Would you like a cold compress to put on that ankle?" I ask. "It might help reduce any swelling or bruising that may come up later."

"Oh, I'm fine," she says, leaning her head on my shoulder and resting her hand on my thigh. She's suddenly become very 'familiar' with me.

"Are you sure you're ok?" I ask as I gently remove her hand from my thigh and put it on her lap. This is a bizarre and very swift change in character.

"How can I not be ok? I'm in this beautiful place, with thish beautiful man…."

Is she slurring? I pause for a second and then it all makes sense. She's drunk, very, very drunk. I look around us. We're surrounded by families, young children. How the hell am I going to get her out of here without making a scene? She starts typing something on her phone and I can't help but look. She's doing a google search, 'Hwo muc mooney does a vet ern'. I can only assume she means 'how much money does a vet earn.' Her typing skills clearly show her level of drunkenness. Shit. I need to get her back to the car and fast. I stand up and slowly assist her to the same position so she can lean on me. I pick her open bag up from the table and there it is. I can't tell if it's gin or vodka, but it's definitely alcohol in an unlabelled glass bottle.

"Right," I say more loudly than is needed, "let's get you back to the car so we can get that ankle checked." I'm hoping people will assume that's the reason she's hanging off me and not that she's blind drunk.

I'm not entirely sure how I get her back to the car in one piece. I've worked up quite a sweat. She's talking non-stop, and I barely understand a word of it. She's literally hanging off me, but we're here and she is safely in the passenger seat. Then I realise I have a problem. I can't take her to her car. She is in no state to drive, and I don't know where she lives. I walk a few feet away from the car and call Dan.

"Dude, you're on a date, why are you calling me? Is it over already?"

"I have a bit of a situation," I say, looking towards the car to make sure she's still safely in it.

"You're my best friend, but there are some things you're on your own with. Take a little pill and give it 20 minutes," he says, sounding amused.

"Dan, listen, she's drunk, absolutely wasted."

Dan starts laughing hysterically. "She had to be drunk to go on a date with you. You are losing your touch, my friend!"

He's clearly not getting the severity of the situation.

"She's been disappearing off to the ladies frequently. I saw a bottle of something in her bag. She's now almost passed out in the passenger seat of my car. We met in a car park where she's left hers. I can't take her back there, and I don't know where she lives. What should I do?"

Finally, he sees my predicament. "Bring her here to the bar. We can sit her in the back room. I'll get Laura to sit with her and we'll wait for her to sober up." Laura is one of the bar staff there; it's actually a sensible idea to have a female sit with her. She'll certainly feel safer than being alone in a room with me or Dan. I get into the driver's side and start the journey back. I decide parking out the back of The Meeting Room will be a much better idea than walking through a crowded bar with her. People may get the wrong impression. Laura comes out to help me get her inside and I leave them in the back office with a couple of very large coffees.

"Bloody hell, mate," says Dan handing me a coffee at the bar, "How the hell did this happen?"

I tell him about the day. "I saw the signs but didn't put them together. I don't know if this is a one off or if it's a problem."

We sit there for another half an hour before Laura comes in. "She's a little more with it. She's asking to speak to you, James."

I stand up to walk towards the office. "Will you stay in the room, Laura? She's drunk and being alone with her now could lead to trouble. I'm sure it won't, but it'll give me peace of mind and maybe her too."

"Of course," she replies, following me.

"How are you feeling?" I ask as I sit on a chair opposite her.

"I am so, so sorry, James. I never meant for this to happen. I was so nervous, I really wanted to make an impression. I just wanted a few sips to relax but, clearly, that escalated. I am so embarrassed," she says, pressing the palms of her hands to her forehead.

I can tell by the smudged eye make-up and her red cheeks that she's been crying. "It's ok, please don't worry. I'm sorry I had to bring you here, but I couldn't take you to your car and I have no idea where you live."

"I need you to know this is not a regular thing for me. I'm not a big drinker, just socially usually, I just need you to know that," she says as she starts to cry again,

"Thank you for being so kind, both of you," she says, looking at Laura.

"We need to get you ho…" Before I can finish, Laura interrupts me.

"I'll take her, I'll get her in safely, I think that's the sensible option here," she says, giving me a discreet nod.

She's right. Lizzie may have sobered a little but she's still drunk and I'm not going to put myself in a situation where things could be misunderstood. "Thank you, I really appreciate that. I'll stay here and help Dan out until you get back."

I walk out to Laura's car with them and make sure Lizzie is safely in. "I owe you one," I say to Laura as she gets in the driver's side of her little Peugeot.

"Well, that's a date you won't forget in a hurry," says Dan, handing me a bottle of beer. "Will you see her again?" he asks. He knows full well the answer to that question. I know he's mocking me. Before I get a chance to tell him where to go, Justin walks in and joins us at the bar.

"How was the date, my friend?" he asks as he gives my shoulder a squeeze.

"Pull up a chair," says Dan handing him a beer, "and he'll tell you all about it."

Chapter 7

Isabelle

It's the morning after what can only be described as the worst date in history, ever, in the world. And I am not being dramatic. I rang Eve on the train on my way home last night and gave her a brief run down. She has taken it upon herself to arrange brunch with Jess and Rebecca so I can relive every painful detail from start to finish, purely for their amusement and entertainment of course. I was hoping I'd wake up to find it's all been one horrible dream, but the several texts from Jason this morning confirm that it was not.

I received the first one within 5 minutes of getting on the train to come home the previous evening.

'My beautiful Izzy, thank you for the most wonderful day, I could never have imagined it would be so fabulous. You have stolen my heart. Please tell me when I can see you again. XXXXXXX'

I did not reply.

20 minutes later.

'Are you ok. Did you get the train ok? XXXX'

I did not reply.

An hour later.

'Maybe your battery has died. Please message me when you get home XXXXXX'

I did reply when I got home. It's not fair to 'ghost' him and I felt it was only right to let him know I was safe.

'Sorry for the late reply, home safely, very tired, it's been a long day, Goodnight'

I then turned my phone off until this morning. The five messages I have received since have all been pretty much the same. Ugh. What was I thinking? Am I so desperate to find love that it's come to this? I'm reminded of Rebecca and Isaac. They are clearly in a very small minority. I know a few people who have tried online dating and they all say the same, 'never again!' When did it get so hard to meet somebody outside of technology?

I quickly call Gina to thank her for holding down the fort yesterday and check that everything was ok at the store. I know I don't really need to; it's always in safe hands with her. I think I'm just trying to put off brunch and the mocking that will come with it. Gina assures me all was well and tells me to relax and enjoy my day off. If only!

I arrive a little late, purposely I might add (that'll teach them), to find all three of them already there.

I stand at the door for a minute, mostly to compose myself, prepare for the onslaught that's coming, but also to admire the décor. The building has been here since the 1800's, and the original stonework is beautiful. The tables are covered with white cotton tablecloths and sitting in the centre of each one is a small vase holding one bright pink and one white peony, simple yet very pretty.

"Hi," I say as breezily as I can as I take the empty seat at the round table. They all just sit there looking at me, and then burst out laughing. They only know the briefest of details and already they are in hysterics. I don't fancy my chances of any sympathy here.

"Are you quite finished?" I ask them, sounding a little like Mary Poppins scolding Jane and Michael in the movie.

They finally calm themselves down and we order our food and a bottle of wine.

"From the beginning, please," says Rebecca bossily, "and don't leave anything out."

"So how are the wedding plans?" I ask in a very feeble attempt to change the subject, knowing full well it won't work.

"From the beginning," repeats Eve.

So, I begin.

I don't get very far before the questions begin.

"So, he had a different accent?" asked Jess.

"Not so much different, just like he was trying to sound upper class, posh even."

"So, you buy a ticket for the tube, continue...."

I go on to tell them about the journey and fits of laughter ensue.

"He was actually stroking your hair on the tube? And calling you darling Izzy?" asks Eve through snorting laughter.

I drink more wine.

"He was so loud, people turned to stare at us. It was mortifying!"

"So, he was a TV presenter? Would we have seen him on anything?" asks Jess a little too seriously.

This time it's my turn to laugh. "You most definitely would not have," I reply and go on to explain about the showreels he'd shown me. More hysterical laughter.

"A shopping channel? What was he selling?" I'm sure Jess is winding me up now.

"I honestly did not pay that much attention, but I think it was kitchenware. It was full on cringe. The sad thing is, I think he genuinely thought he was good. I almost feel sorry for him."

"How embarrassing for him, having his card declined! You'd expect him to make sure he had money in his account, knowing you were travelling up for a date," says Rebecca, sounding shocked and a little amused.

"But in those pictures you sent me," says Eve, "The gardens he was working on looked spectacular. He must be earning decent money; they look like they're in huge grounds and are very well kept, so you would assume the owners would only want the best and be happy to pay for it."

"I'm beginning to wonder if he was telling the truth about that," I reply with a sigh, "How do you go from 'TV presenter' to landscape gardener? I don't know, maybe I'm wrong."

I then tell them about our visit to the royal observatory and how it was advance booking only.

"I thought he told you he had everything planned. That's terrible planning," says Jess.

"That's what he said," I say with a shrug of my shoulders, "He told me the whole day was planned and we were going to have the 'best day ever.' He said it several times, I'm sure it was just a genuine mistake."

Eve is laughing so hard I fear she may pee her pants. "I'm sorry but this is fucking golden, my friend," she says through her laughter, "and also a great reminder of why I don't go on dates."

"No, you just shag," says Rebecca disapprovingly. She's never really approved of Eve's lifestyle choice, but as her friend, she's come to accept it.

"I'm harming no one, we're all consenting adults," says Eve unfazed. "And it avoids all of this…" she says, waving her hand in my direction. She is very used to Rebecca's view on her life choices and it takes it all in her stride.

"But you're happy being alone; these two are happy and settled," I say nodding towards Jess and Rebecca, "You're all content with your lives. I just feel like something is missing."

"So does the story end there or is there more?" asks Jess, clearly hoping for more.

"Oh, there's more." So, I carry on, telling them about our disastrous trip to the cable carts. At this point, I have to laugh with them because quite honestly, it really is laughable. If it happened to one of them, I'd be laughing too, so I join in.

"He did take me to a sports bar in Leicester Square because he'd remembered me mentioning I like football and rugby, credit where it's due, he listens, and yes, I paid for the drinks. I also explained the basic rules of rugby to him; it's safe to say he is not a sports fan."

"Let me get this straight," says Eve, drawing her head back slightly, "You not only paid to travel to London by train for what you were told would be a 'wonderful day with everything planned,' you also paid for everything there?"

I don't need to reply. The look on my face said it all.

"I'm guessing he won't be your plus one at my wedding then?" asks Rebecca, trying not to laugh.

Maybe if they keep laughing, we'll get thrown out for making too much noise and I can hide away at home and try to forget all about Jason and our date from hell.

"How did you leave it with him?" asks Jess.

"Don't judge me but I completely chickened out of telling him I didn't want to see him again," I say, cringing at my own behaviour, "the day had been bad enough and I just wanted to get away, especially after his attempt at kissing me...."

"You didn't let him kiss you?" asks Rebecca, almost squealing at me as she swats my arm.

"OW!" I say a little too dramatically, rubbing where she'd made contact. "He just kinda went for it, tongue everywhere. He had no idea what he was doing; it was awful. I immediately pulled away." I literally shudder at the memory. "Stop it, you two," I say waving a hand at Eve who is sitting next to me. She and Jess are almost uncontrollable again.

"Oh Iz, you need to tell him. I'm assuming you've heard from him since?" asks Rebecca. She's doing well at holding her laughter in.

I take out my phone and show them the messages, another three of which have appeared since I got to the restaurant.

"He's persistent, I'll give him that. Do you need a restraining order?" asks Eve. I'm sure she's only half joking. "Bec is right, you need to tell him, and sooner rather than later. You've stolen his heart, it's only fair...."

And they're off again. I give up and let them have their fun.

For the rest of our time together, we discuss Rebecca's upcoming nuptials, and all compare pictures of outfits, shoes and bags. I'm quite glad the focus is off me and onto something more positive and exciting.

We soon leave the restaurant and Jess and Rebecca head off in taxis whilst Eve and I take a walk through the town.

"So, what's next?" she asks. I've known Eve the longest, and whilst we're a close group, I can't help but feel there's a bond between us that isn't quite there with the other two.

I look at her blankly, not understanding what she's referring to.

"With dating," she continues, picking up on my confusion.

"Ah, you think I'm going to put myself through that again? Oh, hell no," I say with some confidence.

"Oh, come on, you can't let one bad date put you off."

"One bad date? Bad? It was worse than bad. Were you not there when I relived every painful moment? I'm quite sure you were. I can still hear you laughing now!"

"I'm sorry, but you must admit, it is funny. Can you not see the funny side yet?" I actually can and I laugh with her.

"You haven't answered my question," she says once we have controlled ourselves, "Have you been chatting to anyone else?"

"There were another two but I cooled off once I'd arranged a date with Jason. I didn't think it was fair."

"So, pick it up again, and don't be so damn nice. Do you think these guys are only talking to one person at a time? You had a bad date, ok, awful date, laugh it off, put it down to experience and move on. You never know, Mr Perfect may be sitting in that little app somewhere just waiting to be found."

I hate it when she's right, and she is, often. She sees the look of defeat on my face and puts her arm around my shoulder, pulling me into her.

"Tell me about these other two guys, and you do know you don't have to wait for them to message first right? Browse the goods, do a little window shopping and when you see someone that takes your fancy, just send a message."

"And if I don't get any replies?"

"Then on to the next. Don't take it too seriously, get on with your life and just have this going on in the background." I wish I had Eve's confidence and laid-back attitude. She just shakes everything off, takes it with a pinch of salt.

"First though, you need to get rid of this one," she says, referring to Jason.

"Ugh, I know. I'll text him tonight and just be honest, maybe not too honest. I'll just say that I didn't feel a connection and wish him well."

"Maybe a little honesty wouldn't hurt," says Eve, "It might help him in the long run, stop him making the same mistakes again, stop some other poor girl from going through the same torturous date."

"When did you get so caring?" I ask, mocking her. It's a running joke that she has a cold heart when it comes to men. "You're probably right, but I'm not going to be the one to tell him. No way. Hopefully he'll figure it out by himself."

We spend the rest of the afternoon wandering the shops in the sunshine and partaking in a little retail therapy before saying our goodbyes and heading home.

When I get home, I sit out on my balcony and think about what Eve said. She's right, of course; she always is. Why do I need to take this dating malarky seriously? Maybe I should just have a little fun but leave myself open to what could happen. You never know, Mr Right could just walk into the store one day. I think of Jonathan and immediately shake that image from my mind. I decide to take her advice and do a little 'window shopping', but first, I have to text Jason.

'Hi Jason, I'm sorry for not getting back to you sooner, I have been out for brunch with the girls....'

No, I don't need to explain myself.

'Hi Jason, my apologies for not replying sooner. I have been thinking about our date and I don't think we should see each other again. I just didn't feel a connection between us. I wish you well on your dating journey,

Isabelle.'

I really hope he takes it well but something in my gut tells me that won't be the case, and before I have a chance to do anything else, I get that ping from my phone informing me there is a message waiting.

'Izzy I can't believe this! After I gave you a beautiful day out in London and treated you like a queen you just throw this at me. How could you not feel a connection? Our chemistry, that kiss. I'm truly astounded. I urge you to please reconsider your decision.

XXXX'

'There is so much wrong with that message, I don't know where to start. Ping. Oh god, I just know it's him again. I delete the message without reading it. Ping. Enough now. I block his number. I'm not proud of this, but I feel I have no choice

Against my better judgement, I take out my phone, open the app and start 'browsing'. I look at my inbox and come across the messages I exchanged with Ben. I didn't reply to the last one. I take a deep breath and start typing.

'Hi Ben, how are you? I'm sorry for not replying to you sooner, work has been chaos, which is of course a good thing, but leaves very little time for much else, I've also been helping my friend with her wedding arrangements, it's not far away now so there's a lot to do and as I'm providing the flowers for the big day, it's been nonstop. I was wondering if you would like to meet for coffee one day this week?

Isabelle'

I can't decide if I'm being stupid or brave. Time will tell.

As it turns out, I only had to wait 45 minutes to find out.

'Isabelle, how lovely to hear from you. I have been busy also so please don't apologise. It sounds like you've had quite a week of it, so how about something stronger than coffee? Wine instead? I'm free tomorrow evening?

Ben'

'That sounds great, shall we say 6.30? There's a bar called The Meeting Place, do you know it?'

'I do indeed, see you there.'

Brave. I'm going with brave. I text Eve to let her know I've taken her advice.

Chapter 8

James

It's Monday morning and the surgery is busy. There's clearly been a lot of poorly animals over the weekend. We've got everything from ferrets to a tortoise, along with the usual cats, dogs and hamsters, with all manners of ailments.

The morning passes quickly. Both myself and Erica are in today, but we've decided we need to hire a locum vet to help with the workload, so I get Rachael on the case of advertising for us.

I decide to sit outside and eat lunch today. The weather is glorious, and the views are stunning. Halfway through my sandwich, I see Tim running towards me, clearly trying to get my attention.

"James," he says breathlessly, "we need to get theatre ready; we've just had a call, a little dachshund has been run over. It sounds bad; the poor little thing got hit by a truck!"

Ok, that does sound bad. I run inside, throwing my lunch away as I pass the bin and help Tim get the operating theatre ready. I have no idea what to expect. We only know that he's still breathing but in a very bad way. I hate cases like these, but also you can't beat the rush of adrenaline that comes with it. I do know that the little guy is in the best possible hands and has some of the most modern technology on his side. That alone gives him a fighting chance.

Two minutes later, Emily comes running in carrying the tiny limp body and we get to work. His abdomen is distended, and he has trouble breathing. I fear internal bleeding which is never good. He clearly has a broken back leg. Then he starts to seize; my guess is a concussion. Erica scans his abdomen, and we can clearly see blood, a lot of it. We put our lead coats on and x-ray his leg. He has a broken femur, though that's an understatement. It's completely shattered.

"We need to stop this bleeding or he'll bleed out," I say to Erica. She nods in agreement and everybody gets to work. Tim and Emily start setting up sterile trolleys and preparing the poor little mite for major surgery.

"This won't be easy," says Erica through her surgical mask as we're scrubbing ready to operate. "Do you think he's too weak for theatre? And that leg will need surgery."

"Let's try to stop the bleeding first. If we don't control that, he won't be needing his leg," I reply sadly.

Dogs can die within just a few hours if internal bleeding isn't stopped quickly. We both know this. We're working against the clock, and boy, do we know it.

"Do you think we should try to fix the leg at the same time? Save putting him under twice?" asks Erica, but she knows the answer. She knows we have to stabilise him first. I give her the look that she knows so well, one that is sympathetic but asking her to think with a vet's head and not her heart.

"I know, I know. I'm just trying to save him more misery and pain," she replies.

"Ready?" I ask, my gloved hands raised in the air as I walk into the operating theatre.

"Ready," she says following me.

For an hour and a half, we work nonstop trying to find and stop the cause of all the blood in his abdomen, and finally we're done.

"Do you want to stitch, and I'll go and speak to the owner?" I know Erica much prefers animals to people, and she does not do well with upset pet owners. She usually sends one of the nurses to speak to them, but this has been big surgery and he still needs his leg fixing, so I feel it's my place to deliver the update.

"If you're ok with that, thank you. I much prefer the blood to dealing with people."

I take off my mask, gown and gloves and scrub my hands before heading out to reception.

"Rachael, where are the dachshunds' owners? I need to give them an update."

She points to a woman sitting in the corner with her head in her hands. Even though I can't see her face, I can tell she's crying.

"How is he?" asks Rachael, looking concerned.

"Alive, for now," I reply as I head over to the owner.

"Hello," I say as I gently touch her shoulder, "My name is James, my team and I have just operated on your dog."

"Billy," she says without looking up, "His name is Billy."

Rookie mistake, James. Idiot. Always learn the patient's name before speaking to the relative. Yes, I'm using the word relative because most pet owners see the animal as part of their family. "I'm sorry, I didn't get a chance to catch his name when he got here. He was in a bad way and we needed to get straight to work. I have an update on Billy for you."

She turns to look at me, and despite the mascara that has run down her cheeks, there is no mistaking who she is. I don't react; that would be unprofessional. She is a worried dog owner. That is all that matters now.

"How is he? Please tell me he's ok. He just ran out into the road, he's never done that before," she says as she tries to wipe the mascara from under her eyes with the pad of her finger.

"He had internal bleeding…" I begin but she interrupts me before I can finish.

"James?" she asks, looking at me as though she's inspecting my face to confirm what she already knows

"Hi Andrea, yes, it's me," I say, holding her gaze. "How are you? Sorry, silly question," I say as I take a deep breath before continuing, "Billy had a lot of internal bleeding which we had to stop quickly. He also has a broken femur that will need surgery and I think he has a concussion. The next 24 hours will be critical but I'm optimistic. Once he's stable, he'll need surgery to fix his leg. We'll need to keep him in for a few days, possibly longer."

I should probably explain who Andrea is. She was my university girlfriend. We were together for two years; she was studying law whilst I was doing my veterinary degree. She had a brilliant and intelligent mind. I knew she would go far. We were serious for a long time, our families spent time together holidaying in France, but we were young and both very ambitious. We mutually agreed to go our separate ways. She came away with a first-class honours degree and bagged herself an incredible job with a very prestigious law firm.

"Can I see him?" she asks with tears threatening to start again.

"Of course, but please remember, he has had major surgery. He'll be groggy but I'm sure he'll be pleased to see you. Emily will take you through." I gesture to Emily that it's ok to let Andrea into the recovery unit. "Just five minutes though, he just needs to rest and recover."

"Thank you, James," she says, squeezing my arm as she walks past me. What is Andrea doing here in Wiltshire? Surely by now she is a big shot lawyer working in London, terrifying the defence. I decide now is not the time to ask her.

After about ten minutes, she emerges from the recovery room, clearly upset.

"Can I get you anything?" I ask, "Tea, coffee, water...."

"No, thank you, I'm holidaying down here with a few friends. It's meant to be a few days away from work stress to relax." I'm sure there's sarcasm in her tone, understandably. "I'll head back and leave him in your very capable hands."

"At least let me drive you back. You're in shock; you can't possibly drive in this state. You can leave your car here and collect it when you come and visit Billy tomorrow." I can't let her drive. She's visibly shaking and still crying.

"I couldn't ask you to do that, I have no idea where I am but I'm sure we're a good 40-minute drive if not more from where we're staying," she says, gazing through the windows as if she's taking in her surroundings for the first time. "I can call one of my friends from the lodge to come and get me," she says as she starts to sob again.

"You didn't ask, Andrea, I insist. Please let me drive you. It'll save you waiting around here for them to get here."

I can see her thinking about it for a minute. "Ok, thank you, if you're sure it's no trouble. Aren't you needed here?"

"They'll manage, don't worry. Make sure Rachael at the desk has all your contact information and I'll meet you back here in a few minutes."

I walk through to the back rooms and explain to Erica where I'm going.

"She's pretty," she says with a wink, "and there's something familiar there." It's not a question but she sounds inquisitive.

"How very astute! Are you some kind of witch?" I ask with a little humour.

"You have no idea," she replies laughing.

I grab my keys and head back out to reception to meet Andrea.

"All set?" I ask as I lead her out towards the car park.

"They will call, won't they? I mean if anything changes, they will keep me updated?" Andrea asks. She's clearly reluctant to leave and I understand that. We see it all the time.

"I promise I will call you personally with an update later today, and I will continue to do so until we can discharge him. He really is in the best hands here," I say, trying to reassure her. "Now come on, let's get you back."

She gives me the address of her lodge and we drive in silence for the first few miles.

"So how have you been, James? It's been a long time," she says, sounding sad, "How did you end up here in Wiltshire?" She's sitting with her hands in her lap, picking at a loose thread on her jeans.

"You've seen the practice. It's incredible. I was offered an opportunity too good to turn down. It's a beautiful place to live and work, a far cry from London, but I don't miss it at all. Give me rolling fields and countryside over the big city any day," I reply honestly. I was a typical city boy the last time we saw each other. I thought I'd never be convinced to leave the bright lights, but here I am, and I don't regret it for a second.

"It really is beautiful, that's why we chose to come here," she says, looking out at the passing fields, "one of my colleagues at the law firm suggested it. She grew up here and said it was the perfect place for a quiet getaway, long walks, country pubs... and she wasn't wrong."

"How long have you been here?" I ask.

"Since Friday, we're due to leave Wednesday." She looks back down to the loose thread and sighs. "I won't be going anywhere until Billy is fully recovered. I can't go back and leave him here."

"I understand that. You could be looking at several weeks, Andrea." Honesty is needed here; if she really doesn't want to leave him, she will need to put plans in place to stay, and I can't give her a definite time scale, not yet.

She starts to cry again.

"We could see how he goes over the next few days and see about transporting him back to…" I realise I have no idea where she is living.

"North London," she says, finishing for me.

"We could maybe get him stable after his surgery, see if he's well enough to cope with the journey. We could splint his leg and keep him sedated. Between myself and Erica, we can find the best orthopaedic surgeon in the area for you so you can return home with him." It wasn't the best option, but it was a possibility.

"Can we just see how the next few days go? I really can't think straight right now. I can take a few more days leave, maybe even work on some cases from here for the rest of the week and then make a decision. Would that be ok?"

"Of course," I reply, "the longer he is with us, the better it will be for him. Travelling back may not be an option; we won't know for a few days."

"Thank you," she replies in almost a whisper.

We travel the rest of the way in silence. I don't push for conversation; she is clearly distraught. It's been a shock seeing her again after so long. I have no idea how her life has been since we went our separate ways all those years ago. I don't see a ring but that doesn't mean she isn't married. I'm guessing no kids as she is away with friends, but I may be wrong. She was always on the fence when it came to discussing our future and children, but we were so young. All she wanted was to finish her degree and get the 'big' job.

I pull up outside of her lodge and get out to open the passenger door for her. One of her friends opens the door of the lodge to greet her.

"Thank you so much, James," she says, hugging me. I hug her back. "Not just for taking care of Billy but for driving me back. That's above and beyond, I know that, and I appreciate it."

"It's no trouble at all," I say, releasing her from my arms, "I'll call you later today with an update, but feel free to call the practice at any time if you want to check on him for peace of mind."

She thanks me again and heads inside. I sit in the car for a few minutes, gathering my thoughts. It's been quite a morning. The scent of her perfume is lingering, and it sets off a sensation in me. I'm not sure what it is, nostalgia, maybe? I decide to call Dan on my way back to work to tell him what's happened. It turns out he's as shocked as I am. We arrange to meet at the bar tonight so I can fill him in properly on the day's events. I pull up outside the practice and brace myself for Erica's inquisition.

The rest of the day passes quickly. We're constantly checking on Billy, taking it in turns to check for bleeding from his wound, changing his IV drugs. The poor little guy is totally zoned out but that is the best way for him right now. Before heading off for the day, I ring Andrea to let her know he is stable and doing as well as can be expected. Erica is on call tonight so she decides to sleep at the practice to keep an eye on him. I of course offer to stay but she insists. Today has taken its toll and she can see that.

"Go and see Dan. Try to get a good night's sleep. I'll call you if anything changes, I promise," she says, practically pushing me out of the door.

I arrive at the bar at around 6.30 and it's busy. It's the perfect place for post-work drinks and food. It's as busy through the week as it is at weekends. Dan only closes on Tuesday evenings for his meetings, which takes place in the function room upstairs, away from any temptations. They use the entrance at the back of the building so they don't have to walk through the bar. It really is like this place was designed perfectly.

"Sounds like you've had quite the day," says Dan as he hands me a bottle of beer. "And I don't think it's about to get any easier," he says, nodding towards the door.

And there she is, walking into the bar with a friend. Crap. I don't know how I feel seeing her again. Maybe I can turn back around to face Dan and pretend I haven't seen her. Will she recognise him? They met of course; they were both a big part of my life at one point. It's too late to make that decision now. She puts her hand in the air to indicate she has spotted me and walks in our direction; she spots Dan and immediately starts smiling.

"Well," she says as she approaches, "This is a surprise! Seeing James was enough but you as well, Dan! How are you?"

Dan walks around from behind the bar to give her a kiss on the cheek. They chat for a few minutes before he heads back to carry on serving.

"He's running a bar?" she asks, clearly a little shocked. She's fully aware of his background.

"I know. Trust me, it wasn't something his parents or I thought was a good idea, but he's turned things around. He's clean and sober since what happened with Raz, and as you can see, he's made a real success of this place."

"Good for him," she says with a genuine tone of admiration, "I'm so pleased he's turned his life around."

"What brings you here?" I ask.

"Sarah," she says, nodding towards the table where her friend is sitting perusing the menu, "decided it would be a good idea to get out for something to eat. She's put up with my tears all afternoon so she's probably in need of a large glass of something strong, and apparently this is the place to be." Of all the bars, she had to walk into this one. "How is he?" she asks, referring to Billy.

"No change since I called you. Erica will call me if there is any need but I'm quite optimistic for him." I'm hoping my words will reassure her. She looks as beautiful as ever, with her golden hair falling around her shoulders, framing her face, but I can see the tears and shock have taken their toll.

She takes me to her table to introduce me to her friend and I leave them to enjoy their evening. To be honest, I need to escape and clear my head. Unfortunately, Dan has other plans. One of his staff has called in sick so I step in to help behind the bar. I've helped him out so many times, I'm quite the pro now.

A little while later, I see Andrea walking towards the bar. "Multi-talented, I see," she says with a smile. "I just wanted to say goodbye. Sarah is ready to leave. I'm not quite ready to face going back there without Billy, but she is my driver," she says, "Is Dan around? I'd like to say goodbye and compliment him on the wonderful food."

"He's in the cellar, he shouldn't be long. If you want to stay, I can drive you back." I regret the words as soon as they leave my mouth. I'm not sure how I feel about being alone with her again.

"Really? Are you sure? I just can't bear the thought of going back and him not being there; we've never spent a night apart."

Dammit.

"Of course, it'll give you a chance to catch up with Dan. I'll probably be done in about an hour when it starts to quieten down."

"Perfect! I'll just let Sarah know, and could I have a large Sauvignon Blanc, please barman?" she says with a wink.

As I pour her drink, I wonder what the hell I've done. This is not a smart move.

At around 9.30, the place starts to quieten down. "Thanks man, I don't know what I would have done if you weren't here tonight," says Dan as I get ready to leave.

"You would have called me to come and help," I reply, "me being here just saved time!"

He laughs as he pats me on the back. "You're a good friend, Lowry!"

I let Andrea know that I'm leaving and she says goodbye to Dan. "It's been so lovely to see you, Dan," she says as she hugs him, "This place is fantastic. I'm so pleased for you."

"Thank you!" he replies proudly, "It sounds like you might be here for a few more days yet so feel free to stop by again before you leave."

She puts on her coat and heads for the door.

"Good luck," says Dan as I turn to follow her. "Don't do anything I wouldn't do!" he says, chuckling.

I give him a look that says more than any words can and follow Andrea out to my car.

We chat easily. The conversation is light and comfortable; she asks after my parents and brother, and I reciprocate.

"I feel we've both been avoiding important questions, James," she says as she turns to look at me.

I keep my eyes firmly on the road. "We have, well, I have. I didn't feel it was the time to ask certain questions about your life; you've had a shock and focusing on Billy was my priority."

"Ever the thoughtful gentleman. I'm glad to see you've still got the same morals. It was one of the many reasons I loved you," she says with a hint of sadness.

We're heading into dangerous territory here, but I have to admit, I am curious, and clearly, she is too.

"To answer the unasked question, I am single, never married, came close once but she found it too hard with my job, being called out at night, weekends. It took its toll on our relationship, and we amicably went our separate ways."

"I'm sorry to hear that," she replies with sincerity.

"Don't be, it was obviously never meant to be. It was a long time ago. What about you?" I ask, turning the focus away from myself and my disastrous love life.

She seems to hesitate before answering. "I just broke off my engagement a few months ago."

"I'm so sorry, Andrea, and now this with Billy...."

"Can you pull over please?" she interrupts before I can finish.

I drive a little further up the road and pull into a little layby spot.

"Are you ok?" She's had a few glasses of wine, but I don't think she's drunk. Maybe she needs to throw up. She undoes her seatbelt, leans over, and kisses me. The kiss is warm, and her lips feel so good on mine. I undo my seat belt and take her face in my hands, pushing my fingers through her hair as the kiss becomes more intense.

No. I pull away. This is wrong. She's vulnerable and I feel like I'm taking advantage of that.

"I'm sorry, Andrea, I shouldn't have done that. You're upset; you've had a shock today…"

"You didn't do anything, James. I kissed you because I wanted to. It's all I've been thinking about since I walked into Dan's bar and saw you there," she says, looking at me with those beautiful green eyes.

I run my fingers through my hair and let out a loud exhale. "I think I should take you home so you can get some rest. I have to be in early to relieve Erica and check on Billy." It was a lame excuse and we both know it, but she doesn't argue.

"Sure, of course," she says, pulling her gaze away.

We drive the rest of the way in silence until I pull up outside the lodge.

"I'm not sorry I kissed you, James. Thank you for the lift home. I'll be in first thing in the morning to see Billy if that's ok?"

"Absolutely, anytime from 8," I say, trying to sound business-like and professional. I get out of the car and walk around to open the passenger door for her.

She kisses me on the cheek, lingering close for longer than necessary. I can smell her perfume. I can feel her hair against my face. It's taking everything I have not to kiss her again.

"Goodnight, I'll see you in the morning," I say as I step back to put some distance between us. I watch to make sure she gets in safely before driving home. I need to clear my head. What did that kiss mean? If anything at all. What would happen tomorrow when she came to the practice? I know I have a sleepless night ahead of me.

Chapter 9

Isabelle

I arrive at the bar just after 6.30 and it's busy. I've been here a few times before and it's yet to disappoint. I spot Ben sitting at a table in the window and head over. He looks handsome in a casual shirt and smart jeans. His dark blonde hair has a natural wave, giving him a surfer-type look. I made a little more effort than usual this morning. Usually my work outfit would be any old pair of jeans and a T-shirt. Being a florist isn't the cleanest or most glamorous job, so there is no point in making too much of an effort, but I knew today I wouldn't have time to go home and change, so this morning I opted for a pair of cropped skinny jeans with a loose summer blouse. Gina made a comment, of course. That woman does not miss a thing. I told her I was meeting the girls for a drink, but I could tell from the look she gave me that she didn't believe me.

"Of course dear, have a lovely time," she said with one raised eyebrow. She knows me far too well.

"Isabelle," Ben says as I approached the table. He kisses me on the cheek. "It's so lovely to finally meet you."

"You too, Ben. I'm sorry if I've kept you waiting. It took a little longer than usual to close the store." This was a little white lie. I was actually waiting for everyone to leave so I could quickly touch up my make-up in the loo.

"Please, I've only been here a few minutes myself," he says, gesturing for me to sit down as he pulls the chair out for me. "I would usually bring flowers on a first date but ya know…" he says, and I laugh. "So instead, what can I get you to drink?"

A gentleman, I like that. It's a concept lost on many men these days (this is not an assumption; I can confirm this from the disastrous dates of the past) so it's refreshing to see that old-fashioned chivalry is still out there somewhere.

As he walks off to the bar, I glance around, taking in the atmosphere. I like it here. The décor is modern but relaxed, with a few large brown leather sofas scattered with cushions sitting around low coffee tables. There is seating for diners and high stools line one of the far walls with a big wide wooden shelf to put drinks on. Simple candles in plain jars sit on each table. The music is low so you can hear it but still have a conversation. I'm no expert but I'm guessing it's a relaxed jazz playlist.

Ben returns to the table and hands me my drink. "I'm intrigued to hear about how you became a florist," he says, taking a sip of his beer, "Well, not how you became one, more of what made you want to become one."

I tell him all about my grandmother and how I spent my childhood with her there. "They are some of my happiest childhood memories. I loved the smell of the fresh flowers when they were delivered. I still do. Every morning after our delivery, I stand in the cooling room and just take in the scents and colours. It sets me up for the day. I guess it's my own version of morning meditation," I say, smiling.

"Well, it sure beats sitting in traffic on a morning commute. That's how my day starts, unless I'm working from home, and it does not help the stress levels, I can tell you."

We take a sip of our drinks. I can see we've both visibly relaxed. My shoulders have slackened, and I notice his have done the same.

We spend the next hour chatting easily. He tells me all about his job, which sounds pretty good fun, and some stories from his university days.

"Would you like something to eat?" he asks, "Sorry, I don't mean to be presumptuous. I'm just aware you've come straight from work and may not have eaten."

Thoughtful. That's another tick in the box for him. I can feel the two large glasses of wine taking effect. I think food is probably a good idea, but I also think now would be a good time to end the date. Not because I'm not having a good time, I'm hoping he'll ask to see me again, I just don't want us to drag it out and end up having nothing to talk about.

"How about we do food another time?" I reply, "I have to be at the store early for the flower delivery and two glasses is more than enough for me on a school night," I say, hoping he believes me and doesn't think I'm just trying to escape. "I have had a really lovely time."

"Of course, I totally understand. Maybe I can take you for dinner next time, maybe Thursday evening?" he asks with a hopeful tone.

"That would be lovely, Ben. I'd really like that," I reply as I pick up my bag from the chair next to me and stand to leave.

"Great, I'll text you over the next few days to plan, but for now can I call you a cab?" he says as he stands to join me.

"That's very kind," I reply, "but I think I'll walk. It's not too far and the fresh air will do me good." It's still light and there are plenty of people around so I know I'll be ok, plus it's not the first time I've walked home from here after a few drinks.

"If you're sure. Will you let me know when you get home safely?"

"Of course. Thank you for a lovely evening. I'm looking forward to Thursday," I say, and I genuinely mean it.

"It's been my absolute pleasure," he says, kissing me on the cheek. "I'll see you Thursday."

With that, we go our separate ways and I head towards home. I order a pizza online to be delivered (I really do need to eat) and call Eve to tell her all about this evening. I'm feeling very optimistic, or maybe the wine is encouraging my optimism. Either way, I like it.

The next morning, I visit Luca on my way to work for my daily coffee. It's much needed after last night's wine. We have a brief chat. He tells me he has family visiting from Italy next week. He hasn't seen his grandchildren for two years because of the travel restrictions that were in place with the pandemic and I can see the emotion on his face as he talks about them.

"Luca, I am so happy for you," I say, "I know how much you've missed them."

"Don't worry, Bella, I'll still be here to serve you your morning coffee. I may just have a few extra hands to help," he says with a wink.

"Well, I am very much looking forward to meeting them," I say as I give him a little wave and walk towards the store. I can't help but smile as I walk along the quiet street. It's still early so there aren't many people around yet. I sent Ben a text last night to thank him for a lovely evening and let him know I had gotten home safely. His reply came immediately, telling me how much he is looking forward to our dinner date Thursday. Eve was ecstatic to hear I'd had a first date that wasn't a disaster, and to be honest, so am I. I'm so glad I didn't let the Jason date put me off dating.

I get to the store and deal with the huge delivery for today. The cool room smells incredible. We've had some beautiful white roses in from the Netherlands and they look exquisite. Soon after everything is unloaded, Gina arrives and I know I'm going to have to 'fess up about last night. I just cannot lie to that woman.

"Good morning," I say, trying to sound breezy. I know she didn't believe my story about drinks with the girls. She knows I would happily go to meet them in my usual work get-up, so the outfit was a big giveaway.

"And good morning to you," she says, putting on her green apron. I decided to have them personalised with 'The Watering Can' across the front and our names stitched in yellow into the top left side. I like the personal touch. "How was your evening with the girls?" she asks, putting a little more emphasis on the word girls than is needed and I know I'm busted.

"I think we both know I wasn't with the girls," I say, giving her a knowing look, "I was on a date."

"Oh, really? I wouldn't have known…" she replies, grinning. "So, tell me."

"I'll make the coffees and fill you in," I say, turning to the coffee machine. I treated us to a fancy one for surviving the pandemic. So many small businesses were forced to close, I will forever be in debt to the people that supported us during that time. Just as I finish telling Gina about our date, Dom walks in. I give her a quick 'Mum's the word' look which she acknowledges with a wink.

"Good morning, ladies," says Dom, placing a brown paper back on the counter. I can see it's from Luca's deli. "Breakfast is served!" I bloody love Dom. The three of us sit and eat our pastries and drink coffee whilst Dom tells us all about the latest antics of his children and their new puppy 'Floppy'. He's not actually floppy at all, he's a solid black lab, but that's what the children wanted to call him, so Floppy it is!

"Right, are we ready?" I ask as I open the doors and flip the sign from closed.

The morning is busy. Dom is out delivering our online and telephone orders whilst Gina and I man the store. Some of our regulars pop in and we see a few new faces which is always lovely. This weekend we have a wedding and a christening which we're providing beautiful displays for. I love doing these things. I can get really creative. I'm always a little anxious there will be an issue getting the flowers I've ordered here on time. It hasn't happened to us yet, but I always fear there will be a van breakdown, causing the flowers to get hot and wilt. It breaks my heart to think of beautiful flowers having to be thrown away before they've really had time to bloom into their full potential. I always work with the same distributor and thankfully they haven't let me down. These are special days for our customers. I feel privileged that they've chosen us to help make them memorable, so I'm determined to get everything right. And of course, it's good for future business.

I double and triple check our orders are correct before walking to the deli to buy us all a well-earned lunch. Whilst I'm waiting for our sandwiches to be made, I pull out my phone. I have been so busy, I haven't had time to check it since arriving early this morning. I have two notifications. One is a text from Ben, a simple good morning text wishing me a good day.

'Hi Ben, I'm so sorry for the delay in replying, this morning has been manic, just stepped out for some lunch, I hope you have a good day x'

I keep it short and simple; it's all that's needed.

The second notification is a missed call from my mum. We don't speak often; we have a difficult relationship and have for a long time. It's hard to tell how and why it's ended up this way between us. I have spent a lot of time over the years trying to figure it out. Was it something I did without knowing? Have I not been a good enough daughter? (I don't even know what it means to be a good daughter, but I questioned it anyway).

I'm now in a place where I have made my peace with it. It no longer upsets me and I no longer ask myself those questions. It was taking up too much of my energy and life is just too short. I haven't seen my dad for several years; it became apparent he had no interest in me when he moved away. That is something else I have made my peace with. Maybe he just doesn't know how to be a parent, and I forgive him for that and all the hurt it's caused over the years. Forgiveness goes a long way in finding peace. I've learnt that the hard way but at least it's a lesson I have learnt. I'm an only child so my grandmother was the only family I could rely on. I have my friends and my business, I lead a full and happy life and that's all I can ask for. I decide I'll return her call later and head back to the store with lunch.

At about 4.30, I tell Dom to head home. He hasn't stopped all day. "You need some energy for the children and the puppy," I remind him when he tries to protest at leaving early.

"What are the chances Kate has him fully trained by the time I get home?" he jokes.

"Ha! Good luck with that," I laugh.

"What if I take the scenic route? Add an hour or so on to the drive?"

"Go!' I say pointing to the door.

He takes off his apron and hangs it on the back of the door that leads to the back of the store. "Ok, I'm out of here. Kate will be very grateful! See you both tomorrow."

Just as he's leaving, a delivery man walks in carrying a big white box.

"Hello, can I help you?" asks Gina.

"I've got a delivery for Isabelle Watts," he says, holding up the big rectangular box.

"Oh," I say, stepping forwards, "that's me."

"Sign here please," he says, putting a clipboard in my hand. I sign the paper and he hands me the box.

"Are you expecting something?" asks Gina, "That box looks fancy!"

"Nope. I've not ordered anything," I say, feeling a little confused.

"Open it then!" Gina pretty much squeals at me.

"Ok, calm down, woman," I say with a laugh.

I open the box carefully to find beautiful red crepe paper inside with a big white ribbon tied around it and a little card tucked inside. I take it out, open the envelope, and pull out the card. The stationary is beautiful, ivory with gold etched wording. My first thought is that I must find some for our bouquets.

Isabelle,

For Thursday evening, I hope you like it,

Ben x

"What is it?" asks Gina impatiently.

I carefully open the delicate paper and lift out the contents. It's a dress. A beautiful black shift dress, V necked with a lace covering. It looks exquisite. And expensive.

"Well, blow me down!" says Gina, "That is beautiful."

I'm a little lost for words. I have to be honest, I'm not entirely sure how I feel about this. I check the label and see that it's from an exceptionally beautiful boutique in the neighbouring town, and it's my size. I stand staring at it, taking in the soft fabric, running my fingers over the intricate lace.

"Say something," says Gina.

"I'm not quite sure what to say," I reply.

"Well, that's a first…" I give her a look to say that now is not the time for jokes. I'm genuinely stumped by this gift. Should I be happy? Offended? Worried? Is it weird? Is it generous and kind? Thoughtful? Obnoxious? Sexist? I lay it down on the box and sit on the chair by the counter to gather my thoughts.

"You get yourself off home, Gina, I'll close up," I say, not taking my eyes off the dress.

I think she understands I need some time to myself because she doesn't argue. "Thank you, love, I'll see you in the morning," she says, giving my shoulder a squeeze as she walks past me to get her bag.

Once she's gone, I lock the door, switch the sign to closed and take out my phone. The girls are what I need now. I hang the dress up on the back of the door and take a picture.

I open our girls' group chat.

'So girls, I got sent a gift today from Ben……….' I add the photo to the message along with one of the card.

'Not sure how I feel about it. Thoughts?' I type.

Jess: *'Oh how romantic! Looks expensive! Nice one! Can he have a word with Adrian and give him a few tips?'*

Me: *'You don't think it's weird?'*

Jess: *'No, It's very 'Pretty Woman!'*

Eve: *'She's not a bloody prostitute Jess! I think it's a bit creepy if I'm honest. Is it the right size?'*

Rebecca: *'Oooh Iz, that's gorgeous!'*

Me: *'Yes it's the right size and yes it is gorgeous, but is it an acceptable thing to do after one date??'*

Eve: *'He really paid attention to you if it's the right size, I mean would you be able to guess his shirt size from one date? Creepy, I'm telling you'*

Rebecca: *'Did you feel like he was giving you a good once over? Did he seem 'Pervy'?'*

Me: *'Not at all! He was quite the gentleman, it's one of the things I really liked about him'*

Jess: *'So, what are you going to do?'*

Me: *'I'm going to walk home and think about it. Thanks girls, I'll catch up tomorrow xx'*

A flurry of emojis follow, kissy faces, dresses, winks, and a vomit face from Eve. I close the chat and lock up the store. Hopefully I can get a good night's sleep and wake up with the answer.

Chapter 10

James

I arrive at the surgery just after 6 the following morning. Sleep had evaded me; seeing Andrea again and our encounter last night has left me feeling things I don't want to feel, and feelings I can't deal with right now. Getting Billy stable is my focus. I can deal with this array of feelings that are currently taking up residence in my gut when she's gone back to London.

Erica is sitting on the sofa in our little coffee room looking exhausted. Usually when we're on call, we don't have to be onsite, but I know she will have been here awake all night keeping an eye on our special patient.

"Christ, James, you look like you've had less sleep than me. What are you doing here so early?" she asks, giving me a concerned look.

"Thanks!" I reply sarcastically. "I couldn't sleep so I thought I'd come in early so you can head home and get some rest. Anything to report?" I ask. I know he must be stable as she hadn't called me overnight to tell me otherwise.

"He's stayed sedated. I put up another bag of fluids at 4.30 and he's due his next IV antibiotics in an hour. Other than that nothing. Luckily, I've had no call outs, so I haven't had to leave him. I checked his wounds; they look clean and dry. I think the little guy is over the worst of it."

I pour myself a coffee from the machine. I don't offer her one as I fully intend on sending her straight home.

"So, you wanna tell me about Billy's owner? I can tell there's something there," she asks as I join her on the sofa.

"There was, a long time ago. I will tell you all about it but not now. Get yourself off home. I'm sure Fi will be pleased to see you."

"If you're sure, I'm not going to argue. We find out in the next few days if our latest round of IVF has worked so we're both on edge and anxious. I'm not sure how many more times we can put ourselves through this," she says, looking down to her hands that are folded in her lap.

I turn to give her a hug. "I have faith. You will make the most amazing parents. I just have a feeling it's going to happen for you," I say optimistically, "Give Fi my love. Now get out of here."

"Thank you. Emily will be in at 7. She's running the puppy vaccine clinic this morning, lucky girl!" Everybody loves puppy clinic. There's no sadness or bad news, just cute little puppies to play with all day.

After Erica has left, I head into the recovery unit to check on Billy. We'll start to reduce his sedation this morning to see how he copes. He looks so tiny and vulnerable laying there hooked up to IVs but thanks to the sedation and pain meds, he's peaceful and pain-free.

I get started setting up for the day. I have a few farm calls to make but I don't mind. It's nice to get out of the clinic for a while into the fresh air. I have to interview a locum to help us out. I'm praying he's suitable; our workload is increasing, and we really need the help. Emily arrives at exactly 7. I put up Billy's next IV and we have a quick chat about the day ahead over coffee before getting started on our tasks for the morning. Half an hour later, I can hear banging at the door. We don't open until 8, so I'm not sure who it could be. A delivery maybe?

"Ah, Mrs Richards," I say as I open the door. She's carrying Dougie. "What can I do for you?" I don't point out that we don't officially open for another half an hour and are only here for emergencies at this time. She would take no notice anyway, and this time it could well be an emergency.

"It's my Dougie, Dr James, I think there's something wrong with his breathing."

I take the dog from her arms and call Emily to help me get him assessed.

"You take a seat, Mrs Richards, and we'll be back with you shortly," I say, gesturing to the waiting room that she knows so well.

"He seems a little lethargic and his breathing feels a little erratic, but I'm not overly concerned," I say to Emily as I grab my stethoscope and press it lightly to his little chest.

"I think he's got a mild heart murmur. Let's get a chest X-ray to confirm it and rule out heart failure," I say, removing the stethoscope as I give him a little stroke to reassure him.

"Shall I update Mrs Richards?" she asks as I put on my lead coat and get the machine ready.

"No, not yet, let's get a confirmed diagnosis first. That way we can give her all the facts and put a plan in place."

"Good idea. I'll make her a cup of tea while you finish your examination."

A little while later, I walk into the waiting room. It's decorated in neutral tones to try and give a calming effect. Framed pictures of the local countryside furnish the walls, along with a lovely dedication to Dr Simmonds. "Mrs Richards." She looks up from the cup of tea she's nursing in her hands. "Come on through with me." There are a few people in the waiting room now so it's not the place to be giving her Dougie's diagnosis.

She follows me through to the examination room and looks like she's about to cry when she sees him.

"Oh, my boy, is he ok? What's wrong with him?" she asks as she strokes his head affectionately.

"He's ok, but we have found something. Now I don't want you to panic or worry, he's going to be ok. Have a seat," I say, leading her to a little stool next to the examination table.

She sits down, dabbing her eyes with a tissue.

"Dougie has a mild heart murmur…." I can hear her take a sharp intake of breath, but I continue. "He is going to be fine," I say, putting my hand on top of hers, "It's mild and if managed properly, he can have years ahead of him with no issues."

"What do I need to do?" she asks, suddenly sounding very composed and focused.

"I'm going to prescribe a medication called Vetmedin. It's a tablet that's commonly used for these conditions; it works very well. You'll just need to find his favourite food to mix it into to ensure he digests them properly. Cheese or sausages work best but you'll know what his favourite food is more than me, and you should think about reducing his exercise slightly. He'll need six monthly checks but other than that he doesn't need any intervention."

I don't need to worry about the six monthly checks, I know we'll be seeing him a lot more frequently than that with this new diagnosis. We see him almost weekly already. We say our goodbyes and I pack them off with his medications and more words of reassurance. I silently place a bet with myself that they'll be back within the next three days.

"James, are you happy for Billy to have a visitor?" I hear Emily ask; I was so deep in thought I didn't even hear her come into the exam room.

Andrea must be here. "Of course, take her through and I'll be in shortly to update her."

I take a few minutes to gather my thoughts. I won't mention last night. I'll keep it strictly professional; we'll only discuss Billy, nothing else.

"Andrea," I say as I walk into the recovery room. She's sitting with Billy on her lap. He's wrapped in a blanket; she looks exhausted. "How are you?"

"I'm ok. More importantly, how is he?" she says, looking down at the dog lovingly. "The nurse said it was ok to hold him for a few minutes as long as I'm careful of his tubes and the splint on his leg. Is it ok?" she asks, wanting to confirm what she'd been told by Emily.

"It's fine. It'll do him good to be close to you. It can only be for five minutes though. He's had a stable night; he's still on fluids and IV antibiotics. I'd like to start trying to reduce his sedation today to see how he copes."

"But won't he be in pain?" she asks, sounding tearful.

"He's on strong painkillers so he'll still be sleepy once the sedation has worn off. He shouldn't be uncomfortable. Once we're happy, we'll start to reduce those and then we can think about the next step of fixing his femur."

"Thank you so much, James. You have no idea how much he means to me. I don't know what I'd do if he didn't pull through."

"I'll give you a few minutes with him, then we'll have to put him back in his bed," I say as I turn to leave the room.

"Before you go, about last night…"

"It's fine, honestly. We don't need to talk about it. Emotions were high. Let's just focus on Billy's recovery," I say as I continue to walk away.

I walk outside to get a bit of fresh air; it's been quite the morning and it's not even 9 am. After a few minutes, I head back inside. "Good morning, Rachael," I say as I pass the reception desk.

"I hear we had a visit from Mrs Richards. Emily told me about Dougie. It sounds like he'll be ok. She'll be more worried than ever now. I best stock up on the custard creams," she says, sounding sympathetic. Rachael is so good with the owners. She understands that their pets are family; she listens to them and is never in a rush to get away. I often joke that we should add the word 'Counsellor' to her name tag.

I head off to my exam room to get ready for my first patient, an African grey parrot called Reggie.

"Wow," I hear Rachael say. "Look at that beast," she says walking to the window.

A brand-new Maserati is pulling into the car park and it's quite a sight.

"Very impressive," I say, "I'm clearly in the wrong job!" I'm intrigued to see who owns the motor. We're used to beat-up old farm land rovers here; we don't see many like this.

"Now that is one handsome man!" says Rachael, tilting her head to get a better look as the driver steps out of the car.

She's not wrong, even I can see it. He must be well over six feet tall, he's impeccably dressed, and his shoes are so shiny he could use them as a mirror to check his perfect hair.

"He must be a sales rep; he doesn't have a pet with him," she says.

"Tell him we're busy right now, but if he leaves details of what he's selling and a card, we'll contact him if we're interested, and Rachael, try not to drool all over him!" I say, laughing as I head off to the back, leaving her to happily deal with the handsome man.

I finish up with Reggie. The poor thing is picking out his feathers, probably down to boredom. It's the most common cause so I've suggested more toys and stimulation. Next up is Lou the beagle. We see a lot of beagles with that name thanks to the movie whose main character is a dog of the same breed and name. I walk into the waiting room to call them in and notice the Maserati driver sitting in the waiting room.

"Rachael, he's still here?" I ask quietly, standing at the desk.

"Oh yes, he's not a sales rep," she says, "He's waiting for Miss Johnson, Billy's owner. I've let her know he's here."

I suddenly develop a feeling in the pit of my stomach that I can't quite describe.

"Andrea," I say as I walk into the recovery room, "Billy needs his rest now." I'm relieved to see he's back sleeping soundly in his bed; we want to keep his movements to a minimum with his leg still only in a splint. "We'll start reducing his sedation and one of us will call you later with an update." I take a deep breath. "There's somebody here waiting for you. Would you like me to show him in so he can see Billy briefly?"

"That won't be necessary," she says, clasping her hands tightly in her lap, refusing to meet my gaze. "James, that's Will, he's… he's my fiancé."

And there it is. That's what my gut was telling me. My lack of response forces her to continue.

"I'm so sorry, James, I should have told you. I was just so upset, and seeing you just brought up so many emotions and memories. I'm sorry," She begins sobbing.

I'm a little lost for words. I need to keep things professional.

"I'm very happy for you, Andrea, congratulations. Emily will call you later to let you know how Billy is." That's all I can manage right now. "Emily," I call. I need the safety of another person in the room. "Could you please show Miss Johnson out?" I say as she joins us in the room. "I've told her you'll call her later with an update."

"Of course, follow me, Miss Johnson, and don't worry, he's in very safe hands," Emily says, guiding Andrea to the door. Thankfully she seems completely unaware of the huge cloud of tension hanging over the room.

"James...."

I don't let her finish. "We'll be in touch. Goodbye, Miss Johnson," I say, closing the door behind them.

The rest of the morning passes without any issues. I work through lunch, getting my farm visits done. It's a relief to be out of the clinic and into the fresh air, although being alone with my own thoughts in the car as I drive between locations is not where I want to be right now. I go to call Dan to see if he's free tonight, but I remember Tuesday nights are when he holds the meetings for recovering addicts, so I call Justin instead. I haven't known Justin anywhere near as long as I've known Dan, we only met a few years ago through a mutual friend of Dan's at a boys' poker night, but I liked him straight away. He's always up for a laugh but he's also as genuine and honest as they come. He'll be a good one for advice.

"James," he says, answering my call, "how are you, bud?"

"Honestly, I could be better. Are you free for a beer tonight?"

"You, my friend, are in luck. Steph has had a friend cancel on her so I'm not on babysitting duties. Should I be worried?" he asks, sounding concerned.

"No, it's nothing serious. I could just do with some solid sound advice. Actually I don't even need advice, more just someone to vent to," I say honestly.

"I'm intrigued. Am I right in assuming this vent is regarding a woman?"

"Right on the money!" I reply laughing, "We can't go to Dan's; he has his meeting tonight. Shall we meet at The Bell?" The Bell wouldn't be my first choice by a long shot; it's an old hotel that hasn't seen a lick of paint for about 20 years, and I'm sure I can still smell cigarette smoke on the walls. It's what we refer to as the 'old man's pub', but the beer is good and it's quiet so we can chat.

"7.30? I can get Lucy bathed and to bed and then Steph is free to put her feet up with her reality TV rubbish that she loves." Lucy is their 2-year-old, adorable daughter.

"Great, see you there, and the first round is on me," I say before hanging up.

I pull up outside Cornerstone Farm and wait to see what's in store for me.

I arrive back at the surgery just after 4 pm to find the locum waiting for me. I realise I'm late; our appointment was half an hour ago.

"I'm so sorry to keep you waiting," I say, shaking his hand, "You know how these farm visits can be; you go for one thing and end up treating the entire herd."

"Please don't apologise. I completely understand. Jim Peters, nice to meet you."

He's not an overly tall man, shorter than me. He's balding and wears little round spectacles. He looks much older than his 42 years.

"James Lowry. Come on through to the back and I'll show you around."

I get us coffees from the machine, and we take a walk through the grounds.

"Your CV is quite impressive; you've worked in one of the biggest animal trauma centres in the country." I'm referring to the Queen Mother Hospital for Animals in Hertfordshire. It's one of the biggest teaching hospitals in the UK. "What brings you to Wiltshire?"

"Honestly? A messy divorce. I need some peace and quiet for a while. Please don't think I'm belittling this place at all. I've done my research; it's magnificent. I mean the quiet of the countryside where I'm not bumping into everyone who knows my business better than I do," he clarifies.

"Ah I see. Well, there's plenty of countryside around here as you can see," I say, gesturing to the vast fields behind us.

We chat a little longer about his experience and what he can expect here. I like him. I can't officially offer him the position without speaking to Erica, but I have no doubt she will like him too. And I tell him as much.

"This could get confusing, James, Jim and Tim all working under the same roof!"

"Well, if it helps, I'll answer to anything," he says, laughing.

"I'll speak to Erica tomorrow and get back to you by the end of the day, how does that sound?"

"Great, I look forward to hearing from you," he says, shaking my hand again.

I see him back to his car and walk back inside to finish up. It's my turn to be on call tonight so my day isn't officially over, but I don't need to be onsite, so I head home and get ready to meet Justin.

Chapter 11

Isabelle

It's Thursday evening, and against my better judgement, I'm getting ready for my dinner date with Ben. Eve thinks I've lost my mind, and right now, I'm inclined to agree with her.

I called him the evening I received the dress thanking him. I told him I couldn't possibly accept the gift, that it was too much, but of course he insisted I keep it. I have deliberated for the last few days over whether I should see him tonight, but we had such a lovely evening on Monday, I'm going to overlook the possibly inappropriate gift. Maybe I'm mistaken, and I'm completely misreading the situation. What if it is just a really nice thing to do and that's what I should see it as? I shake Eve's comments about sexism away and finish touching up my make-up. Apart from my drink with Ben, when I kept it minimal, I haven't really worn make-up since before Covid. I haven't had the need. I've also attempted some version of a French twist in my hair; it's not perfect but it works. It's got that untidiness to it that looks intentional. This dress deserves some effort so I had to try. I slide my hands over my hips, feeling the softness of the intricate lace fabric. I'm quite sure this is the loveliest dress I've ever owned, and I can't deny that I feel like a million dollars in it. I had to make a mad rush to Rebecca's last night to borrow a pair of heels and an appropriate bag, neither of which I own. I really must go shopping.

What woman doesn't own a pair of black heels?! I've agreed for him to pick me up from home tonight. I wasn't sure when he suggested it, we've only been on one date, but I'm always going on about chivalry, so it was hard to say no when he suggested it. I apply one last slick of lipstick just as my buzzer beeps at me, letting me know he's here. I take one final look in the full-length mirror in the hallway before grabbing my bag and heading down the stairs to meet him.

He's leaning against his glistening black BMW, and I have to admit, he looks incredibly handsome. He's dressed in beige chino-type trousers, a white shirt and a navy jacket. He looks impeccable.

"Isabelle, you look beautiful," he says as he comes towards me to kiss me on the cheek.

"Thank you," I say, blushing slightly. Get a grip, Iz! "I think I have you to thank for that; this dress is just stunning," I say, subconsciously stepping back so he can get a good look.

"It's all you," he says, smiling at me, "You'd look incredible in anything."

I can feel my cheeks flush. What is wrong with me?

He walks to the passenger side and opens the door for me to get in, then takes his seat in the driver's side.

"So, where are we going?" I ask. I notice we're heading out of town and my curiosity has crept in.

"You'll see," he says with a grin, keeping his eyes on the road.

I feel a flutter of excitement. This is a far cry from my day trip to London. I actually feel like I'm on a date, a proper grown-up date. It's been so long, I'd forgotten what that feels like.

The sun is shining; it's a glorious evening. I notice the rolling fields as we travel through the countryside. The sunlight peeking through the trees that line the lanes only adds to the romance of it all and I can't help but smile. We chat easily about our day. He tells me about a new project he's working on, and soon enough we arrive in the next town. I have been here several times. There are some lovely restaurants. It has its usual chain bars, burger joints and chicken diners linked to the cinema complex, but the locally-owned places are by far the best.

He parks up in one of the car parks and comes to open my door for me. My excitement is mounting, although I have relaxed a little on the journey here. Ben seems incredibly chilled out. He's clearly not nervous at all, and why would he be? It's not our first date. I suddenly feel silly for feeling the way I do and try to force myself to relax more. He takes my hand easily and we start walking.

"Are you hungry?" he asks, "Or would you like a drink before dinner? We have time."

A drink sounds like a great idea.

"How about a drink first?" I reply, "There's a great little wine bar just up the road." Where did that come from? Me, taking control on a date?!

"Show me the way," he says as he puts his hand out gesturing for me to take the lead.

The bar isn't too busy so we get a table easily. It's still light outside but tealights are lit on every table alongside a little vase with a single red rose in. It's very romantic, maybe too romantic for a second date? Why am I thinking like this? It's a wine bar. I come here with the girls. It doesn't feel romantic then. In fact, we have been known to sing along to the music playing on occasions when a few too many wines have been consumed.

"This is lovely," remarks Ben, "I'm assuming you've been here before."

"A few times with the girls. Our brunches have a habit of turning into dinners and late cocktails. We like it here, we're usually surrounded by couples. One night we ended up celebrating a wedding anniversary with two guys who were celebrating their first year of marital bliss. I did not feel great the next day," I say, almost cringing at the memory of that hangover. We'd gone onto another bar where we were drinking very expensive champagne at their insistence. I can't help but wonder where they are now. I hope they're still together and as blissfully happy as they were that day.

"They sound like a fun bunch!" he says, laughing as the waiter brings our drinks.

I go on to tell him about the girls and how our friendship group came about.

"Eve sounds like somebody you would not want to mess with, she terrifies me, and I've not even met her," he says, feigning a look of fear.

I laugh, "I have seen grown men almost in tears in the courtroom, but to me, she's just the girl I grew up with, the girl who used to play in my back garden and have sleepovers. I'm incredibly proud of her. She followed her dream and is living her life exactly the way she wants."

We finish our drinks with easy conversation before he says we should move on to our dinner reservation; he pays the bill and takes my hand as we leave the bar and walk towards the bottom of town.

The temperature has dropped a little but there is still a warm breeze. I can hear live music playing from a bar close by, accompanied by the smell of food being cooked outdoors. It gives me the feeling of being on holiday and I like it. As we walk further through the town, I try to figure out where we might be going. We've walked past most of the nicer restaurants, so I'm intrigued. Maybe there are places I don't know of? That happens a lot here, new businesses struggle to stay open and they are quickly replaced. We start to head towards the cinema complex; maybe a new restaurant has opened there. There was a lovely Thai place a few years back, but it didn't last past its first year unfortunately.

"Here we are," he says proudly as we approach Moonrakers.

Moonrakers is a burger diner, named after the historical people of Wiltshire.

I look around. What am I missing? Is there a secret door? Is it one of those places that is so discreet you don't even know it's there?

He walks towards the small desk at the door of the diner and says words that I can't hear to the girl standing there. I'm still trying to figure out where we could be going.

"Yes Sir, right this way, the rest of the party are already here. Please follow me," she says, flashing him a flirty smile.

Rest of the party?

He looks towards me, clearly not picking up on my confusion. "Are you coming? It sounds like everyone else is here," he says, walking towards me, taking my hand again.

I'm in a state of utter confusion. As he leads me through the doors, I glance around. It's full of families and groups of youths laughing and joking. There's the odd couple but this is not what I was expecting. Everyone is dressed very casually, and I feel like all eyes are on us. We approach a table that is occupied by three men.

"Fellas," says Ben, announcing our arrival, "Sorry to keep you." They all stand up to greet us and start talking at the same time. There's laughter and banter but I can't take it in. I just stand there like a deer caught in headlights. I feel like my feet have taken up root on the spot.

"This is Isabelle," he says as they all turn to look at me, "Isabelle, this is Dave, Jer and Mark," he says as he points to them in order. They all say hello and shake my hand in turn.

My throat is dry, but I manage a feeble, "Hi, nice to meet you all."

I quickly start thinking back to our phone calls and messages. There haven't been many but I'm sure I would have remembered if he had said our date would be with three other people. I don't have a problem with casual restaurants for a date at all, I quite like the lack of pressure that comes with them, but everything over the last few days, the dress, his discreteness, all pointed to something much more sophisticated and intimate.

He pulls out a chair for me and I take a seat. I feel incredibly overdressed and out of place.

"What would you like to drink?" he asks, turning to look at me from the seat next to me. The other three are sat opposite, deep in conversation about the day's events. They've been to a rugby match from what I can gather. At any other time, I would be quite happy sat chatting about sports over a few beers, but I've been caught off guard here, and I'd rather be doing it in jeans and a T-shirt! I can't help feeling I've been incredibly misled about the evening's plans and a feeling of disappointment washes over me. I could leave, be honest and tell Ben that I feel uncomfortable, but as we discovered with the last one, I'm not very good when it comes to walking away from a bad date. I'm far too polite, or so Eve says. So instead I ask him for a glass of wine and peruse the menu. As he heads off to order our food and drinks (nope, not even table service), his friends make polite conversation with me.

"So, you two met online, huh?" asks one with a grin. I can't remember which one is which; this is going to be painful.

"Yes, we did," I reply with a forced smile. They've clearly been enjoying the bar at the rugby, and again, at any other time, I'd find this quite amusing and be joining in the banter, but I have just met them, I'm dressed like I'm going to a frigging opera, and I'm sat in a restaurant (I'm using that word very loosely) surrounded by rowdy youngsters.

Ben returns with our drinks and drapes his arm across the back of my chair in a casual manner. He's removed his jacket, so his attire is much more fitting to our environment; this only adds to my serious discomfort. How can he not see that I look out of place here? Surely, he must sense that I'm feeling uncomfortable. How could he not tell me we were meeting up with his friends? And why the hell did he buy me this dress if he knew all along where he was going to bring me? Did he want me all dolled up to meet his mates? Is he showing me off in some way? My head is swimming with questions but I push them aside.

As the evening continues, I try my best to join in the conversations. I listen to their stories, ask them about their jobs: one is an architect, one a sports coach and the other is a teacher. I couldn't tell you who does what or even who is who, but no matter how hard I try to relax and enjoy the evening, I just feel miserable. I nod in all the right places. I briefly tell them about my store when they ask what I do, but they soon lose interest when I start talking about flowers so I just sit there quietly. Ben, however, is having a great time. He's laughing as they share tales from their university days. Other than names and jobs, no further information was offered on Dave, Jer and Mark so I can only assume that uni is where they all met.

Finally, Ben says we should probably leave and relief sweeps over me. I can't wait to get back to the comfort of my own quiet, cosy home and out of this damn dress. We say our goodbyes. There's lots of bear hugs and handshakes. I feel like it's another hour before we eventually step outside.

"Did you have a good time?" Ben asks as he puts his arm around my shoulders and tilts his head close to mine.

I'm not quite sure how to answer that question. "I didn't know we'd be meeting your friends," I say, trying to sound casual, "That came as a bit of a surprise." Understatement.

"I assumed you wouldn't mind," he replies, "It's not like it's our first date or anything."

Oh. I don't really know how to respond to that. He really doesn't see that he put me in a very uncomfortable position.

"I have to say, I did feel very overdressed for our surroundings." I'm trying my best to sound light-hearted so he doesn't pick up on my disappointment.

"You look stunning, babe," he says, planting a kiss on my cheek.

I can tell I'm fighting a losing battle here, and it's right at that moment that I decide I won't be seeing him again, so I see no point in telling him how I feel about this evening. It will only make the journey back unbearable for us both. I know I'm taking the coward's way out again and I should probably tell him, but honestly, what will it gain? Nothing, apart from unnecessary tension and awkwardness. Part of me was hoping he'd tell me this was a last-minute arrangement, that he didn't want to pre-warn me in case I backed out, or some other flimsy excuse. At least then I'd know it wasn't planned this way. I can't help feeling that I've, unintentionally, been made to look silly and my heart sinks a little.

We get back to the car, he opens the door for me, and we start the journey home. He's such a gentleman in some ways. How could tonight have gone so wrong? I felt like an overdressed spare part, that glossy new tyre that sits in the boot of your car until you need it.

"You're very quiet," he says, interrupting my thoughts, "Are you ok?"

"I'm fine," I lie, "just a little tired. It's been a long week."

"Aren't the boys just a blast?" he says laughing, "The stories we could tell!"

He then spends the rest of the drive telling me them, most of which I have already heard over my chicken burger.

"Here we are," he says as we pull up outside my apartment building. I take off my seatbelt and he turns to face me. "I've had the loveliest evening, Isabelle. When can I see you next?"

Awkward.

"I~~'ve~~ got a wedding and a christening this weekend so I'm busy right through to next week," I say. It sounds pathetic but is actually true.

He undoes his seatbelt, and I can see where this is heading: he's going to try and kiss me. He tilts his head towards mine. "It sounds like you'll be needing some TLC after all of that. Let me take you to dinner again," he says as he leans across and strokes my hand.

I quickly snatch my hand away and pick up my bag from the floor, indicating that I'm ready to get out. "Great," I say as I quickly open the door and run towards the safety of home.

Once I'm inside, I take off the dress and throw on my comfy joggers and a jumper, the make-up comes off and I let my hair fall loose. I pour myself a glass of wine and settle into the recliner on my balcony. I need to just sit and take in the night's events. It's dark now and the town looks like it's gone to sleep. There are a few lamp posts lighting up the walkways. I love that they have used old-fashioned lantern-style lights. They give a soft glow, it looks very atmospheric and feels incredibly peaceful. I hear my phone beep to tell me I have a message. I purposely left it on the kitchen counter so I could gather my thoughts without interruption. I'm guessing it's Ben. Even though I don't know what the message says, I do know that I won't know what to say in reply, so I choose to ignore it and enjoy my wine in tranquil bliss.

Chapter 12

James

It's been a few days since my encounter with Andrea and Will, and I have to be honest, I have kept my distance from them when they've been to visit Billy. I am happy for her, but seeing her again, spending time with her, that kiss, it's brought up a lot of memories and feelings that I can't quite explain. I don't have feelings for her; it's just reminded me of the ones I did have long ago when I was that young man who was finding his way in the world, studying, partying (sometimes a little too hard) and figuring out where his life was going. Oh, how things were simple then, even if I didn't realise it at the time.

It's Friday morning, and I'm looking forward to my last weekend of being on call for a few weeks. We have recruited Jim as our new locum. It's his first day today. Erica loved him. His presence is going to make things a lot easier around here for all of us. He's going to come with me over the weekend on any call outs I get, just to get the lay of the land. It was his suggestion and I thought it was a great idea; he's showing commitment.

I arrive at the surgery early. It's a gorgeous morning; the sun is shining over the manor house sending ripples of sunlight through the cedar trees that frame the entrance, the birds singing are the only sound I can hear, and I can feel the early morning sun on my face. It feels so calm and peaceful. I'm the first one here. I decide to sit outside with my coffee and enjoy the quiet before the day starts. As I sit on one of the benches near the entrance, I see Erica pull up in her black mini cooper. She was on call last night, but she looks well rested so I'm guessing she wasn't called to any emergencies.

"Good morning," I say as she steps from the shiny black motor.

"It's happened, James, it's actually happened!" she says, running towards me, arms waving around above her head frantically. Her sunglasses fall to the floor from her face, but she doesn't appear to notice.

"What are you on about?" I ask, looking at her like she's gone mad, "Are you ok?"

"We're pregnant! Fi is pregnant! We're having a baby!!" she says, throwing her arms around me. "Can you believe it?"

I hug her back tightly. "Are you serious?" I ask, stepping back, holding her at arm's length. "I'm so happy for you both!" I say, squeezing her back against me. I can feel her tears on my shirt, and I'm a little emotional myself. "This is just the best news, Erica."

"I can't believe it's happened," she says as she wipes the tears from her eyes with her fingertip. "I feared it would never happen for us," she continued, almost sobbing.

I'm hugging her so tightly to me, I can almost feel her relief slipping away.

"We can't tell anyone yet, not until we're 12 weeks. You have to keep this a secret; we've waited so long for this, James. You have to promise," she says as she pulls away, giving me a stern look.

"I absolutely promise, scouts honour," I say, holding up my hand.

"You were a scout?" she asks, looking surprised.

"Well, no, but still…" I reply laughing, "You know you can trust me."

"We'd love it if you could come for dinner tonight to celebrate. In fact, Fi is quite insistent. Nothing special, we just want to mark the occasion," she says. She is positively beaming.

I walk over to retrieve her glasses from the floor and hand them to her. "Of course! I'd be delighted! Thank you, what can I bring?" I'm thrilled that they have chosen to share their news with me.

"Nothing at all, except maybe low expectations on the food front," she replies, laughing. "Shall we say seven o'clock?" It's a running joke around the surgery that neither Erica nor Fi can cook. We learnt the hard way when Fi surprised us with cookies one day, solid as a rock!

We sit chatting for a while in the sunshine about the wonderful news when I suddenly remember what Dan has asked me, so I put his idea to her.

"Does he really think it'll help?" she asks. I can hear the compassion in her voice. She has met Dan several times and is full of nothing but admiration for him and what he's achieved. She adores him, and I love the fact that my two closest friends get on so well.

"I honestly don't know," I reply, "but I see what he's trying to do. It's coming from a good place, one of desperation but good nonetheless. I can run puppy clinic one day so I can oversee it; that way I can take responsibility. It would be a good way to throw Jim in at the deep end, see if he floats," I say with a wink.

"Let's get Rachael to check where we stand insurance-wise. If he's under 18, his parents may have to sign a consent form and disclaimer, just in case of any bites. I know they're puppies, but those teeth are like needles," she says, wincing at the thought.

"That's what I told Dan would probably happen. I'll call him at lunchtime and see what the situation is with the boy's parents, and we'll take it from there."

"So, while we're sitting here sharing…." she says cautiously, "Are you ready to tell me about Billy's owner?"

I take a deep breath and run my hands through my hair as I exhale. "The short version is that she was my university girlfriend. We were serious, our parents adored each other, and us, on paper it was perfect, but we were both young and ambitious," I say, shrugging my shoulders to indicate there isn't anything else I can really say on the subject.

"And this is the first time you've seen her since then?" she asks, sounding surprised.

"Yes, when I walked out and saw her there that day, it was the first time in 12 years," I reply.

"Something happened, didn't it?" she asks with an inquisitive tone. "Whilst she's been here, I mean, recently?"

"We shared a kiss, but she told me she had called off her engagement," I say as if I'm trying to defend what happened and my actions. "I had no idea until he walked in that day, I was misled, but she was in shock and upset," I say, now trying to defend her, "I shouldn't have offered her a lift home. It was bad judgement on my part."

"Don't be so hard on yourself," she replies with a sympathetic smile. "You were trying to do the right thing, but yeah, terrible judgement call," she says, giving me a playful punch on the arm.

"I've been doing my best to avoid them when they've been in, just to avoid any awkwardness," I say as I start to walk towards the door.

"I noticed," she says as she steps alongside me, "You disappear off to make the farm visits, which is great because it means I don't have to go." She's not a fan of cows after an unpleasant experience involving one almost trampling on her so she's more than happy to let me make most of the visits.

"He's always with her," she continues, "never leaves her side. I find it a bit odd. He literally watches her every move when she's here."

"He's probably just trying to be supportive," I reply, silently hoping I'm right.

"You say supportive, I say controlling, but hey, it's none of my business," she says, raising her hands in the air as if she's surrendering to the enemy.

I get an uneasy feeling in the pit of my stomach, but I do my best to ignore it. Andrea is a grown woman, she makes her own choices, and I can't imagine her being in a controlling relationship. She was always so headstrong and confident. I really hope that's still the case.

The day goes smoothly. I observe Jim with the animals and their owners, and I have to say, he was the perfect choice. He's compassionate and caring. He's patient when he's speaking to worried owners; he doesn't rush them when he's trying to gain information about their beloved pets, and his diagnoses have been spot on. He's everything we could have hoped for.

"So, how did I do?" he asks as we're getting ready to close for the evening.

"You really impressed us today, Jim, both of us," I say, speaking for Erica too.

"Thank you, I've really enjoyed today. I think I'm going to like it here."

"Would you mind locking up?" I ask, dangling the keys from my hand. "I have dinner plans and I need to stop off somewhere first."

"No problem," he says, taking the keys from me, "Erica has given me the alarm codes. I'll be fine. I was actually going to suggest a celebratory beer but maybe another time?" he asks.

"Absolutely but let's wait until Erica is on call so we can make the most of it," I say with a grin.

"Deal! Now, get yourself off, I've got things here."

I quickly walk to the car and drive into town. I want to get some flowers to take to dinner tonight. I've noticed a florist when I've been walking through but never used them before. I haven't had the need lately. Hopefully it's still open. Just as I pull up, I spot an older lady taking in the buckets of flowers from the front of the store.

"Excuse me, am I too late?" I ask after I've parked up.

"Depends on what you want, love," she replies with a friendly smile, "Tell me the occasion and I'll see what I can do."

I explain that two of my closest friends have received some incredible news and we're having a dinner to celebrate.

"Well, we can't let good news go uncelebrated," she says chirpily, "Come with me inside and I'll make you a bouquet."

"Thank you so much…" I pause, waiting for her to tell me her name.

"Gina," she replies. "I can make you one up at a reduced price as it's the end of the day. Don't worry though, they'll last, they were fresh this morning," she says as she sets to work picking different flowers out of buckets, matching and measuring them up.

"Oh, please don't do that, I'm more than happy to pay the full price. I'm just very grateful to you for doing this as you were about to close."

"Just give me five minutes and I'll have you sorted," she says.

I look around the store. It's bigger than it looks from the front. The décor has a vintage feel to it; it's cosy and welcoming. There are two women sitting behind the counter looking over photos of floral displays. From what I can gather one of them is getting married shortly; the excitement is obvious from the little squeals I keep hearing. One of them is wearing a green apron similar to Gina's so I assume she works here. It's clear from the way they're interacting with each other that they're close friends.

After a little while, Gina reappears carrying the most beautiful bouquet.

"How's this for you, love?" she asks, "Coral and orange roses, pink lisianthus, greenbell and blue iris to name just a few," she says proudly.

"If you say so," I reply with a wink, and she laughs. "It's beautiful. Thank you so much."

"My pleasure. Would you like a gift card to write on? Just choose one from the stand here and I'll pop it in for you," she says handing me a pen.

I pick out a simple plain one with gold etching around the edge.

'I could not be happier for you both, here's to babysitting duties!'

I turn the card over. It simply has 'The Watering Can' typed on the back. I can't help but think what a creative name that is. I certainly won't forget it.

Gina takes the card from me, places it in a small envelope and attaches it to a little stick in the centre of the flowers.

"Gina, you are a gem," I say handing over my credit card, "My friends will love them."

"It's my pleasure; enjoy the rest of your evening," she says cheerily as I take my card and head back to my car. I make a quick stop at my apartment to shower and change my clothes before making the short drive to Erica's.

"James," Fi says as she answers the door. She's dressed in her usual bright colours, pinks, blues, greens; she's quite the sight but I'm used to it now. "How are you?"

"All the better for hearing your news," I say as I step inside, kissing her on the cheek. "These are for you," I say as I hand her the beautiful bouquet.

"Gosh, they are stunning, you shouldn't have!" she says taking them from me.

"Well, it's not every day I find out two of my closest friends are having a baby," I reply. I feel genuinely happy for them and it's such a nice feeling. "What's cooking?" I ask as we walk into the kitchen where Erica is looking harassed.

They have a gorgeous little cottage just on the edge of town. It has its natural oak beams throughout the downstairs, but my favourite feature is the inglenook fireplace. It has the original brickwork still in place. I have spent many a winter night here in front of that fire on the old brown leather sofa with an array of cushions thrown on it, drinking red wine. It's so homey and welcoming; it's my absolute favourite place to be.

"Something half edible, if you're lucky," is the reply that comes from the kitchen, and I chuckle to myself.

"Drink?" asks Fi as we head to the little dining room. The table is set with candles and bamboo placemats. I can't help but feel instantly at home. I always do here.

"I'm on call so just a water thanks. I'll have a small wine with dinner but that's it for me," I reply.

"Good idea, you'll need the alcohol to wash down whatever is being concocted in there," she says, nodding towards the adjoining kitchen.

"I bloody well heard that!"

Fi and I laugh as we walk in to join Erica.

"Thank you for the flowers, James," she says, leaving the oven to kiss me on the cheek, "They're beautiful."

We chat easily in the kitchen whilst Erica finishes cooking before sitting down to eat.

We talk about the baby news, our new locum Jim and how we're both massively impressed with him already. Fi tells me all about a new exhibition at the gallery.

"I'm having an open night for him in a few weeks. You must come," she says enthusiastically, "I'm so excited about this one; it's a new artist I came across recently, and in this town would you believe! His work is incredible."

"I'd love to," I reply, "just tell me where and when."

"Maybe you could bring a date," says Fi sheepishly.

"Fi!" says Erica, interrupting her, "Ignore her, James. I'll be your plus one for the evening."

"What?" asks Fi innocently, "I was only saying he's welcome to bring somebody."

"Thank you, Erica," I say, jumping in, "I'll happily take you as my plus one." I can see her give Fi one of 'those' looks that's telling her she's not impressed.

"This is delicious, Erica, what is it?" I ask changing the subject, and we all start laughing because it's terrible. The chicken is overcooked, I feel like I need a chainsaw to get through it, and there is a strange mixture of herbs somewhere in it. "Please don't feel like you have to tiptoe around my dating. You're like family to me. I know you only have my best interests at heart."

"We just want to see you happy," says Erica, "I can see how much the Andrea situation shook you. I think we'll be able to transfer Billy early next week. I've found a brilliant surgeon in her area."

"It certainly will make things easier once they've travelled back and I'm not worried about bumping into them at the surgery all the time."

"Do you think her fiancé knows who you are?" asks Fi.

"I have no idea," I reply, "If he does, that might explain why he stays by her side during their visits; it might make him uncomfortable."

"I still think something is off there," says Erica, "He always has to be touching her, a hand on her shoulder, or around her waist. It's unsettling to see. Can't you ask her? See if she's ok?"

"It's not my place, you know that," I reply sadly, "She's a grown woman."

"I know, I know," she replies, "I just don't like the thought of anyone being in that kind of relationship."

We sit in a comfortable silence for a minute or two, possibly all thinking about Andrea and what could potentially be a sad situation that she is in.

"So," I say, changing the subject. "I am going to be Uncle James, right?" I ask with a wink.

We chat for a little while longer before I decide I should make a move and leave them to celebrate privately. This is a huge thing for them; they have waited so long for this.

"Thank you again for the beautiful flowers," Fi says as we're standing at the door saying goodbye. "I might use that florist for the open night at the gallery. It's good to support local businesses."

On the drive home, I feel content, happy. I may not have found the person I want to spend the rest of my life with yet, but I am blessed, between Dan, Justin, Fi and Erica, I have all the people I need until I find her.

Chapter 13

Isabelle

I awake to the sound of my alarm beeping away. It sounds unnecessarily ferocious for six am. I lean across the bed to switch it off. The sun is shining through my window already and I can tell it's going to be another glorious day. I have a little stretch in bed before I get up and walk to the kitchen and switch on the coffee machine. Whilst it's whistling away and doing its thing, I walk through my little cosy lounge and open the double doors that lead to the balcony. I can feel the warm sun on my skin and it brings a smile to my face. I have managed to avoid speaking to Ben since our date on Thursday, but I know I need to tell him soon. We've exchanged a few messages; I've told him I'm extremely busy this weekend so we'll catch up properly early next week. It isn't fair to keep him hanging on, and it's not intentional, but I have to focus on this weekend's events. These are big contracts for the business so they need my full attention. I don't quite know what I'm going to say yet. I'm not going to think about that today. I don't want anything to ruin this early morning moment for me. I stand there for several moments before heading back inside. I grab my coffee and get ready for the day ahead.

"Good morning, Luca," I say as I step inside the doors of the deli. "How are you today?" I ask as he turns from whatever he was preparing behind the counter.

"Bella, good morning. I am well, my friend, and you?" he asks with that lovely smile on his face as he starts to prepare my coffee. Another customer enters the store and asks for a bottle of water, an early morning runner it looks like, and a rather handsome one at that! I shake my head and remind myself of the last two dates. Ok the one with Ben wasn't quite as bad as Jason's attempt but it's up there!

"Good morning," I hear a voice say, interrupting my thoughts. Oh, it's him, and he's talking to me! Gosh, he is dreamy. "Morning," I reply, trying my best to give him my 'flirty' smile. I'm sure I look like I've got wind.

Luca and the handsome runner exchange a few friendly words before he takes his water and walks off up the hill.

"I will be closing early today, Bella," says Luca excitedly, "I'm going to the airport to pick up my family."

Embarrassingly, I notice I'm leaning back slightly to get a better look of the handsome runner out of the window.

"I can't wait to meet them," I reply, hoping Luca didn't notice my blatant perving. "Have a safe trip," I say as I take my coffee and head to the store.

Gina is already there. She's agreed to come in early to help with the wedding flowers; we did most of the preparation yesterday, but there's still lots to do today.

"Morning, Gina, how are they looking?" I ask as I walk into the cool room where she is standing admiring our work.

"Aren't they just stunning, love?" she asks, "If only your grandmother could see this," she continues as she puts her arm around my shoulder.

I give her a warm smile. "No time for sentiments; we've got work to do."

The wedding isn't until three 'o clock. I've been assured the rooms where the flowers will be displayed are all air-conditioned so they won't wilt in the heat. It means we can get there early to set up without worrying about anything happening to them.

Dom arrives an hour later with Kate and the van; Kate is going to man the store whilst we set up. The van is small so it will take a few trips, but I would much rather that than squash them all in the back just to get it done in one go. Once the first lot of displays are loaded, we head off to the venue. I go in the passenger seat with Dom, and Gina follows in her car. I really need to think about investing in a bigger van.

The venue is just stunning. It's a big country estate with breathtaking grounds. It has an orchard, orangery, walled garden and its own lake. It's the epitome of romance. I can't help but feel a pang of disappointment at my own ill-fated love life as I look around at the beautifully decorated deck.

Dom gets to work unloading as Gina and I set up the flowers in the room where the ceremony will be taking place. I'm running out of words to describe how beautiful it is here. The room has a high arched roof with windows from the ceiling to the floor that look out onto the lake, the sun is glistening off the water, and there isn't a cloud in the sky. Everything looks so perfect. I can't imagine how the bride-to-be, Libby, is feeling right now. We've met several times to discuss her wishes for the displays and bouquets. We visited the venue together so I could get a real feel of the surroundings. After lots of deliberation, she opted for pale pink and white roses bound together with thick white ribbon, simple yet elegant. Just as Dom heads off to pick up the next lot of flowers, Libby turns up to see how we're getting on.

"Oh Isabelle, I could cry," she says, almost doing so. "They are everything I wanted and more, I don't know how you do it," she says as she glances around the room with a look of complete awe on her face.

"It's my pleasure," I reply. "How are you feeling?" I ask as I put the flowers down that I'm holding and walk over to her.

"So nervous!" she says as she fiddles with the delicate necklace around her neck. "It's silly really. I could not be happier to be marrying Rob, and we've been together for over six years, so there's nothing to be nervous about."

"It's your special day, of course you're nervous. I see brides all the time who feel the same," I say, trying to reassure her, "I think it's perfectly understandable you want the perfect day."

"Thank you," she says as she gives my forearm a gentle rub. "You're right of course. I just want everything to be perfect."

"And it will be. How can it not be in such a beautiful place?" I say as I glance around the room. "And just look at this weather, did you put an order in for this?" I say with a smile as I gesture to the window.

She lets out a little laugh. "It really is wonderful, isn't it? I'm going to leave you to get on. I'm not sure if I'll see you again today but I'll call in the shop next week before we go on our honeymoon just to make sure everything we owe is settled."

"I'm quite sure it is but feel free to stop by and show me some photos." I love to see photos from weddings we've been a part of, how our bouquets look against the dresses, guests sat around tables laughing with our centrepieces taking pride of place, knowing our flowers will be seen in years to come when they look back on their wonderful day. It takes job satisfaction to a whole new level.

Over the next two hours, we transform the dining tables and entrance hall into something spectacular. There are podiums on either side of the entrance to the ceremony room bursting with the palest pink roses and lilies, the table for the guestbook has a simple vase of bright pink begonias for contrast, and the most exquisite floral table runner I think I've ever made lays across the top table. Just before leaving, the three of us take a walk around to admire our handy work.

"I think you've outdone yourself this time, Iz," says Dom proudly, "I don't think you've produced a more beautiful wedding setting in all the time I've been working for you."

"We," I correct him, "we produced a beautiful setting. It may be my name above the door and on all the bills," I laugh, "but we are very much a team. I couldn't have done this without you two." I feel immense pride and gratitude as I stand there with them.

Once I'm happy everything is ready, we all drive back to the store to finish the day. I feel a shift in my attitude as the day goes on. I'm not quite sure what it is. My mood feels lighter somehow. Maybe it was all the romance of the day, but I feel like there's a happy future ahead for me. I have no idea who with, or how we'll meet, but I just know it's going to happen.

"Who's coming for a celebratory drink?" I ask as we get ready to close the store for the day. "First one is on me as a thank you for all the hard work today."

"Ooooh, I could go for a G and T," replies Gina, "One won't hurt before going home and cooking dinner for his lordship." She's referring to her husband Len. They've been married for nearly forty years, and despite what she says on occasion, they still adore each other. It warms my heart to see them together. Don't get me wrong, they bicker like two children, but the warmth, love and respect is always there between them.

"He's welcome to join us," I say but I already know the answer, or a version of it.

"Gawd no, I see enough of him as it is! Thank you but he'll pass this time," she says with a wink.

"How about you two?" I ask looking towards Kate and Dom, "Do you think your parents will babysit for another hour?"

"I reckon so," says Kate, "I'll give them a quick call just to check but I can't see it being a problem."

"Excellent," adds Dom, rubbing his palms together. "I could murder a pint right now; it's thirsty work all that driving and lifting."

Kate confirms her parents are happy to babysit for a while longer. "They're even going to feed them so we may squeeze in two drinks," she says, nudging Dom with her elbow.

"Blimey, quick, let's get going before one of the little buggers throws a tantrum over what they want to eat and they change their minds!" he replies.

We all laugh and set off for The Meeting Place to reward ourselves for a job well done.

The bar is busy, not surprising given it's a gorgeous Saturday evening, but we manage to find a little table tucked away in the corner.

"What's everyone having?" I ask as they get themselves settled. I take their orders and head to the bar.

"Hi, what can I get you?" asks the guy behind the bar.

"A pint of lager, two gin and tonics, and a Sauvignon Blanc, please."

"Coming right up," he says. There's something familiar about him but I just can't place it. He's incredibly handsome, and he has the most gorgeous, friendly, open smile. I'm trying hard to figure out where I could have seen him before, probably in here on one of the many occasions I've visited. Or maybe he visited my dreams, because I am not kidding, this guy is seriously hot! Actually, hot is the wrong word. He's handsome, tall, dark and so handsome. As he comes back over to me with the drinks, I can't help but notice his eyes. They're an incredible shade of blue, almost indigo. Dark hair and blue eyes, that's quite the combination.

"So, anything else?" he asks, and I realise this is the second time he's asked the question. I can feel my cheeks redden. Was I staring at him?

"Umm, no, thank you, that's all," I say as I hand over my bank card.

"Thank you, enjoy your evening," he says with a smile.

I pick up the tray of drinks and walk back to the table, feeling a little flustered. Where the hell have I seen him before? Maybe he's been in to buy flowers for his significant other. Just my luck.

We spend a pleasant hour discussing the wedding. I show Kate the photos on my phone that I'd taken whilst we were there.

"Why didn't we get married somewhere like that?" she asks Dom with a dramatic frown. "I had to make do with a registry office and a cheap buffet!"

"And you loved every minute," he replies, giving her a kiss on the cheek, "You would have hated the pressure of a big day." He's right. I know Kate well enough to know she hates a fuss. She doesn't even like us mentioning her birthday, let alone celebrating it.

I can't help but feel happy sitting here with my team. I'm fortunate enough to be able to call them my friends.

"Right, love, I need to make a move. Len will want feeding, heaven forbid he cooks for himself or for me," she says with a roll of her eyes, but I know she would not change a thing about him. They have been blessed with two children, grown up now of course, and five grandchildren. I'm not even sure she needs to work; I think she just loves the store and what she does. "I'll be in tomorrow to help with the christening," she continues, "around eight o' clock; does that work?"

"You really don't have to," I tell her, "I can manage this one on my own. It's a fraction of the size of today's wedding. I can have everything set up in an hour." I know that Sundays are family days for her, big Sunday roast and boardgames. It's also the only day we're closed so I really don't expect her to come in and help. "Most of the prep is done anyway."

"Well, if you're sure. How about I open Monday morning? Give you a morning to yourself to make up for working on a Sunday?" She really is the sweetest person.

"That's really kind of you. I'll call you tomorrow and let you know if that's ok. You know I don't like to put on you."

"I'll go in and help out," says Dom, "You take the morning to relax, and we'll see you at lunchtime with some of those meatball sandwiches from Luca," he says winking at me.

"It's a deal," I reply with a laugh.

"We should probably make a move, get the kids home and to bed," says Kate, "Thank you for the drinks, Iz. It's nice to get together like this; we should do it more often."

"I agree," I say as I glance across to the bar. He's laughing and joking with another of the barmen. I can't help but feel a little kick of something, excitement maybe.
As they all leave, I decide to sit for a minute and finish my wine. I wonder about today's wedding and I really hope the day has been beautiful for them. Every bride and groom deserves a special day. Looking at the weather, I can't see how it could have been any other way.

"I see your friends have all left." There's no mistaking that voice. I turn to see him standing next to my table. "Can I get you another?" he asks with that gorgeous smile.

I can feel my face flush a little. Damn wine. I'm blaming the alcohol, but I think it's a combination of that and my attraction to him. Compose yourself, Iz.

"I'm fine thank you; I'm just going to finish this, and I'll be leaving," I reply with that attempt at my flirty smile again, and then it hits me. I know where I've seen him: the Deli this morning. He was the hot runner!
"Well, enjoy the rest of your evening," he says as he takes the empty glasses from the table and walks towards the bar.
How have I not seen him here before? He obviously works here. Maybe he's new? I could sit here all night looking at him and drinking wine, but I have the christening tomorrow, and he'd probably think I was some weirdo stalker, so I pick up my bag and head for the door. A takeaway and a movie are on the cards tonight instead.
"Goodnight," he says with a wave from behind the dark wooden bar.
I swear my tummy is doing backflips. All I can manage is a pathetic raise of my hand in response as I walk quickly out of the door.

Chapter 14

James

I wake up to another beautiful morning. The birds are chirping away outside my window, and I can feel the warmth of the day already. I pick up my phone and see that despite the sunshine creeping through the window, it's still early. As I lay there, I think back to last night's events and the wonderful news the day brought, and I can't help but smile. I know Erica and Fi are keeping the news to themselves until they hit the safety of 12 weeks, but I just know everything is going to be ok, and that before we know it, they'll be bringing home a healthy new bundle of joy. I get up and walk to the kitchen to switch on the coffee machine then change my mind. I didn't get called out last night which means I'm well rested, and for the first time in a long time, I feel full of optimism, so I decide to go for an early morning run instead.

I put on shorts and T-shirt, lace up my trainers and head outside into the glorious sunshine. As I run through the streets towards the river, it strikes me how peaceful it is at this time of day. I run along the river path, watching the swans, cygnets, ducks and even a heron as I go. A few people are sitting outside their canal boats, enjoying coffee in the morning sunshine, making the most of the peace no doubt before the paths get busy with cyclists, dog walkers and families. It's a popular spot for picnics; you often see paddle boarders and canoeists on the water, but not this morning. Other than the odd early morning dog walker and resident, I'm alone and it is perfect. Before I know it, I'm on the return journey and almost seven kilometres in. I stop on a bench overlooking a field of sheep and stretch off. I'm sure I'll be feeling today's efforts tomorrow, but right now, I feel great.

As I walk back towards home, I stop in a little deli to buy water. I usually bring some with me when I run, especially in this heat, but in my eagerness to get out into the glorious weather, I completely forgot this morning. I've passed this place many times before but never been in. It looks lovely from the outside. It's obviously Italian. The front is painted in neutral browns and beiges, and it gives it a welcoming and friendly look.

"Good morning," says the man behind the counter, finishing his conversation with the only other customer in there. "What can I get for you?"

"Morning," I reply, "just a bottle of water please." I turn to look at the other customer and offer a polite "Good morning" in her direction.

"Morning," she replies. I can't help noticing what a lovely smile she has.

"Lovely morning for a run," says the man behind the counter as he reaches into the fridge. "I was quite the runner back in my younger days, couldn't do it now though!" he says with a chuckle. I can tell by his accent he's Italian so I'm guessing he's the owner. "I have trouble keeping up with the grandchildren, well, trying to anyway," he continues.

"I'm sure running around with little ones is much more fun, although it was beautiful along the river path this morning, very peaceful," I say as I pay for my drink. I don't know what he's baking but it smells incredible. My tummy gives a little growl at the smell of food. I must come back here and try out the delicious-looking food he has on display.

"Oh, I'm sure it was. Best time of the day if you ask me," he says with a smile. "Enjoy the rest of your day."

"Thank you, you too," I reply as I leave the deli and head up the hill towards home.

Once I'm showered and changed, I make myself scrambled eggs on toast for breakfast. My thoughts wander again to my love life, or rather lack of it, to how lovely it would be to have somebody to make breakfast for, to sit here on the stool next to me at my little breakfast bar planning our day, but they are soon interrupted by the work on-call phone ringing.

"Hello," I say, answering it, "James Lowry." I hear the familiar voice of one of our regular callers, Anthea. She owns a livery yard but also has several of her own horses. She describes the symptoms of one of her mares to me. She's quite right in guessing it's probably colic. She's had this problem with other horses in the past, so she knows what to look for.

"She's sweating profusely and violently rolling around on the floor," she tells me, "I'm quite sure it's colic."

Given her experience and knowledge when it comes to horses, I'm inclined to trust her judgement. "Try to keep her walking around if you can. I know it's difficult, but as you know, it will help. I'll be there in about twenty minutes," I say, picking up my car keys before I've even hung up. Colic, if left untreated, can cause death in horses so time is of the essence. I ring Jim from the car and tell him we've got a call and he agrees to meet me there. I give him directions to Foxglove Stables and hang up. Luckily the roads are still quiet, so I make good time and arrive fifteen minutes later. Jim arrives five minutes after me. I give him a quick rundown of the horse and her symptoms, and we get to work. I listen for sounds from the horse's stomach with a stethoscope whilst Jim checks her vital signs. I notice how well we work together.

"You don't think it's displacement colic?" he asks as he strokes the horse's bloated abdomen to try and calm her. That type of colic needs immediate surgery but I'm sure that's not needed this time.

"No," I reply standing to join him, "I think we can get away with a nasal tube," I say feeling thankful. Operating on a horse this size is no mean feat and takes an awful lot of planning. I stand back to look at the beautiful mare. She's a stunning chestnut colour with a white strip down her nose; the shine on her coat is dazzling. "Is she one of yours?" I ask as I turn to Anthea who is watching anxiously from the stable door.

"She is my pride and joy," she says attentively, "Will she be ok?"

"She will," I reply reassuringly, "we'll put a stomach tube in to relieve some of the gas. Is she halter trained?" Jim gives me a hopeful look; he knows that we have a good chance of tubing her without sedation if she is.

"It was the first thing I did when I got her," Anthea replies, "so it shouldn't be a problem."

"We deal with all your horses, but I've not come across her before. Is she new?" I ask as we set up to get her tubed.

"No, I've had her for four years. Erica has been out to her a few times."

"Right, are we all ready?" asks Jim as we get set. Anthea has seen this before so she's a great person to have help us. "You halter her, and we'll get this done as quickly as we can."

Ten minutes later, the tube is in. We all take a step back and observe the beautiful mare for a few minutes.

"I'll stay in here with her today and through the night to make sure she doesn't try to get it out. I won't sleep anyway," says Anthea wearily.

"We'll come back tomorrow morning to see how she's getting on," I say as we start to pack up our equipment, "but if you have any concerns before then just call me. If she gets worse, or distressed, we need to know straight away." I feel a bit patronising telling her all of this, she knows what to look for, but it's good to reiterate it.

"Great work," I say to Jim as we head back to our cars, "I think we're going to make a great team."

"Thank you, I appreciate you saying that," he replies as we stand and take in our surroundings. Foxglove Stables are set on a huge estate. Horses are their main business, but they have been known to hold the odd wedding here to help with the extortionate costs of running the place.

"Fancy a little stroll around before we leave?" I ask him.

"Absolutely, lead the way."

We walk up the gravelled drive towards the main house. It's built of old natural stone; wisteria climbs the walls and frames the door. Just to the back of the house there are two small cottages. I've never been in them, but they look tiny. I assume it's where employees lived years ago. There are curtains and trinkets in the windows, so they must still be in use, holiday lets maybe. Huge oak trees give a perfect amount of shade from the morning sun. One of Anthea's assistants is walking a horse around the training ring with a small child on the back, clearly a new student. His parents stood watching proudly from the side, mobile phones out snapping away to capture the moment.

"There are far worse places to get called out to on a sunny morning," says Jim, shielding his eyes as he looks around.

"Oh, there are, and trust me, you will get to visit them all during your time here," I reply with a laugh.

"Can't wait," he replies with a hint of comical sarcasm.

On the drive home, my phone rings. I can see it's Dan.

"Dan, how's it going?" I say as I answer.

"Mate, I need a favour," he says, sounding desperate, and I know what's coming. "Two of my staff have called in sick; any chance you could help out tonight? Just a few hours to get us through the rush? I'll throw in one of our burgers for your dinner," he says hopefully, knowing how much I love the food there.

"I can, but I'm on call so I may have to leave if anything crops up. That's the best I can offer."

"Amazing! I bloody love you," he replies, sounding relieved, "I owe you big time."

"I'll add it to the list," I say jokingly. I don't mind helping him. It beats sitting at home alone in my apartment with take away pizza waiting for the phone to ring. "What time?"

"We usually get busy around five o' clock, but I'll take whatever you can give me. Thanks again, man, I really appreciate it." I know he means it.

As I drive through the lanes back towards town, I can't help but think how lucky I am to live in such a beautiful place. The old farmhouses are spectacular, as is the countryside and fields that stretch for miles and the sun peeking through the trees. My thoughts are again interrupted by my phone ringing. I press the handsfree button to answer.

"James, hi," says the familiar voice at the end.

"Andrea, what can I do for you? Is Billy ok?" We discharged him just yesterday; his leg is plastered to keep it stable and in position for when he gets transferred to the clinic in London for surgery. I haven't dealt with Andrea at all. Erica kindly agreed to take over all aspects of Billy's care, including liaising with her and Will. He's been given antibiotics and pain meds to take to keep him comfortable and infection free.

"He's fine, doing great actually. He's eating and seems comfortable. I was wondering if you were free for a coffee today. We travel back to London Monday, and I'd really like to meet up before we leave. You've been so wonderful with Billy, it doesn't seem right to just leave."

I inhale deeply and run a hand through my hair in the hope it will delay my response. Is this a good idea? Is there anything left to say between us?

"I'm on call this weekend so I may get called away, but I could meet you shortly. I'm just heading back into town now." James, you idiot, I silently chastise myself.

"Perfect, where?"

I give her the name of a little quiet café in town, and we agree to meet in half an hour. It's a chance to say goodbye properly, let her know there are no hard feelings between us, and wish her well. I don't want to leave things the way they are now, so I decide this is a good thing and retract my self-chastising.

I arrive at the café before her. I find a table and order coffee. It's a lovely little locally owned coffee shop. The décor is simple with wooden tables, fake flowers in little vases, and plastic wipeable menus. It's one of the few places that survived the pandemic.

I soon see her walk through the door. She, as always, looks beautiful. The stress and worrying about Billy have gone and she looks radiant. She has her glow back, the one that I knew so well all those years ago.

"James," she says as she kisses me on the cheek, "Thank you so much for meeting me. I know you must be busy if you're on call."

"I'm just back from a visit so I'm hoping for a little reprieve before the next one," I say as I pull out the chair for her.

The waiter takes her order of a coffee, and we settle into a few seconds of comfortable silence.

"I didn't want to just leave without saying goodbye, and thank you, for all that you have done not only for Billy, but for me too. You have gone above and beyond, and I am so grateful, James. I'll never forget your kindness," she says, looking at me attentively.

"There's no need to thank me. I was just doing my job, and part of that is making sure the owners are supported," I say truthfully.

"Oh, come on," she says with a hint of a smile, "How many owners do you offer to drive home?"

"Ok, you've got me there," I reply with a little laugh, "I wouldn't do that for just anyone, but you aren't just anyone. You were a huge part of my life, the biggest part of my life for a long time."

She takes a deep breath before replying. "I also wanted to explain about Will…"

I cut her off. "There's really no need. You were upset, distraught, it doesn't matter," I say, taking a sip of my coffee.

"It matters to me," she continues, "I need you to know that I didn't purposely mislead you."

I don't respond. I just let her continue. She clearly wants to explain her situation.

She looks down at her hands folded in her lap. "Will and I have been engaged for just under a year. Before coming to Wiltshire, I told him I needed some space. He can be a little intense sometimes and I felt like I couldn't breathe." Her eyes have a sadness to them as she's speaking. "But I know he loves me, and we'll have a wonderful life together. When I told him about Billy, he travelled here without me knowing and just arrived at the lodge. I was upset and agreed to give things another try. I am so sorry I wasn't completely truthful with you." She clasps her hands around her cup as though she's looking for some kind of comfort.

Her words concerned me. She said he loved her, but not once did she mention her feelings for him. "Can I be honest with you, Andrea?" I ask cautiously.

She nods her head slowly, not meeting my gaze.

"He may love you, but do you love him?"

Her pause is long, and it feels intense. "In my own way, yes, I do. We have fun, he treats me so well, we'll have such a wonderful life together."

I stay silent, forcing her to continue.

"I'd like to have children one day soon and he'll make a wonderful father."

I'm not satisfied with her answer, and by the way she is constantly avoiding my gaze, I know that she knows it, but it's not my business and I realise very quickly that I shouldn't have asked.

"I'm sorry for asking; it's not my place. I just want to see you happy," I say, and I genuinely mean it. She deserves to be happy.

"I am happy," she says with a sad smile, but I don't believe her for one minute.

"I should probably go. I've promised Dan I'll help him out at the bar tonight," I say, realising there really is nothing left for us to say to each other.

"You're a good friend to him. I'm so glad to see that you are still as close as you were all those years ago. It's incredible how he's turned his life around," she says with a genuine warmth to her voice. "Please tell him I said goodbye; we need to get ready to leave so I won't have a chance to call in and see him myself."

I'm sure this isn't true, and that she would make the time, but she wants to avoid any awkwardness and I get that. I also appreciate it.

We both stand to leave at the same time. She picks her bag up from the table and puts it over her shoulder. We stand and look at each other for a moment before I step forward and put my arms around her. I know this is the last time I will see her.

"Take care of yourself, Andrea," I whisper quietly into her ear.

"You too, James," she replies as she pulls away, wiping a tear from her eye. "You are going to make one lady very lucky in the not-too-distant future, I just know it," she says with an affectionate smile.

And with that she's gone. I feel a sense of sadness wash over me, not for myself, but for her.

A few hours later I walk into The Meeting Place, a little earlier than I planned, but I need to keep my mind occupied after seeing Andrea.

"Am I glad to see you," says Dan as I walk behind the bar, he throws a bar towel at me, which I catch, and I know it's my cue to get to work.

I remind him that I'm on call so may have to leave but his appreciation at me even being here is clear.

"How's the day been?" he asks as he pulls pints, "A busy one?"

"Not workwise, no, just the one call so far, but I did see Andrea today," I say, trying to sound nonchalant as I load the glass washer.

"We need to discuss this further," he replies, still pouring drinks, "but obviously not now. Are you ok?" he asks with a hint of concern in his voice.

"I'm good," I reply honestly, "Closure, my friend, closure."

A little while later, I see a familiar face walk into the bar, it's that lovely lady from the florists last night, what was her name? She's with a few other people; should I go over and say hello? She was incredibly helpful, but I decide against it. I doubt she'd remember me anyway. One of her companions comes over to order drinks; she looks familiar too, maybe I saw her whilst I was in there buying flowers. She's very cute. She has a friendly warmth to her which I feel drawn to, but the place is packed so I don't have time to chat to her and I can't help but feel disappointed. Over the next hour or so, I catch myself glancing over to their table. I can't figure out the dynamics between the four of them, but they look relaxed and happy. I take a quick break and sit in Dan's office to eat the delicious burger I was promised. It sure beats another takeaway or meal for one, which is what would have been waiting for me at home. When I return to the bar, I notice she is sitting alone. She looks deep in thought. The empty glasses on the table are a perfect excuse to go over.

"I see your friends have all left," I say as I approach her table. "Can I get you another?" I say nodding towards her almost empty glass of wine.

"I'm fine, thank you; I'm just going to finish this, and I'll be leaving," she says with a smile.

Why would she sit here alone when her friends have gone? She's probably got a husband or partner at home waiting for her. I bid her a pleasant evening and take the glasses from the table back to the bar. Just a few minutes later, I see her walking to the door to leave.

"Goodnight," I say with a wave and a big sigh to myself as I carry on serving thirsty customers.

Chapter 15

Isabelle

I am so grateful that Gina offered to open the store today, giving me the morning off. Yesterday's christening turned out to be harder work than I thought. The child's grandmother was incredibly demanding, and his poor mother spent the entire day looking defeated and worn down. I've met her a few times to discuss her requests and she has been lovely, but her mother-in-law was a force to be reckoned with. My plan to be in, set up for an hour, then home was severely scuppered. By the end of the day, I felt like her personal assistant. Nothing was good enough: the flowers were too pale, there wasn't enough 'green stuff' in them (her actual words), she didn't like the shade of blue of the ribbons holding the bouquets together, the vases weren't shiny enough…. It went on and on. I explained several times that I had gone over every detail with Gail, the boy's mother, but I was told in no uncertain terms that she should have been involved in the planning. Four hours after arriving, I left with my patience completely vacant and a major headache. Poor Gail, her life must be made very difficult by that woman. She apologised to me profusely as I left for the behaviour of her mother-in-law and my heart went out to her. She looked close to tears. Her day had been ruined, a day when she should have been celebrating with her family and enjoying her role as a mum. I was extremely grateful to get home, pour a glass of wine and find a trashy romance to watch on TV. I went to bed feeling much more relaxed and hopeful of finding love. God bless Netflix.

This morning I'm making the most of my break and I'm meeting Eve for breakfast before she heads for court. She's desperate to hear about my date with Ben. She knows it was yet another disaster but I have withheld the details so far, for two reasons really. One, I just haven't had time to fill her in properly, and two, I haven't really wanted to relive it, but I think it will be good to talk about it now, get another perspective on the way he behaved, though maybe Eve isn't the best one of my friends for this. She's a bit of a feminist so I can imagine what's coming when I give her all the gory details.

I have also agreed to meet Ben tonight after work. I can't keep putting him off. I'm still not sure how to handle this one. Part of me wants to give him the 'I just didn't feel it' speech that I'm all too familiar with, giving and receiving, but the other part of me wants to be honest about how he made me feel, to find out if it was intentional or not on his part. I'm hoping I'll figure it out as the day goes on.

"So," says Eve as we sit at a table and wait for our breakfast and coffee. "Is this another one I'm going to really dislike? I mean, I wasn't his biggest fan after the dress stunt so I'm wondering how much worse it could have gotten," she says, looking at me intently.

"It wasn't the most romantic of evenings, that's for sure. I got quite excited when I saw the direction we were heading, but guess where he took me?" I say with a hint of humour. She starts to reel off some of the fine dining establishments she is very familiar with in the next town. She dines out with clients on a regular basis. "Not even close," I say, holding my hand up to interrupt her on her fifth guess. "Think burgers, teens having a bite before a cinema trip, families having a quick dinner out before putting the kids to bed…."

I don't need to go on.

"Moonrakers? No way?! Are you kidding me?" she replies, looking infuriated. All I can do is laugh in response and nod my head slowly.

"And you went all out in that dress to go THERE?!" The young girl serving us doesn't quite know where to look as she puts our plates and coffees in front of us from the tray she is balancing. I smile at her enthusiastically as she hurries off.

"Yes," I reply as I take a sip of my coffee, "I felt ridiculous, like everyone was looking at me, but it gets worse."

She gives me a nod to continue as she tucks into her eggs benedict.

"He'd arranged to meet some old uni friends there who were here for a rugby match…."

"And he didn't tell you?" she asks, interrupting me.

"No, he did not. I wouldn't have minded so much had I been dressed a little more casually and he'd told me. They don't get to see each other much so it wouldn't have been an issue, and they were actually good fun, a little inebriated, but nice guys."

She puts her fork down and sits a little taller in her chair. "Let me get this straight," she says, sounding serious, "he buys you a dress, a stunning one I'll admit, sends it to your place of business, leading you to think he'll be taking you out for a sophisticated dinner but ends up taking you to a teen hangout to meet his drunken friends?"

I think about it for a second before replying because that's exactly what he did. Hearing Eve put it like that makes me feel the humiliation of the night all over again.

"So, he dressed you up like a bloody doll to show you off to his friends? Christ, what a prick! I'm so mad for you, Iz."

"I was mad too," I say, giving her a little smile, "but I'm over it. I've been putting him off since then, but I've agreed to meet him tonight after work. I need to tell him we won't be seeing each other again. It's not fair to keep him hanging."

"What he did to you wasn't fair!" she replies with a renewed anger in her voice.

"I know, I know, but maybe it wasn't intentional. Maybe he just didn't realise how it would make me feel."

"I've said it before and I'll say it again, my friend, you are just too damn nice, always trying to see the good in people. It's admirable, but this time I think you're wrong. I think he knew exactly what he was doing."

"Really?" I say, wrinkling my nose at her.

"Yes really. You need to be straight with him about this and how he made you feel. He should know, and don't you dare worry about making him feel bad. I know what you're like; you'll come away feeling like the bad person. Well, I am telling you, Iz, HE deserves to feel terrible and guilty; don't you hold back when you speak to him!"

I decide to change the subject before she blows a gasket and goes looking for him herself, so I ask about her court case today and we finish our breakfast whilst debating how far a person should go to protect their family from an intruder in their own home.

I get to the store just after 11. Gina is busy chatting to a customer. She's put together the most beautiful white bouquet and I can't help but feel proud of what we have become. It's a feeling I've become very familiar with and one I won't ever take for granted.

"Hello, love," she says as she waves off the happy customer, "how was the christening?"

I give her a look that she knows well, one that demonstrates exactly how the day went without the need for words.

"That bad huh? I best get the coffees," she says as she heads to the back of the store.

Later that afternoon as I'm washing down the coolers, we hear the screech of tyres on the road outside. I run to the door to see what's happening, promptly followed by Gina. We get there just in time to see a car speeding off down the road.

"What the…" says Gina but before she can finish what she's saying we spot a cat in the middle of the road. Together we rush over to see if it's ok.

"It's breathing, but not really moving," I say as I stroke its little ginger head, "There, there."

"What should we do?" asks Gina as a small crowd gathers around us, "We can't just leave it."

"I have an old blanket in my boot," says a man who has pulled over to see what's happening, "We could wrap it in that to keep it warm."

"Perfect, thank you," I reply as I try to think what to do next, "We need to get it to a vet. Pop the closed sign in the window and lock up," I say to Gina, nodding towards the store. "Grab the van keys and we'll take it up to that vet's, the one in the old manor house. I think that's the closest. You drive and I'll call them on the way so they know we're coming."

As Gina heads off to get the van, I wrap the little cat up in the blanket and scoop it carefully into my arms. A minute or two later, we're flying through the lanes on our way to Cedar Lodge. I'm holding the poor little thing close to me as instructed by the vet nurse I just spoke to; she said it will help keep it warm and minimise any movement just in case anything is broken. I keep stroking its head trying to keep it calm. I have no idea if it's helping or not. Its tiny body starts shaking profusely in my arms. I assume it's caused by the shock. Looking down at its little face covered in blood, I feel so helpless.

Five minutes later, we arrive at the surgery and head inside with the little bundle.

"Hi, I'm Emily, we spoke on the phone," says the nurse as she gently takes the cat from my arms, "Thank you for bringing this little one to us; you've probably saved its life," she says with a gentle smile. "I'm going to take it to the back now so James our vet can take a look. As there's no tag, we'll check for a microchip so we can inform the owners. Would you mind leaving your details at the desk before you leave? It's just standard procedure for our records."

"Of course, will it be ok to call later to see how it's getting on?" I ask anxiously.

"Absolutely, I have to get him checked now. It's a boy, but we'll speak later, and thank you again," she says as she disappears through some double doors.

I leave my details with the receptionist, and we head outside into the warm air.

"Blimey," says Gina as we sit on a bench to gather our thoughts. "That's not how I expected the day to go! I hope the little thing is going to be ok," she says as she takes a deep breath.

"I hope they manage to find his owners," I reply thoughtfully. "It's beautiful here," I continue as I look around our surroundings, "and the building is stunning. I wonder how they managed to get an animal hospital here."

"I think it was left to an animal charity by a rich old vet when he died and they turned it into this. It's got quite a reputation for the work they do here. From what I've read in the local paper, it's one of the best in the southwest," says Gina, almost proudly.

"Good, that means we have left him in very capable hands," I say as I stand up and stretch. The sun feels great on my skin. "Come on, the store won't run itself and we have orders to put together," I say as I give Gina's arm a little nudge.

The rest of the afternoon passes without any further drama and before I know it, we're getting ready to close for the day. I pick up my phone and call the vet to check on our little friend.

"He's doing well," I say to Gina as I slide my phone into the back pocket of my jeans. "A broken rib and a few cuts; he's one lucky kitty!"

"Any luck finding the owners?" she asks as she picks up her bag ready to leave.

"Unfortunately, the microchip has a phone number on it that's no longer in use. Emily said he'll have to go to the rescue centre once he's well enough. Hopefully the owners will look there for him."

"Let's keep our fingers crossed then, love. I'm sure he'll be reunited with them soon enough. I'll see you in the morning. I'm off to make his Lordship his favourite tea before spending a riveting evening in front of the telly," she says with a roll of her eyes. She doesn't fool me. I know she wouldn't want to be doing anything else this evening. I'm keeping the faith that I'll find my 'favourite tea and telly' companion, but for now, I have to meet Ben and put some closure on our date.

We've arranged to meet at a little coffee shop that stays open in the evening. I thought this would be better than a bar; that would feel too much like a date and this is definitely not one of those. He's already there when I arrive. He looks so damn handsome. Do not get distracted, stay focused on the matter at hand.

"Hi Ben," I say as I approach the table, "how are you?" He stands to kiss me on the cheek. We order coffees and make small talk for a few minutes.

It's a cute little coffee shop. It's got a French bistro feel about it: wooden chairs in a mix of dark and light wood, little tables with a marble style finish, and vintage framed pictures are dotted around the beige walls with French writing. It's quite lovely.

"I'm sensing I'm about to be told thanks but no thanks," says Ben, cradling his coffee cup in his hands. "It's nice here but this doesn't feel like date number three," he continues, sounding a little apprehensive.

Ok, here goes…

"I have to be honest, I felt quite uncomfortable on our date last week…"

"It was the mates, wasn't it? They made you feel that way. I'm so sorry, Isabelle, I'll speak to them…" he says, interrupting me.

I hold my hand up to stop him. "Please, let me finish." Eve would be proud.

"It wasn't quite what I was expecting. You sent me that gorgeous dress which indicated to me that we were going somewhere, umm, a little more…sophisticated, so I was quite surprised to end up where we did. I felt incredibly overdressed amongst all the teens and families; it felt like everybody was looking at me." Don't stop now, Iz, you've started so you have to finish. "I had no idea we were meeting your friends which only added to my feeling of embarrassment. Don't get me wrong, I liked them, they seem like great guys, and if the situation had been different, I probably would have had a really pleasant evening, but I just felt humiliated, like you'd sent me that dress knowing I'd make an effort, just to put me on show in front of your friends." I can feel my cheeks redden a little at the memory.

We sit in silence for what felt like forever but in reality was probably only about ten seconds. I wasn't going to say anymore, so I sat there waiting, almost forcing a response from him.

He's staring down at his cup. "I'm sorry." It was said in such a muted tone I barely heard him. I don't respond. I need more than that.

He slowly raises his head to look at me. "In hindsight, I think that's exactly what I did. Sitting here listening to you saying it like that, yeah, that's what I did." He looks back down towards his cup. The confident, assured guy I'd met on our first date seemed to vanish before me. He looks unsure and anxious.

"I was going to ask why, but it really doesn't matter now. I just wanted to be honest with you rather than brush you off with the usual excuses. I didn't think that would be fair," I say, looking at him sadly. Seeing him like this, I can't help but feel that the image I was presented with on our first date was just a façade and this is the real Ben, the one sitting in front of me now.

"I really am so sorry," he says with genuine intention as he stands to leave. "Goodbye, Isabelle."

"Goodbye Ben, take care of yourself," and with that, he's gone.

I'm not concerned that there was no explanation. I don't need one now; it's done. I'm extremely proud of myself for not taking the easy option. Honesty was definitely better. I don't like that I made him feel bad, if that's even the case. He seemed genuinely sad and sorry. I really hope that he finds happiness.

Before I head home, I type a quick text to Eve.

'All done, you'd be proud of my bravery, I was totally honest with him. Hope court went well, speak soon xx'

I take a slow walk back to my apartment. The town is alive with the sounds of laughter, al fresco dining, soft music and chatter. The air is warm, and I can feel a light breeze on my face. I can't help but think about our little kitty friend from today and wonder how he's doing. I make a mental note to call tomorrow and check on him, but for now it's PJ's and a microwave meal for one in front of the TV.

Chapter 16

James

Monday morning arrives and it's another beautiful day. Despite a few call outs over the weekend, it's passed quickly and pleasantly.

Today is the day the young, troubled teen, Dylan, is coming to attend puppy clinic. We've received written consent from his parents, basically saying they agree not to sue us if he happens to get nipped by one of the little pups. It's highly unlikely it would be taken further if it did happen but that's what the insurance company wanted, so that's what we've provided. Unfortunately, it's highly likely he will walk away with a nip or two. I'm still not sure what Dan is hoping to achieve by this. I mean, I see the thinking behind it, but if Dylan really does see the world as a bad, terrible place, then I don't see how a few cute puppies will change that, but like Dan said, maybe a day away from his troubles might just help, even if it's only temporary.

"Good morning," I say as I walk into the reception area of Cedar Lodge. "How was your weekend?" I ask Rachael as she sips her coffee behind the desk.

"Morning, James," she replies with a smile. "It was fine, thank you. There's somebody here to see you," she says nodding to the seats behind me.

I turn to see a young boy sitting there. His hair is in dire need of a cut. He can barely see through it hanging over his eyes. I can see he's tried to make an effort with his clothes; a red and black checked shirt that is about three sizes too big for him hangs over black trousers that are a little on the short side, and he's wearing black shoes that look like they might fall apart at any moment. Dan told me he comes from a very disadvantaged background and my heart instantly goes out to him.

"Dylan?" I ask as I walk towards him and offer my hand out to shake.

He stands up and shuffles uncomfortably on the spot as he reaches for my hand. "Yes," he says quietly.

"I'm James, it's lovely to meet you. Dan has told me a lot about you," I say as I pull my hand back, "I'm sorry I wasn't here when you arrived. I wasn't expecting you until 9.30." I don't point out that he's an hour and a half early.

"My brother dropped me off on his way to work. I didn't have the money for the bus," he says, looking at the ground.

I try to ignore the tugging feeling in my chest. He's clearly embarrassed so I move away from the subject.

"I assume you've met Rachael. She's our receptionist but really she does a whole lot more than that; the place wouldn't run without her," I say, giving her a wink.

"I'm glad you've noticed," she replies with a laugh. I notice Dylan smile slightly at this.

"As you're here, how about you help me get set up and I'll tell you what's involved in the puppy clinic," I say, trying to sound upbeat, but honestly, my heart could break for this kid. There's a real sadness around him, like something has just sucked all of the happiness and joy right out of him. "I hope you've had a good breakfast; these puppies can be hard work!"

"I didn't eat yet," he replies almost inaudibly.

I'm not one to judge at all but something tells me Dylan doesn't get regular meals.

"Is anyone else in yet?" I ask Rachael.

"Tim is out back," she replies, "and I think Emily has just pulled up." She looks at me quizzically.

"Perfect," I say as I pull out my wallet and hand her a few notes. "It's my turn to buy breakfast today, remember?" I say giving her a look that she instantly understands.

"Ah yes, I do believe it is," she says with a knowing look, "Bacon butties all round?"

"Dylan, how does a bacon sandwich sound?" I ask casually.

"Wow, great, thanks," he replies, smiling, "Are you sure?"

"Absolutely, it's the best way to start the day in my humble opinion!"

As Rachael heads off in her car, I introduce Dylan to Tim and Emily before we start setting up the clinic.

"So, you like puppies?" I ask as I hand him a spray bottle and cloth to clean the surface we'll be putting the pups on. It's not all fun; he needs to do some of the actual work too.

"Always wanted one," he says as he sprays the countertop. "Was never allowed one" he replies sadly.

"Well, they are a huge responsibility, as you'll find out today," I say as I get the injection packs ready.

Just then, Rachael appears with breakfast and we all head to the staff lounge to eat together. The team is great with Dylan. I briefed them about his background a few days ago. I thought it was only fair that they all knew what to expect, as much as we could know anyway. I wasn't even sure what to expect. Dan gave the impression of an angry young man filled with hate but I'm yet to see that. The conversation is kept light, no mention of school, friends, family or future careers. Dylan is engaging and polite. He takes a real interest, asking about the strangest animals we've treated and our favourite patients… So far he's a pleasure to have around. He seems so different already to the boy sitting waiting for me only an hour ago.

"Ummm, what's going on here?" asks Erica as she walks into the lounge. "Special occasion, is it?" she asks as she looks at the empty wrappers and plates from our breakfast on the table. "Where's mine?"

"Snooze, you lose, early bird catches the worm…" I reply as everyone starts clearing the table. "Dylan," I say as we both stand from our seats, "this is Erica, my partner. Erica, this is Dylan."

"Nice to meet you, Dylan," says Erica with a warm smile. "It's lovely to have you here with us. Don't let James work you too hard, always thinks he's the boss," she says, winking at the young lad.

"Ok ok, enough," I say laughing. "Come on then, let's get this clinic started," I say as Dylan follows me down the corridor.

"So, she's your girlfriend?" he asks shyly.

It takes a second to register what he's just asked. "Oh good lord no," I say laughing, "she's just a work colleague and a very good friend."

"Oh," he says, sounding embarrassed, "you said she was your partner, so I thought…" He tails off before finishing.

"In business only, we run the practice together," I reply with a laugh. "I love her dearly but purely as a friend."

Our first puppy of the day is a 10-week-old Cockapoo named Charlie. Adorable is an understatement. Dylan is clearly taken with the little ball of fluff. He watches intently as I place treats on the counter and inject the puppy without so much as a flinch from him.

"Doesn't it hurt them?" he asks as Charlie and his owner leave the room. "I hate injections."

"Did he look like it hurt him?" I ask, "He was so focused on the treats in front of him, he didn't even notice. They just need a distraction, and puppies are easily distracted, especially with treats."

"Yeah, I guess that makes sense. He didn't even move when you put the needle in him," he replies with a subtle little shudder.

I check the computer to see who our next patient is. "Would you like to call our next patient from the waiting room? Her name is Willow, just walk out and ask for her and bring them through."

"Oh, ok, I can do that," he replies as he heads off to the waiting room.

When he returns, he is closely followed by the most gorgeous little whippet puppy. She's a beautiful grey colour and, those eyes, it's like they can see right through you, right into your soul.

I go through the formalities of introducing myself to her owner, and explaining that Dylan is observing today. It's always polite and professional to introduce everyone in the room.

"Here, now watch as I put the treats down, she'll be so focused on eating them, she'll be injected before she's even swallowed them," I say as I quickly squeeze her skin together and put the needle in and out again.

"And just like that she's done," I say, patting the little pooch.

"Can I hold her?" he asks, looking at me hopefully.

"We'd have to ask her owner that. Mrs Peters, would you mind?"

"Not at all, she loves a cuddle. She'll be a real lap dog, I can just tell already."

I watch closely as Dylan carefully picks up the dog and brings her into his chest.

"She's so tiny," he says as he nuzzles into her neck with his nose, "I feel like she might break."

I can't help but wonder how much affection he gets shown at home. I know he's a teen but all children, no matter their age, should be shown love.

"Right, we have other puppies to see. I'm afraid you need to pass her back now," I say with an exaggerated comical frown which is met with laughter from both Dylan and Mrs Peters. "Any problems, you know where we are," I say as we wave them off.

"You have the coolest job," says Dylan enthusiastically as we wipe down the counter before calling in the next one. "You get to do this every day."

"Well, not quite this every day. I'll show you around when the clinic is finished, give you a better idea of what really goes on. This is just a tiny bit of what we do here."

As the morning passes, Dylan's confidence grows. He chats to the owners, asks every single one if he can hold their dogs. He's polite, calm and courteous. He really is a pleasure to work with. When we have seen our last puppy of the morning, we clean and tidy the examination room before I give him a tour of the building.

"So, some old rich dude just left the building to you?" he asks as we walk around the grounds in the sunshine.

"Not to me personally no, to a charity who then turned it into this hospital which is exactly what he wanted it used for. I then moved here from London to work here. I fell in love with the place as soon as I saw it," I say looking around proudly, "I've been here ever since. I could never go back to living in London now."

"London sounds insane! I would love to live there!"

"You may think that, but after a while, it loses its appeal. Well it did for me anyway; some people love it and could never imagine leaving."

We chat a little while longer about the practice and what we do there. "How are you getting home?" I ask, suddenly aware he is only meant to be with us for the morning and it's already gone one.

"I don't actually know," he says, all of that confidence suddenly gone. "I think I'll be walking. My brother doesn't finish work until tonight." I notice he's looking down to the ground and I sense he's embarrassed about his situation.

"I have a few errands to run in town. Why don't I drop you off on my way through?" I don't have errands to run and I have no idea where he lives, but the look on his face tugs at my heartstrings.

"I don't need pity," he says a little angrily, "I know why you got me breakfast earlier, and now offering me a lift. I don't need your charity." I notice a sudden change in his whole demeanour. It's subtle but obvious enough for me to know I've hit a nerve. I need to find a way to calm the situation down before it escalates.

"I don't pity you, Dylan. I just want to make sure you get home safely; you'd have to walk the country lanes and I've seen how people drive around them. I'd only worry about you all afternoon, so you'd be doing me a favour, not the other way around."

"Why would you worry?" he asks gruffly, "You've only just met me; you don't know me."

"You're right, I have only just met you. I would worry about anyone walking these lanes, and technically you are still on my watch so it's my responsibility to keep you safe," I say, hoping that's enough to diffuse the situation. "Plus, you've met Dan, can you imagine what he'd do if I didn't get you home safely? He thinks a lot of you, and everyone else from the youth centre, so basically, I have to take you home whether either of us likes it or not. I value his friendship too much not to," I say with a hint of humour.

"I guess when you say it like that…" replies Dylan as he shades his eyes from the sun with his hand.

"Cool car!" he says as I open the passenger door for him, "Really nice ride, man."

"Thank you, though you wouldn't say that if you saw it covered in mud from all the farms I visit. It's recently been cleaned so you're seeing it at its best today."

He gives me his address and I let the satnav do the rest. It's a part of town I don't know so I'm happy to be guided. I try to keep the conversation light, but I want him to know how much I've enjoyed today.

"It's been a real pleasure working with you today, Dylan, you've certainly got a way with animals, they loved you."

"I'd love to be a vet," he says quietly, "but I'm too stupid, not clever enough for that. My dad says I'm no good at anything."

I can feel my jaw clench and my grip on the steering wheel tighten. I take a minute to choose my next words carefully. I can't outright say his father is wrong, that wouldn't be appropriate, and I'd hate to bring any trouble to the practice if my words were repeated to him. "You can be anything you want to be if you put your mind to it and put in the hard work. I genuinely believe that." He doesn't respond, so I decide not to say anything more on the subject. We finish the drive in silence.

"You can just drop me here," he says as we approach a block of flats on the outskirts of town. "I can walk from here; there's no more lanes, it's just around the corner." He's already undoing his seatbelt so I pull over.

I open the glove box and pull out one of our business cards. "If you ever want to visit or need anything, that is my mobile number. Just give me a call, we'll gladly have you back," I say, handing him the card.

"Thanks for the ride," he says as he takes the card and gets out of the car. I have no idea if he'll keep it or not, but I had to do something. I drive back to the surgery with a heavy heart and a lump in my throat.

"Good timing, James," says Rachael as I walk through reception, "Somebody is bringing in a little cat that's been run over. It's not hers, it happened outside of her store. No tag so fingers crossed it's chipped."

"Thanks for the heads up. I'll get the exam room ready. No Erica or Jim?"

"Both on call outs," she replies, "Hence your good timing. Emily spoke to the lady so she might know more about the cat's condition."

I find Emily already getting the exam room ready. "I don't really know much, sorry," she says before I have a chance to ask her. "They just heard a car screech off and found the poor thing in the road, covered in blood but breathing."

"Well, that's something," I say as I wash my hands ready for the imminent arrival, "I'll finish getting everything ready here. Why don't you wait out the front for them?"

A few minutes later, Emily walks back in with the cat wrapped in a blanket. I can see a lot of blood around its face. Emily lays him gently on the exam table and I get to work checking him over. It turns out he has a broken rib and a few cuts, one nasty one to his mouth which needs stitches. He's one lucky cat; it could have been so much worse. Due to an out of date chip, we can't trace his owners so he'll be off to the rescue centre once he's recovered and well enough. Jim is on call tonight so he'll be here to keep an eye on him.

As I drive home that evening, I can't stop thinking about Dylan and his situation. I don't know how Dan does this all the time, how he deals with the emotions that working with these kids on a regular basis must bring. I decide to call in and see him at the bar to let him know how today went.

"Hey, man," he says as I walk into the bar. It's busy but not manic so we'll have time to talk. "I was going to call you later to see how today went with Dylan. You saved me the trouble," he says as he walks out towards me from behind the bar.

"I knew you'd want an update," I say as we sit at a couple of bar stools. I go on to tell him about my morning with Dylan and give him a rundown of what happened when I offered him a lift home.

"That sounds like Dylan alright. I really feel for the kid, but I can only do so much."

"I have no idea if he'll keep my card or if it's in a bin somewhere. I couldn't just leave him there," I say, running my hands through my hair. "I don't know how you do it, my friend, I take my hat off to you."

We chat a little while longer about Dylan before he brings up the subject of dating.

"So, what's next on the agenda on the dating front?" he asks, trying to sound casual but failing miserably.

"Nothing. Nada. No thank you," I say with confidence, "I think it's time to take a break again for a while. It's exhausting to be honest."

"No more online hookups?"

"There have been no hookups as you well know," I say, doing my best to sound stern. "On that note, I'm going to leave you to it and head home for my pasta meal for one."

"You're not getting any younger, James…" he calls after me as I walk through the tables towards the door.

"Don't I know it," I mutter under my breath.

Chapter 17

Isabelle

It's been a busy week, but Friday is finally upon us. Rebecca has popped into the store to discuss all things wedding. She is positively glowing; she's oozing happiness.

"So, you've got your outfit sorted, even shoes?" she asks, sounding surprised.

"Yes, even shoes, with a little help from Jess, but I have them, and a bag!" I reply with a look of mocked shock.

"You just need your plus one now then," she says as she sips her tea.

"There will be no plus one, I'm afraid. You have been here the last few weeks, right? You were there when I retold every painful detail of my date with Jason, and you know what happened with Ben! How can you possibly want me to continue this perilous path of online dating? Or any dating for that matter."

She put her cup down to respond.

"And before you tell me how online dating worked for you and Isaac," I say before she has a chance to start talking, "you two are an exception, I'm sure of it."

"I just want to see you happy, Iz. I don't want to watch you give up on love and happiness."

"I am happy," I say, and I genuinely mean it. "Yes, it would be lovely to have somebody, I admit that, but I can't keep going on these awful dates. It's hard work. I'd rather keep my sanity and stay single."

We sit in comfortable silence for a minute or two.

"Oh, I haven't told you. I'm thinking of getting a cat!" I say excitedly. I go on to tell her about our incident on Monday with the stray cat. "Nobody has claimed him, so the poor thing is at the shelter. I went up on Wednesday to see him. They don't think he's even a year old. He can be our store cat."

"Please don't tell me you're going to turn into an old cat lady, you know the ones who have like twenty cats and no life?" she asks. I'm not entirely sure if she is serious or not. "And don't you prefer dogs?"

"Of course not, he'll spend his time here at the store. I'll have a cat flap put in the back door so he can come and go as he pleases," I say smiling at her, "and yes, I do generally prefer dogs, but this little kitty has stolen my heart. Plus I can't really have a dog in the store. It's fate," I say, dramatically holding my hand over my heart.

"Eve is going to love this...." she replies laughing. "What do you think, Gina?"

Gina has been pottering around the store quietly, but no doubt listening to every word intently.

"Oh pet, it doesn't matter what I think. She's already picked out names for him," she says, rolling her eyes dramatically.

"Names?" she says, looking at me.

"Sage, Thistle or Juniper. I can't quite decide," I say thoughtfully.

Just as we're saying our goodbyes, a customer walks into the store. "I'll leave you to it," says Rebecca as she kisses me on the cheek. "Think about what I said, and no more blooming cats!"

"So, he can't be my plus one for the wedding?" I ask with a wink as she walks out of the door. "Can I help you?" I ask the lady. "Or are you just browsing?" I can't help but notice her colourful clothing and bright smile. She looks like somebody's favourite aunt, warm, comfortable, and trustworthy. I can't quite guess her age. I feel like the baggy, colourful clothes she's wearing make her appear older than she is.

"Hello, yes, help is definitely what I need," she replies, looking around at the array of flowers on display.

"I'm Isabelle," I say holding out my hand, "I own the store. What can I help you with?"

She takes my hand and shakes it warmly. "Fi," she says, "artist, and complete flower novice. Pleasure to meet you; you have a beautiful store."

"Thank you," I say proudly. "Let's have a seat," I say as I guide her over to the counter and pull out a stool for her.

"I own a gallery just down from here, 'The Galleria', it's on the corner near the little Italian Deli."

"Yes, I know it. I pass it every day. Coffee is my vice so I'm in the Deli almost daily," I reply with a smile, "I often stop to look at the beautiful artwork in your window."

"Oh, you must pop in some time and I'll show you around," she says beaming, "Sorry, I digress. I'm holding an art show next Friday. I know it's short notice, we've had to bring it forward due to the artist involved having family commitments he can't change. I need a few flower arrangements to go on the tables and maybe a big one for the entrance. I'm not quite sure really," she says laughing, "Art I have an eye for, but flower arranging is out of my comfort zone. I can paint them but that's my limit."

Before I have a chance to tell her how busy we are at the moment, she carries on.

"A friend of ours gave us a beautiful bouquet from here and I just knew I wanted you for the job. They were stunning."

I'm a sucker for a compliment about my work. "We are extremely busy at the moment, it's wedding season and it is very short notice but flattery gets you everywhere,"

I say with a smile. I walk around to the other side of the counter and pull out our portfolio.

"You'll do it? Thank you so much," she says, standing to hug me, "You are my saviour!"

I have no idea how, but I'll do it.

We spend the next twenty minutes looking at pictures and finalising a few choices. She tells me about her wife Erica who is a vet.

"We needed one of those recently, poor little cat got run over on the road just out the front there. We took him to that beautiful old manor house that's now an animal hospital," says Gina, "I can't remember what it's called now."

"You mean Cedar Lodge? That's where Erica works," says the lady, "He was certainly in the best hands if that's the case."

"I'm thinking of adopting him. He hasn't been claimed yet, and he was just adorable. I hate the thought of him stuck in a rescue centre," I say, joining in the conversation again.

"Well, wait until I tell Erica that. She'll be down here thanking you personally," she says, laughing. "Joking aside, what a lovely thing to do."

"My friend is now concerned I'll turn into a bitter old cat lady who has given up on love so I'm not sure she'd agree but thank you," I say as Gina walks past and rolls her discreetly eyes at me. "Wouldn't hurt you to settle down, love," she says as she starts cutting some rose stems and putting them in a vase on the counter.

"Never give up on love," says the customer, putting her hand gently on top of mine. "Keep your heart open to possibilities, you never know what's around the corner," she says with a wink.

"Do you know nice bachelors?" says Gina laughing, "Before she adopts any more cats!"

"My matchmaking days are behind me. That's gotten me into trouble too many times. I prefer to leave it up to the universe now, much more reliable if you ask me," she says with a hearty warm laugh.

We say our goodbyes and I promise to call into the gallery tomorrow to have a look around and get the lay of the land for the flowers.

"What a lovely lady," says Gina as she continues to arrange the roses, "She has a kindness about her."

"She really does. I like her a lot. Right, I'll be out the back having a clean up if you need me," I say as I head to the back of the store to wash out the flower containers.

A little while later when I'm completely lost in my chores, Gina pops her head around the door. "You've got a visitor," she says, looking at me apprehensively.

I give her a questioning look. "Your mother," she mouths without any actual sound coming out.

Oh no. I forgot to call her back the other day, and now she's here. Gina can see the look of anguish on my face. "No rush, love, I'll make her a cuppa and keep her busy for five minutes. You do what you need to do."

"Thank you," I say to her quietly as I make a prayer gesture with my hands.

I can hear them chatting away as I wash my hands and try to flatten the loose bits of hair I know are floating around my face. I know exactly what's coming. The same interrogation I've had for the last few years. The answers remain the same.

"Mum," I say as I walk towards the counter where she's sitting with Gina sipping her coffee. "How are you? I'm sorry for not returning your call, we've been flat out here the last few weeks," I say, giving her a kiss on the cheek.

"Me? I'm fine, dear, it's you I'm worried about. What have you been doing back there?" she asks as she holds me at arm's length to 'inspect' my appearance. "Surely as the person in charge here, you should look more presentable. More like the boss?" Before I have a chance to respond, she holds my hands in hers. "And those nails. Let me take you for a manicure. I'm sure Gina can manage, can't you, Gina?" she asks.

I look at Gina's bemused face and shake my head subtly, letting her know not to agree.

"How will you ever meet a man when you walk around like this all day?" she says, waving her hands at me. I take stock of her appearance before replying. Her perfectly blow-dried hair, French manicured nails, the cream linen suit that is completely free of wrinkles....

I can't help but sigh before answering. "Please don't, mum, we have this conversation every time. I'm at my happiest like this. I don't want to walk around looking like the 'person in charge'. I want to walk around looking like a florist, one who enjoys her job." I can hear Gina audibly take a deep breath.

"Fine," she replies haughtily, "Can you at least freshen up a little so I can take you for a coffee? Would *that* be ok?" The emphasis on the word 'that' is not lost on me.

"Gina, can you manage for half an hour whilst I have coffee with my mother?" Please say no, please say no.

"Of course, love, take your time," she says, giving me an apologetic look.

"Give me five minutes," I say as I head to the back to remove my apron and find a brush.

"Why don't we get a take away coffee and sit down by the water?" I ask as we step out into the sunshine.

"Or we could find a nice little café that does proper coffee and has a decent seat," she replies.

I feel myself sigh again and I resist the urge to defend Luca's fantastic coffee. It's not worth the hassle, so instead we head to one of the many little coffee shops to find a 'decent seat'.

"So, tell me the latest dating news?" she says excitedly as the waiter puts our drinks in front of us. "You really need to start focusing more on settling down and less on that little shop of yours."

I can feel myself tense in my seat. I silently remind myself to at least try and rise above her comments. I should be more than used to them by now. "That little shop as you call it is my livelihood," I say calmly. "It was your own mother's pride and joy, and now it's mine."

"What about me, Isabelle? Have you thought about me? I'd rather like to be a grandmother myself whilst I'm still young enough to enjoy it," she says almost sulkily.

Please God give me strength, I plead as I raise my eyes to the sky above. I resist the urge to point out that she would never be one to roll around on the floor playing with grandchildren or take them to the park for fear of getting anything on her perfectly clean clothes. "I'm sorry you feel that I'm not considering your feelings when it comes to my future." I don't mean it to sound sarcastic, but I think it came out that way. Or maybe I did mean it, I'm not entirely sure. "I'm not going to just settle when it comes to love and my future happiness." I again resist the urge to say something completely inappropriate; that wouldn't help the situation at all.

My mother remarried soon after my dad left, but she married for money and stability, not love. Richard is never there, always away on business to God knows where. Her life consists of lunches with women who I don't think are even her friends, wives of Richard's business acquaintances I think, shopping, and trips to the salon to keep up her appearance. I was eight when they married. As soon as I turned eighteen, they decided they were moving away from Wiltshire, and I moved in with my grandmother. They live in a beautiful house in West London, far too big for just the two of them; they have a live-in housekeeper so at least she has a bit of company when Richard is away. I make her sound shallow, but she's not. I think she just married too young, and Richard provided what she needed when she felt abandoned and feared being a struggling single parent. I don't believe she is entirely happy; she must get lonely. I've tried spending more time with her, but she does not make it easy. I always come away feeling flat and deflated so I've been keeping my visits brief lately, hence the surprise trip to see me today. Maybe now isn't the best time to mention that I don't think I'll be having children anytime soon, but I may be getting a cat…

"How's Richard?" I ask, keen to change the subject.

"You'd know if you visited us more," she replies with that sulking tone again. "He's fine, thank you for asking. He's in Dubai for a few weeks. I'm not sure when he's back."

Let it go, Iz, let it go.

When we've said our goodbyes and I've walked her back to her shiny little Mercedes convertible, I decide to walk in the sunshine for a while. I love my mother but it's draining being in her company. Of course I want children, she knows that, but seeing the way she's chosen to live her life has shown me exactly how I don't want to live mine.

"Is your sanity still intact?" asks Gina when I return to the store.

"I love her, but she does test my patience," I say with a sigh, "At least any visits between us are usually planned so I have time to mentally prepare; she caught me off guard today. I know she must be lonely, but she does make it very hard to enjoy spending time with her." I can feel guilt creeping in. Should I try harder? Should I make more effort to see her?

"I know what you're thinking, love," says Gina, reading my mind. "I also know how hard you've tried with her over the years. Trust me when I say you've got nothing to feel guilty for. She is a grown woman who has chosen a certain lifestyle; she can't expect you to change who you are to accommodate those choices," she says, giving my arm a squeeze. "Please tell me you told her about the cat?" she says with a wicked grin. I can't help but laugh at that.

As we start getting ready to close for the day, Jonathan comes in for his weekly order. "Hello ladies," he says with a smile that is filled with smarm and overconfidence, "Looking as lovely as ever."

He makes me want to throw up. "The usual," I say, handing him the bouquet.

"She'll love these, she's been so busy this week with the children and school events. I feel rotten that I've been away for most of it working."

I'm quite sure you don't, you jerk. "Enjoy your evening," I say as I hand him back his credit card.

Later that evening, I sit out on my balcony enjoying a glass of wine in the early evening sunshine. I think back over the day. I think about my mum. I realise I actually feel a little sorry for her. I know she made her choices, but I don't think she made them thinking she'd end up lonely (which I doubt she would ever admit she is, but how can she not be.)

Loneliness. Ugh. I pull out my phone and reluctantly open the dating app. I'll just have a little browse for now. What harm can it do? Then maybe over the weekend, I'll pay a little visit to Sage, or Thistle, or Juniper. I still haven't quite decided what to call him yet.

Chapter 18

James

Hello Friday, am I glad to see you. Don't get me wrong, I love my job, but a weekend ahead without being on call is a very welcome thought after a busy week. Not that I have any plans. It'll be like most of my weekends off, go for a run or two, catch up with Dan and possibly Justin if family commitments allow, and then wallow in loneliness and self-pity. I won't do that of course, it's not in my nature, but I may get lost in a box set to pass the time.

"Morning, sunshine," says Erica as I walk into the coffee room at the surgery. She is positively beaming.

"And good morning to you too. You look like you got out of bed on the right side today. How's Fi doing?" I ask as I make a discreet round belly motion.

Erica laughs. "Great actually. No sign of morning sickness or anything so far. We have tons of appointments coming up. Carrying a baby at 42 comes with risks, which we knew of course, but it's still all a bit daunting. I'm determined not to let it take away any of our joy; we've waited so long for this. She's taking every pregnancy supplement under the sun, eating all the right things, avoiding everything she's been advised not to have. We just have to leave the rest up to nature."

I honestly could burst with happiness for them.

"Oh, before I forget, she's asked me to let you know that the art show is now happening next Friday."

"Art show?" I'm a little puzzled for a second.

"The one she mentioned at dinner. I'm your plus one, remember?" she says with a cheeky wink.

"Ah yes, I'll have to check my ever-expanding diary to see if I have any hot dates that night…"

"Hey, are you saying I'm not hot or a date?" she says with a teasing tone.

"Ha! You are my only date that night, hot or not!"

"You cheeky beggar," she says, giving me a not so gentle thump to the arm.

"Of course I'll be there, and I wouldn't want anyone else as my plus one, unless Julia Roberts is free…."

"Dream on, my friend, dream on! Right, let's get the day started." She grabs her coffee and heads out of the door just as Jim arrives.

"Nothing personal, but I think I have a budgie waiting for me," says Erica.

"I've been turned down for worse," he says with a grin. "Morning, everyone."

"Morning Jim, I'm not sure what's waiting for me, but I best go and find out. Catch you later," I say as I head towards reception to see who my first patient of the day is.

Lizzie. It turns out Lizzie is waiting for me. She's sitting in one of the big tub chairs in our waiting room. She doesn't appear to have an animal with her, so I have no idea why she's here. I can't help but notice how tired and pale she looks. She's looking down at her hands clasped tightly in her lap. "I was just coming to find you," says Rachael as I approach the desk, "You have a visitor."

"Thank you, Rachael. Is my first patient here yet?"

"Nope, you've nothing booked for half an hour."

"Lizzie," I say as I approach the chair. She jumps a little.

"Sorry, I was miles away. How are you, James?" she asks as she stands.

Do I hug her? Kiss her on the cheek? I opt for a brief kiss on the cheek.

"I'm great, thank you. This is a surprise. What brings you here?"

"I was hoping I could talk to you, I know you're busy. I promise I won't take up too much of your time." She looks sad, lost even. Definitely not the Lizzie I'd met previously.

"Why don't we take a walk outside? I don't have anything booked for half an hour. It's too nice to sit in here."

We walk out into the sunshine. There's a welcome gentle breeze; it's the perfect summer morning. We walk slowly towards the back of the building. We could go for miles from here. She pulls her sunglasses from the top of her head to shield her eyes. I'm not sure if she's keeping them from me or the brightness.

"I owe you an apology," she says sadly, "I'm so ashamed of my behaviour that day. I thought I'd never be able to face you again, but I had to do this in person. I'm sorry I didn't call or text first, but I was worried you would make an excuse not to see me."

"You don't have to apologise. Honestly, it's forgotten, it's in the past. Please don't feel ashamed."

"I also want to thank you for your kindness. Some men would have taken advantage of that situation, but you were a complete gentleman, and your friends too. You were all so lovely to me. I realise now I have a problem. I lied when I said it wasn't a regular occurrence to drink that much. I'm not just a social drinker. I'm a daily drinker. I drink excessively every day. I'm an alcoholic, James, I just didn't know it." She stops to pull a tissue from her bag and wipes her eyes under her glasses. "That date made me realise I cannot go on like this. I've spoken to my doctor who has been wonderful. I won't bore you with the details of my planned recovery, but I know I'm on the right path and I know I can do this. I'm determined to do this."

"Lizzie, I am so sorry you are going through this. I think you are being incredibly brave. Reaching out and getting help isn't easy, and I can't imagine what it must have taken for you to come here today and tell me this. Do you have support?" I remember her saying her dad not being present and her difficult childhood, but I'm not sure about other family relationships. I instantly think of Dan.

"I have only told one friend, and my boss. I had to tell him. I had no choice. He suggested I take a month off to focus on getting well, which I've agreed to do, and now you of course. My doctor says once I forgive myself and get over the shame I'm feeling, I'll feel more confident in sharing what I'm going through with others, but for now, I don't want anybody else to know. I'm at the start of my journey and it's very personal. I'm worried I'll be judged by friends and family, and I can't deal with that just yet."

"I understand that, but please know that anyone who loves you won't judge you. They'll support you and be there for you."

"I really hope so," she replies sadly. I can see the tears falling below her glasses.

"I have a friend; he's a recovering addict, he's completely turned his life around. There's no pressure, but if you want, I can put you in touch with him. He holds meetings for addicts once a week but if you don't feel ready for that yet, I'm sure he'd be happy to meet one to one, just for a little support from someone who's been there." I don't want to mention that it's Dan. I can't even remember if she met him that day, and I know there are huge confidentiality issues around these meetings. I know he'll be more than happy to meet with her, but she has to be ready to accept the help.

"I guess it couldn't hurt to meet with him. Do you think he'd mind? What if I'm not quite there yet? I'd hate to waste his time." She looks so despondent.

"Trust me, he won't mind, and I promise you won't be wasting his time. If you're not ready when you meet him, then you just contact him again when you are. There is no pressure at all." I notice we've looped around and we're now back at the front of the building. I hold my hand out towards a bench. "Shall we sit for a minute?"

We sit in silence for a minute or so. She puts her glasses back on top of her head and looks around. "It's beautiful here, what a lovely place to work."

"I never take it for granted," I reply, following her gaze around the fields that surround us.

"I should probably go, no doubt you have a busy day ahead. Thank you again, James," she says as she puts her hand on mine. "I can't thank you enough for your kindness, not only that day, but now. I knew you were special the day we met, and this meeting today has only reinforced that."

"No thanks needed, please just take care of yourself. Are you happy for me to pass on your number to my friend? It's totally your call." I'm keen to emphasise again that there is absolutely no pressure from me.

"That would be great," she says as she stands to leave, "Thank you," she says again as she kisses me on the cheek before walking to her car.

I sit there for a while, taking in what's just happened. I'm full of admiration for what she's done and will continue to do. I know if anyone can help her, it's Dan. I think about calling him, but I decide this is probably better discussed face to face. I sit for five more minutes before heading back inside to see my first patient.

As I'm getting my exam room ready, Erica pops her head around the door. "And who was that?" she asks quizzically.

"You don't miss a trick! That was Lizzie." She gives me a baffled look. "We went on a date, and she had a little too much to drink…."

"You really aren't narrowing this down for me," she says laughing. I give her a stern look. "I'm joking, yes, I know who you mean now. What was she doing here? I saw you talking outside; she looked upset. I know you're a looker and totally charming but you can't have broken her heart that quickly!"

"Funny," I reply, "She was here to apologise; she's getting help for her drinking. She confessed she drinks every day and has spoken to her doctor. She didn't know, or maybe didn't want to admit she had a problem until what happened on our date."

"Well, don't I feel like an absolute jackass now for making jokes, sorry."

"Don't be, you didn't know."

"But what did she want from you? Another chance?" she asks.

"I honestly don't think she wanted anything from me. She just wanted to apologise, maybe she wanted somebody to confide in, I don't know, but there was no mention of anything further between us, and as a newly diagnosed addict, that would be the last thing she needs right now. She needs to focus on herself, get help, and get better."

"That's a lot for her to tell you. It must have taken some balls for her to come up here."

"That's exactly what I said, although I didn't quite phrase it like that, of course. I told her how brave she is for reaching out and getting help, and that she shouldn't be ashamed. It's an illness like any other. I'm going to put her in touch with Dan, with her permission of course, and then when she feels ready she can reach out to him."

"You really are a lovely human being, do you know that, James Lowry?" she says as she hugs me, "You didn't have to be so understanding; some men may have reacted very differently."

"I think when you've seen somebody you love struggle with addiction, it makes you more empathetic. I just hope she recovers. I've seen Dan do it, and we all know what dark place he got to, so I know it's possible. Ok, let's change the subject now, something lighter please." I smile as I say it but my heart feels heavy for Lizzie.

"Oh, I've got some news that will put a smile back on that handsome face of yours," she replies excitedly.

"Go on, I'm all ears."

"So, Fi went to that florist to ask if they could put together some arrangements for the art show, which they have agreed to do so she's ecstatic. Turns out that's the store that poor little cat got run over in front of on Monday, apparently nobody has come forward yet to claim him so the owner there is thinking about adopting him! Isn't that a lovely thing to do?!"

"It really is. I think I met her when I went to buy the flowers, lovely older lady, Gina, if my memory serves me correctly."

"I'll keep you posted. Fi will be seeing her a few times over the next week so I'll ask her for updates. Right, stop chatting and get some work done," she says as she leaves the room with a spring in her step.

After work, I drop my car off at my apartment and walk into town to see Dan. When I arrive, the bar is busy but I know he'll make time for a quick chat.

"Hey, I wasn't expecting to see you tonight," he says as I approach the bar, "Beer?"

"Please," I say, taking a seat on one of the bar stools. "I was actually hoping to have a chat with you about something," I say as I take a sip of the pint he's just poured me. The coolness of it is feels wonderfully refreshing.

"Here or out back?" asks Dan.

"Maybe out back will be better."

"What's up?" asks Dan as we sit in his office, "You look troubled."

"I had a visitor at the practice today. Remember Lizzie? The date I had to bring back here?"

"Really? Now I'm intrigued, go on."

"It turns out she has a drinking problem. She came to apologise again and to tell me she's spoken to her doctor and is getting help."

"Wow, that must have taken some courage. So that day wasn't a one-off then?"

"Apparently not. She said she drinks daily and to excess. She's taking a month off work to focus on recovery."

"She'll need a lot longer than that unfortunately. Do you know what her recovery plan is? Is she going to rehab?" he asks, looking concerned.

"I honestly don't know. It didn't sound like rehab was on the cards. She said she didn't want to bore me with her plans. I was wondering if you'd meet with her, just to chat, offer a little support and make sure she is getting the right help," I say, giving him a very hopeful look.

"Of course, but does she know you're speaking to me about this? You know she has to be ready; it has to be on her terms, I can't push anything."

"I asked if she'd be happy for me to talk to you about it; she said it was ok. I didn't mention you by name, I just said a friend. I didn't go into details about your past, that's not my place, she just knows you've been there and you hold meetings, but I said if she wasn't ready for that, maybe you could meet one to one for now. I know you're busy, and I'm sorry to put this on you, but I knew if anyone could help, it would be you. I don't think she has much support; I know she's told one of her friends but other than me and her boss, that's it."

"Don't apologise mate, this is what I do. I'm more than happy to help, but I think you should pass on my number to her so she can contact me when she's ready. If I contact her first, she might feel pressured into meeting with me. She's at her most vulnerable with regards to her recovery journey. Tiny, baby steps are the way to move forward. How did you leave things with her? I'm worried you're going to feel obligated to support her through this. I know what you're like, too bloody decent for your own good sometimes. She can't do this on her own, but you can't be the one to help her."

"I genuinely don't think she's expecting anything from me. She said thank you, kissed me on the cheek and got into her car; it felt quite final."

"I know you'll want to keep in touch just to see how she's doing, but for the sake of her recovery, it's best that you don't. If you give her even a hint of anything more, she'll latch onto it and that could be disastrous for her, especially at this stage."

"I'll text her to pass on your number, but other than that, I won't contact her, and honestly, I don't think she'll contact me. She looked beaten down, but she sounded determined."

"I'll do what I can," he says as he puts his hand on my shoulder, "She's got a hard, long journey ahead."

"Thanks, Dan, I really appreciate this."

"So, how's it going with online dating? Any new dates lined up?" he asks as we walk back to the bar.

"I haven't even looked at it for days. I don't think I've been in the right headspace for it to be honest after Andrea turning up like that."

"Yeah, I get that, but she's gone now, she's moved on. Now it's your turn, unless…don't tell me you have feelings for her again?" he says, stopping in his tracks.

"No, absolutely not. I'm sad for her, I don't think she's entirely happy, but that's all; those feelings are long gone. I'm ready to find my own happiness."

"Good, you had me worried for a second," he says as we carry on walking, "So now get back out there, get back on the app, have some fun. What have you got to lose?"

He has a point.

"Want me to get one of your favourite burgers made up for you?" he asks as he gets back to work behind the bar.

"Thanks for the offer, but I think I'll head off now," I say, finishing my drink. "I'm sure I can find something semi healthy in the fridge to cook tonight."

We say our goodbyes and I head off for my walk home. As I walk through town, I think about what he's said. I guess it is time to get back out there.

Turns out my semi healthy dinner is beans on toast with a little grated cheese, just to add a little something special. Even I roll my eyes as I think that.

Ok, here we go again. Feet up in front of the TV, cold beer in hand, I open the app and start browsing. Just as I'm getting bored of the same old bios, someone catches my eye. She's cute, beautiful actually, but not in an obvious way. She has a friendly smile, an almost familiar smile. Isabelle, a florist who lives in Wiltshire. I press the favourite button. What have I got to lose just by doing that? It's not like she knows she's a favourite, I think. I realise I really have no idea how this thing works. I decide that's enough progress for one night and turn my attention to the TV.

Chapter 19

Isabelle

Gina and Dom are watching the store this morning so I can visit the art gallery to see what space we have to work with. They've both agreed to work extra hours this week if needed to help get things ready in time, for which I am extremely grateful.

As I walk through the door of the gallery, I hear a voice I recognise. "Hello, I'll be there in just a minute."

It's a lot bigger than it looks from the outside; it's bright and spacious. Art isn't really my thing; I can see something and like it, but other than that, I do not have a clue. If you asked me what style of art I liked, I wouldn't be able to tell you. I have a few pictures up at home, but they are mostly generic beach hut scenes and a very scenic one of a lighthouse on a cliff. I think they all came from a trip to IKEA with Jess when I first moved in.

The art here is definitely not what you would find in a home store.

Even my inexperienced eye can see that some of these are spectacular. As I walk around, I'm completely in awe of what I'm seeing. The colours and the way they mix, the different styles. Some are landscapes that instantly capture you. The sunsets over sandy coves are breathtaking, the most beautiful landscapes I have ever seen. I never knew there were so many shades of green.

The detail is spectacular; they instantly take you away to another place far away. There is a beautiful collection, clearly by the same artist, all of ladies in long red dresses dancing, their long brown hair flowing as they sway to the music. The expressions on their faces show they are lost in the moment. I imagine them dancing the salsa or something equally as exotic and sensual. I can almost hear the music and feel the beat they're dancing to. How artists can capture movement in a still image just amazes me. Some of the other works are more 'modern' shall we say. I couldn't even tell you what they are meant to be pictures of, but I guess that's the beauty of art; it doesn't have to be a 'thing', it can just be colours or shapes. One in particular catches my eye, a stunning watercolour painting of peonies (it's no surprise that I'm drawn to this one). Blues, pinks, dark purples and greens are blended beautifully.

"You like that one?" asks Fi as she approaches me. "I can instantly tell by the way somebody looks at a piece of art how they feel about it. I think you're quite captivated by this one," she says, smiling.

"I am, it's just beautiful. I'm no expert at all, but this I like," I say, unable to draw my eyes from the canvas.

"It's one of mine," she says proudly.

I look at the ticket sitting beneath it. 'Peonies by Fiona Armstrong'.

"Really?" I say, looking at her, "You have quite a talent. I'd love to be able to produce work like this."

"Thank you. I never get bored of people saying they like my work, especially when their faces reflect it. And can I remind you that you do produce work like this. I do it on canvas, you use the real things. I've seen your bouquets, remember? Art comes in many, many forms, and floristry is one of them. Now, can I get you tea, coffee, water?" she asks.

"Water would be great, thank you." When she returns with the water, I'm still standing in front of the peonies, thinking about what she said.

"Come on, I'll show you around and tell you my plans for the layout I hope to go with for the show. Please do tell me though if you think my arrangement choices won't fit. I'm happy to rearrange anything that needs to be moved."

We walk around for a good half an hour; I can tell a lot of thought has gone into her planning. She talks me through some of the paintings on display and tells me about the artists.

"So will you be showing your own work at the show?" I ask, stopping to look at some more pictures.

"Not this time. I'm working with a German artist, Karl Brandt, he lives here in town. We came across each other at a little craft fair a few months ago, got chatting and here we are. Funny how the universe works. Anyway, his work is just brilliant, but he's struggling to get himself noticed so I thought I'd give him a helping hand. Well, try to anyway. I've invited everyone I know in the art industry; I don't have big connections, but it only takes the right person to be here and see what I see in him."

"What a lovely thing to do," I say out loud. It was intended to be said quietly in my head.

"Everybody needs a helping hand sometimes," she says warmly. "Especially struggling artists!" she adds with a laugh.

We talk some more about plans for the evening. "It starts at 6 pm for drinks and canapés but I'll be here all day setting up so just come and go as you need to," she says, showing me to a couch to sit down.

"You being so close to the store will save on a lot of travel time so hopefully it won't take too long."

"I can rope in a few hands if you need help bringing things across. It's the least I can do seeing as you've helped me out at short notice," she says just as the door to the gallery opens. "Ah, excellent timing. This," she says, standing, "is my wife Erica. Erica, this is Isabelle. She's the wonderful florist doing the arrangements for Friday, my saviour!"

"It's a pleasure to meet you, Isabelle," she says, coming over to where I'm sitting.

"Likewise," I say standing to shake her hand.

"So, you're the lady who saved that poor little cat and brought him up to the practice?" she asks.

"Yes, that was me, and my assistant Gina. He looked in such a bad state, we had to do something," I reply, "I'm hoping to adopt him soon. He still hasn't been claimed. I went to visit him at the shelter, and I was instantly smitten." I can't help but smile when I think about giving him a home.

"Well, he is one lucky kitty. I do love a happy ending," says Fi.

"I should probably get back to the store," I say. I'm aware I've left Gina and Dom there, and they've also kindly agreed to cover an hour over lunch so I can meet Eve and Jess for a quick catch up.

"Thank you again, so much," says Fi as she walks me to the door, "You have my number if you need anything, or you're always welcome to stop by, but I'll see you Friday, if not before. Oh, and you will come, of course, to the show in the evening? I'd love it if you would." She looks at me hopefully.

It's not like I have a hot date lined up, or anything at all for that matter. And I've never been to an art show.

"Really? Thank you, it'll be a first for me so definitely count me in."

Just as I'm heading out of the door after saying our goodbyes, I hear Fi call my name, "And you are more than welcome to bring a guest."

I wonder what Gina is doing Friday evening.

After an hour at the store, I pop out to meet Jess and Eve for a quick bite to eat. I walk into The Meeting Place to find them both already there.

"Sorry," I say, kissing them both on the cheek before sitting down.

"Don't be, you aren't late. I was just keen to escape the kids for an hour," says Jess, looking as elegant as ever. "I'm starving," she continues, "Let's order then we can catch up properly."

Once our food and drinks orders have been placed, we slip into comfortable conversation. Eve tells us about her latest cases at work, Jess fills us in on the children's latest antics with pride, and then, of course, the conversation turns to me and dating.

"I know you've had some pretty crappy dates," says Eve, "but you need to get back on the horse, so to speak. Any more luck with online thing?"

"I've looked at it once since my date with Ben. I just don't know if it's for me," I sigh, "It just feels like a lot of effort. Meeting somebody and falling in love should be the easy part of life, surely? Boy meets girl, falls in love…" I say, nodding my head in Jess's direction.

"I'll admit, we have been incredibly lucky in how our life has turned out. Look at Rebecca though, she couldn't meet us today because she's having lunch with the mother of the man she's about to marry, the man she met online," she says with a raised eyebrow. "It does happen, and I really don't think you're going to meet anyone in this town. If he was here, surely you would have met him already. It's a small place; you must see the same people every day."

She's got a point.

"Did anyone catch your eye on the app?" asks Eve.

"To be honest, I wasn't really paying attention. I had one eye on the TV. Have you seen that new series on Netflix?" I ask, hoping to change the subject.

"Nice try," says Eve. She knows exactly what I'm doing. "Get your phone out, we've got time. Let's have a look now."

"Oh, I don't think…."

"Yes!" squeals Jess, "Come on, we're only looking." Should I remind her that the last time she 'just looked,' she was almost drooling over Ben?

"Fine, here," I say, handing over my phone with the app open. "But absolutely no interaction of any kind with anyone," I say firmly, "You're just looking!"

They pull their chairs closer together and huddle like a couple of schoolgirls sharing a secret.

"Cute."

"Oh, definitely not."

"Ooooh, I like his hair."

"He's got trouble written all over him."

"Is that a wedding ring?"

"EEEWWWWWWWW!"

"Why would you put that in your bio? Weirdo."

"Ok, enough," I say, holding out my hand to demand my phone back. "See? It's not so easy," I say triumphantly, glad I've made my point.

"What about him?" says Jess as she hands me back my phone, the app open on a profile.

"He looks vaguely familiar," I say, staring at the screen, "but I can't place him."

"Let me see," says Eve, leaning in to get a closer look. "Nope, I can't say I recognise him. He's a looker though, and from Wiltshire."

"Wiltshire is a big county," I remind her.

"He's a vet," she continues, clearly ignoring me and my point.

"Oh, that reminds me," I say, putting my phone away, "I have some news!"

"You sound way too excited for this not to be life-changing," says Jess as she tucks into her panini.

"It kinda is, but not spectacularly life-changing."

"Spit it out then," says Eve, "I'm intrigued."

"I'm adopting a cat," I say as I clasp my hands excitedly against my chest.

"Oh dear God, we've lost her," says Eve, putting her head in her hands dramatically. "That's it, you may as well get another ten and be done with it."

"Stop it," says Jess in Eve's direction, "I think it's a lovely idea."

"Thank you, Jess," I say, glaring at Eve in a humorous way, just so she knows I'm not really mad at her. I know her comment was said in jest, or at least I hope it was.

"I am only half joking. Where's this idea coming from?" asks Eve.

I go on to tell them about what happened outside the store and our dash to the vets. "Nobody has come forward for him. He'll probably stay in the store. He'll have a cat flap so he can come and go as he pleases, and I'm there every day, or one of us is anyway. Even on days we're closed, I still go in to do a few things, and if I can't, then I'll ask one of the others to pop in and feed him and check on him. I went up to see him a few days ago. I'm going up again tomorrow to speak to them about it and see what the next step is."

"I can get on board with this if you promise to stop at one. I will not let you turn into an old cat lady."

"Eve, I promise to stop at one and not turn into an old cat lady," I say with my hand on my heart.

"Thank you, that's all I ask," she replies. "That, and please don't give it a silly name. There, I'm done," she says, raising her hands.

"And I promise, no silly names," I reply laughing.

That evening, after I've eaten my dinner of soup and a few crackers, I know, I can just hear Gina now "That's not a proper meal!" I think back to what was said over lunch and think about my options when it comes to meeting somebody. Limited is the word that comes to mind. In fact, throw a 'very' in front of that. Very limited. Ok Eve, you win. I pick up my phone and open the dating app. It's still on the same profile we were looking at over lunch. I press the favourite button. I think that means it'll save his profile and I can come back to him later. James, you're my one and only favourite. I put my phone away and pick up the TV remote to see what I can find to pass the time on this Saturday evening.

Chapter 20

James

I wake to the sound of my phone ringing. 7.15 on a Sunday morning. This had better be good.

It's Jim.

"James, I'm so sorry to call you this early on a Sunday, especially on your weekend off, but I'm with Mrs Richards."

He doesn't need to continue; I know what's coming.

"And let me guess, she wants me or Erica to see Dougie because you're new?" I ask, yawning.

"Bang on the money. I'm at the house. When I spoke to her earlier, it sounded like I needed to be here rather than her bring him to the surgery. I don't think it's anything serious, a bit of an infection in his ear but nothing more." He sounds a little exasperated. "I am sorry to call."

"Don't worry about it, Jim, honestly, we've been dealing with Mrs Richards long enough to know what to expect. Tell her I'll be there in about 45 minutes, or would you rather I didn't? I don't want to step on your toes with this."

"Oh please, I'm not worried about things like that. I just don't think she'll be happy until you or Erica see Dougie. Do you want me to call Erica?"

"No, I'm awake and she likes her Sunday lie-ins; she'll turn into the devil if you wake her," I say with a chuckle. "I'll be there shortly," I say as I leave the comfort of my bed and head for the coffee machine.

"Shall I text you the address?" asks Jim, sounding more than a little relieved.

"No need, I've been there just a few times before." I hang up the phone and pour myself an exceptionally large coffee before making my way to the shower.

Forty minutes later, I arrive at the little cottage that is home to Mrs Richards and the beloved pooch. Jim is sitting outside in the small front garden on a weathered wrought iron chair, cradling a cup in his hands.

"Am I glad to see you," he says as I get out of my car. "I'm not entirely sure she trusts me with him," he says, referring to Dougie.

"Don't take it personally; she's just used to seeing me or Erica. She doesn't strike me as a lady who takes well to change," I say with a little humour. "She's harmless really."

I briefly tell him about the losses she has endured, and he gives me a knowing nod.

The cottage is small and quaint. I don't think it's been redecorated for about 30 years. Pictures of her husband and daughter Charlotte decorate the walls; trinkets from travels around the world are placed on shelves and tables.

I find her in the lounge sitting on the sofa, Dougie next to her on a fluffy blanket that looks well used and loved.

"Doctor James, thank you for coming. Nothing personal to the other man but you know my Dougie and all his problems; he doesn't," she says, stroking the dog's head affectionately.

I go to sit next to her; Jim is standing in the doorway cautiously.

"I understand that, Mrs Richards. But Jim here is an excellent vet; we wouldn't have employed him otherwise. You will have to deal with him along with myself and Erica from now on." I don't want to be too firm with her, but I need to make it clear that she can't expect Erica or myself to come in on our days off. She needs to learn to trust Jim. "Today is meant to be my day off you see…" I say, trying not to sound too harsh.

"Oh, I am sorry," she says looking apologetic, "I didn't mean to ruin your weekend."

"You haven't, but please in future, if Jim is on call, you have to let him see Dougie. If I trust him to take care of your boy, then maybe you should trust him too," I say, giving her a warm smile.

"I'm sorry, Doctor, umm…" she says, looking towards the doorway where Jim is standing.

"Jim," he says, walking towards the sofa where we're sitting. "Just Jim is fine. Now, shall we get little Dougie sorted?"

"Definitely an ear infection," I say after a few seconds of looking into the red, inflamed fluffy ear. "Just as Jim said it was," I continue, giving her a little smile.

"A short course of antibiotics and some ear drops will soon have him right as rain," Jim chips in.

"Thank you both so much. I'm sorry for being an old fuss pot. I really didn't mean any offence Doctor Jim, I just worry about him, a little too much," she says sadly.

"No offence taken, and there's no such thing as worrying too much. He's a very lucky boy to have somebody who loves him as much as you do," he says reassuringly. "I'll leave his medications here and maybe bring him by to see me on Friday at the clinic, just so we can check he's on the mend. How does that sound?"

"That's wonderful, thank you."

We leave her with instructions on how and when to give the meds before leaving.

"Thank you for coming out, and the support in there. I really feel for her," says Jim as we walk outside.

"No problem, I think we brought her around in the end. I doubt you'll have any more issues there," I reply as I get into my car, "I hope the rest of the day passes without any dramas." He gives me a wave as I drive off.

After a late morning run, I decide to pay Dan a visit and treat myself to one of the delicious roast dinners the establishment has to offer. I was thinking about Lizzie earlier. I won't ask him if he's seen her or heard from her, but I'm hoping he'll offer the information anyway.

"Hey," says Dan as I walk towards the bar, "what brings you here on a Sunday?"

"I thought I might eat a proper meal for once and have one of your roast beef dinners and a pint," I say, taking a seat at the bar. "I thought it would be busier today," I say, looking around. It's not empty but it's known for its Sunday lunches.

"It's the sunshine. It's a warm one today and people aren't really up for a big old roast dinner when it's hot, plus the lack of a beer garden doesn't help. It's quite nice having it a little bit quieter today, yesterday was manic," he says as he puts my beer on the bar. "I'll just put your order in and I'll be back. Why don't you get a table and I'll join you if you don't mind some company."

"Of course not, we haven't eaten together in a long time."

"So, what's new?" he asks as he joins me at the table with a lime and soda.

"Absolutely nothing. If you were hoping for some gossip, you've come to the wrong place, my friend," I say, taking a sip of my beer. I used to feel awkward having a drink when I was with Dan, but he assured me constantly that it was ok and had no effect on him at all. Now I don't give it a second thought.

"No dates? No plans?"

"No dates. I am going to Fi's art show on Friday night but that's it as far as plans go I'm afraid."

"Any luck with the dating app?" he asks with a hopeful, optimistic tone.

"I did make a little progress with that actually..."

"Tell me, I'm all ears."

"I favourited a profile!" I reply with a look of feigned shock.

"That's it? Jeez, man, go steady, you'll be buying a ring next!" he says with a wink.

Before I can reply, our plates are out in front of us. "Your lunch is served." I recognise that voice. I look up to see Dylan standing there in a white T-shirt, tea towel thrown casually over his shoulder.

"Well, this is a surprise!" I say, giving Dan a questioning look. "How are you?" I ask, turning back to Dylan. He looks different. His hair is cut and tidy, and he has a lightness to him, like he's no longer carrying the weight of the world on his shoulders.

"Hi James," he says with a broad smile, "I'm good thanks. Best get back to the kitchen, pots and pans to clean! Enjoy your lunch."

I look at Dan raising my eyebrows as Dylan walks off towards the kitchen.

"Ah, I forgot to mention, I have a new kitchen hand," he says as he seasons his roast beef with salt and pepper. "I had a note in the window advertising for a weekend kitchen assistant and in he walked. He's only been here a few days, but he seems to love it, and he's a real grafter. He gets on with everyone; he's fitting in really well."

"He looks like a different kid, and I don't just mean the haircut. It's like something has changed in him," I say as I take a bite of roast potato. I swear these are the best roasties I have ever tasted.

"It's early days but we'll see how he gets on. I agree though, something has changed in him. On another note, and to be clear, I am breaking no rules here, I met with Lizzie," he says, taking a sip of his drink. "She asked me to let you know that we have spoken, and to pass on her thanks. I can't really tell you any more than that, but she's on the right track. She's found a support network which is very important, as you know."

"I wasn't going to ask, I would never put you in that position, but I was hoping you'd tell me something, so thank you for that. It's reassuring to know she's reached out to you. I know you must be discreet, but I really do appreciate it."

"I only passed on that information because she asked me to. What I can tell you is that she is very grateful to you for putting us in touch with each other, that's another thing she asked me to pass on," he says taking a mouthful of food, "Damn this is good, I think I must have the best chef in Wiltshire!"

We finish our meals over small talk about our families. He tells me his parents are visiting soon. We always have a big dinner together whenever they're here. They feel like family to me; I adore spending time with them. Dylan swiftly removes our empty plates and offers us a look at the dessert menu. I rub my stomach dramatically. "I can't eat another thing. I may fall asleep right here. That was delicious."

"Thank you, Dylan," says Dan, "Don't forget to remind the chef to put a plate aside for you when your shift finishes, and dessert, of course."

"Thanks, man," replies Dylan as he walks off with a little spring in his step.

"Perks of the job," says Dan, almost justifying his reason for feeding the teen. "Ah yes, Dylan interrupted us earlier. You were telling me about your *progress* with the dating app." He puts a lot of emphasis on the word progress.

"Can you blame me for being so apprehensive? I don't have the best record when it comes to online dating, well, dating in general really," I say, running my hand over my chin thoughtfully.

"So, tell me about this one on your favourite list, or whatever you call it."

I reach into my jeans pocket for my phone. "Probably easier to show you," I say as I open the app and find her bio.

He scans over my phone for several seconds. "Well, she looks lovely, and normal! Lives in Wiltshire, bonus. Have you sent her a message yet?" he says as he hands my phone back to me. "Give me that back for a second," he says, referring to the phone.

"Oh no, not a chance, you are not sending her a message," I reply, holding the gadget tight in both hands.

"I'm not that much of a dick," he says, laughing, "I just think I recognise her; she looks familiar, let me see."

I hand back my phone, closely watching his every move, just in case he is that much of a dick.

"I can't place her," he says, shaking his head with a puzzled look. "There is something familiar about her."

"That's funny because I actually thought the same, something about her smile...." I look at her photos again, but I just can't place her.

"So, you're going to message her, right? What have you got to lose? It's one message, mate, that's all, one little message..."

I let out an audible sigh. "Yes, ok, I'll message her tonight, but first I want to pop by the gallery and see if Fi needs any help with anything before Friday evening," I say as I stand to leave.

"YES!!" says Dan as he high fives thin air. "I've got a good feeling about this one," he says, looking very pleased with himself.

"You sure it's not wind after all that veg?" I joke as I pull out my wallet to pay.

"Funny! And you can put that away. With all the help you give me around here, you really think I'm going to let you pay? This is on me, you've saved my ass more than a few times," he says, waving his hands at me, gesturing for me to put my wallet back in my pocket.

"You've got to let me pay at some point; you always do this. If you won't take my money then how about I tip the waiter," I say, handing over a ten-pound note. "Pass this on to Dylan, just maybe don't tell him it's from me."

"Deal. Thanks, man, he'll be made up."

We say our goodbyes and I head off towards the art gallery.

"Hi, Fi," I call as I walk through the door, the little bell above it tinkling. I can see her standing at the desk with her back to me, dressed in her usual bright colours. Pink and orange are the choice for today.

"James," she says as she turns towards me. "How lovely to see you. What do I owe this pleasure?" she asks as she kisses me on the cheek.

"I just had lunch with Dan and I thought I'd pop in and see if you need any help ahead of Friday. No lifting anything for you so you can leave all of that to me. I can come down in the afternoon and help with any last minute things." I stroll around, taking in the beautiful artwork. I've seen Fi's work many times before. I can usually pick out which ones are hers; she has her own style. I find her pictures calming, soothing. The way she mixes the colours to create her own unique palettes is just breathtaking.

"These are exquisite," I say looking over a small collection of floral prints. I have no idea what the flowers are but I'm quite sure nature doesn't give them the magnificent colours they have on the canvas in front of me.

"Thank you, James, you are always so complimentary about my work," she says, touching my forearm affectionately. "This is my new collection," she says proudly.

"This one has sold already; you must be incredibly pleased," I say referring to a beautiful watercolour with a sold sign on it.

"Not technically sold, just not for sale. The wonderful florist who is doing the flowers for the show fell in love with it. I'm planning on giving it to her as a thank you for getting everything done so quickly. She has been an absolute gem."

"And adopting the cat, I hear," I say as I continue to browse. "I met her briefly when I picked up the flowers that evening I came to dinner. Lovely lady, reminded me of my late grandmother; she has similar mannerisms," I say, remembering Grandma Lois with fondness. She was my father's mother. She would take my brother and I to run very important errands; this was all a cover to take us to our favourite bakery for jam doughnuts.

"Oh no, that's not her. Isabelle is much younger, late twenties maybe, lovely girl. I'm sure you'll meet her Friday. Anyway, there's nothing needs doing right now, but I could use some help Friday moving a few things around if it's not too much trouble?"

"Of course not, I'll tell Rachael to keep my diary free for the afternoon. I'll be at your disposal," I say, bowing dramatically.

"You're a good 'un, James Lowry," she says, putting her hand on my cheek. "How you've not been snapped up yet is beyond me," she says, giving me a wink.

"Well, if you're sure there's nothing I can do here, I'll leave you to it. I've got a FaceTime date with a beautiful, cheeky four-year-old," I say, referring to my niece.

"Ah, the delightful Ella, such a sweetheart. She must have grown so much since their last visit."

"You would not believe the difference in her, Fi; she's growing so quickly. That reminds me, she has just taken up ballet. Apparently, she loves it and is a natural. I was hoping you might be able to help me find a beautiful piece of artwork for her wall, nothing 'childlike'. I'm thinking something a little more grown up that she can have on display when she's older, if she chooses to, of course."

"I'd be delighted to help, James, leave it with me and I'll do a little research. You know how much I love to pair somebody with the perfect piece of art," she says excitedly.

"No rush. I know you've got a lot on this week. Right, I shall see you Friday if not before, don't overdo it," I say, giving a little nod towards her belly.

I spend a delightful 45 minutes hearing all about Ella's friends at school and their recent trip to the local 'Tierpark', which I know is German for animal park. She tells me about how she fed the deer, saw 'big scary looking birds', zebras and all other manner of animals. Her excitement at starting ballet is adorable; the way her eyes light up at the mention of it just melts my heart. She shows me her ballet shoes and little pink tutu.

"Will you come and watch me, Uncle James, when I'm good enough to be in a show like the other girls?"

"I promise you, sweetheart, I will do my absolute best to be there." This is a promise I am determined to keep.

Later that evening, I remember my conversation with Dan. If I don't send this message now, I never will. Here goes…

Hi Isabelle,

I was going to start this message by introducing myself, but of course you can see all about me on my bio.

Please let me apologise for my lame attempt at a first message, I am not very good at this at all (as you can probably tell.)

I can see we have two things in common already, you love dogs, of course being a vet, this is music to my ears, I think you would love our puppy clinic! And I will happily eat your 4th slice of pizza, and the 5th, and maybe even the 6th! It is so refreshing to hear the words beer and cheesy pizza rather than the usual, wine, dine and I only eat salads.

I would love to know more about you but there is no pressure.

Have a lovely evening,

James x

Chapter 21

Isabelle

I don't think I have ever been so excited for a Monday morning to arrive. Today I pick up Juniper; that's what I have decided to call him (I wonder what Eve will make of that.) I went to the shelter yesterday to discuss adopting him and the staff were delighted for me to take him. He is such a sweetheart; he just loves people and cuddles. I explained about the store and that that is where he'll be staying during the day, but I've decided I'll bring him home with me at night. I don't want him left there by himself, and to be honest, the company will be nice. I had to make a quick dash to the pet store yesterday to get everything he'll need. I probably went a little over the top, but why not? He deserves it after everything he's been through.

I shower and dress at lightning speed. I want to stop in the store first to help Gina open up, then I'll drive up to get him.

"Ciao, Bella," says Luca when I stop in for my usual coffee. His joyous smile is infectious.

"Ciao, ciao," I hear as two little heads pop up from behind the counter.

"Well, hello there," I say as I move closer. "Nice to meet you, I'm Isabelle."

"This is Matteo and Sofia, two of my grandchildren," Luca says proudly, "They're helping me out today." He starts preparing my coffee and I can see the children are eager to help.

"I think I'll take four of your finest croissants please, two almond and two plain," I say to Matteo and Sofia. "Could you get those for me?" They say something to each other in Italian, clearly planning the task at hand. Matteo heads in one direction, expertly picks up two plain croissants with tongs and carefully puts them in a paper bag, whilst Sofia mirrors his actions with the almond croissants.

"Great teamwork," I say to them with a wink, "You've got them well trained, Luca!" I spend a few minutes chatting with them, telling them about Juniper and showing them a picture of him I took yesterday. Their English is superb. Luca tells me they have been raised bilingual. Anyone who can speak more than one language always impresses me. I opted for German at school; it seemed like the easiest of them all. I was wrong and failed miserably when it came to my exam.

"I brought breakfast," I call as I walk into the back door of the store, "Some of Luca's finest."

"I missed breakfast," says Kate as she appears from the cooling room. "Too busy getting the kids ready and dropping the puppy off at doggy day care. Great, thanks," she says, helping herself to a croissant. Kate and Dom have both come in today to help plan for the art show. "You just missed Dom," she carries on through a mouthful of food, "He's gone to collect the flower stands from the supplier."

"Ta love," says Gina as she picks up a croissant mid-flower trimming. "Go on," she says to me, rolling her eyes, "go get that kitty. I know you can't wait; we'll be fine here."

I grab the keys for the delivery car and give her a kiss on the cheek before practically running out of the door. "Thank you!"

As I pull into the car park, I can barely contain my excitement. I'm actually getting to take him home. I grab the pet carrier I purchased yesterday from the back of the car and head inside.

"Hello," I say to the man behind the desk, "my name is Isabelle Watts. I'm here to collect, um, well, his name is Juniper now. The little ginger cat that was run over, I take him home today." I can feel the pride and emotion in my voice.

"Ah yes, I'll just get somebody to bring him through for you." As he picks up the phone to make a call, I look around at all of the wonderful pictures on the walls, animals finding their forever homes, everything from cats and dogs to tortoises and birds. It's so heart-warming to see.

"Lawrence will bring him through in just a moment," he says, replacing the receiver. "Have you got everything you need for him? We have a little store here on-site if there is anything."

"I have everything he needs and then some," I say, laughing, "I think I went a bit OTT but he's worth it."

"People often do when they adopt," he says with a warm smile, "It's not a bad thing at all. All animals deserve love, care and comfort; it makes my day to see our animals go off to their forever homes."

I walk around for a few minutes, taking in the stories of the rehomed animals whilst the man behind the desk carries on with his duties.

"Here we are," I hear a voice from behind me say, making me jump a little. "I believe this little one now belongs to you." He hands me the little ginger bundle and my heart swells.

"Hello, Juniper," I say as I nuzzle his neck, "You're coming home with me."

"What a lovely name. How did you come up with that?" asks the man, who I assume is Lawrence.

"I own a florist in town; he'll be mostly our store cat so I wanted a name that was fitting. Daisy or Rose didn't quite suit him," I say, giving him a little squeeze.

Lawrence gives a little chuckle. "I like it, it suits him. Now we just have some paperwork to sign before we can send him off. Take a seat and I'll be right back."

I sit on a curved sofa with my little bundle. I can't take my eyes off him. He is so soft, and he looks so healthy and well after the accident.

"Right," says Lawrence, returning with a clipboard and pen. "I just need you to sign on the dotted line. I know my colleague Jen spoke to you yesterday so we don't need to go over everything again. Just to remind you, he comes with three months free pet insurance so please remember to renew that or arrange cover with another company before that runs out. He is microchipped now with your details so if you move house or change your number, it's important to let them know; all of the information on how to do that is in this little welcome pack. It also has dates of when he'll need his next worming treatment. It would be wise to register him with a vet in the next week or so. Any questions or problems, please do contact us. We're here to help even after they leave us. We want the transition to be as smooth as possible for both of you."

"Thank you so much. You have been wonderful. I just can't wait to get him home and settled. I know it can take a while, but I'm prepared for that."

I put him in the pet carrier, sign the paperwork and head for the car park.

Ok, first problem. Do I put the carrier in the boot? On the back seat? On the front seat? In the footwell? Oh dear Juniper, what have you let yourself in for? I look around and spot a lady opening the boot of her car. Yes! Inside is a little pet carrier with a puppy in. Boot it is then.

The drive home is a slow one. I don't think I've ever driven so carefully since I first passed my test many moons ago. I'm very aware of the precious cargo I'm carrying. If Eve could see me now.

"They're here," Gina calls to Kate as I walk into the store carrying the crate. "Oh, he's a darling, and look at him! Look how well he is after the accident." She beams. I knew she'd be smitten.

"Let's give him a little space," I say as I put the carrier on the floor near the counter and unlatch the door. "I'll just leave this open and he can come out in his own time. We'll just go about our business whilst keeping one eye on him. I don't want him escaping out of the door when anyone comes in; he's microchipped but I still want to keep him inside, just for now."

"I've put down some water and a few little bits of food for him, I hope that's ok?" Gina clearly loves him already.

Over the next few hours, he makes himself very at home, curling himself around our feet as we work, jumping from counter to counter, chasing one of his many little toys around the floor, and the customers love him. Once I know he's happy and content, I put his little blue collar around his neck. The little tag has my surname and contact number on it. Apparently, it's not the done thing to put the animal's name on them anymore.

"Um. Sorry, love, but that's it? You've put his collar on him just like that?" asks Gina with a look of surprise.

"How was I meant to do it? Did I do it wrong?" I ask her, giving the collar another look and feeling a little puzzled. I look at Kate and Dom, who is back from the suppliers. They shrug their shoulders, clearly as confused as I am.

"No little naming ceremony? Nothing to mark the occasion?" she asks. I hear a stifled giggle coming from Dom's direction. I look across at their bemused faces.

"Honestly, I hadn't given it much thought." I don't really know what else to say. "Did you do that with your puppy?" I ask Kate.

"God no," she laughs, "Collar was on and off he went to play with the kids."

I hear Gina tutting, slightly louder than is necessary, and nothing else is said on the matter.

"I need to get these stands to the gallery," says Dom, changing the subject, "We don't have the space to store them here. I'm hoping they have somewhere."

"I'll pop across now and ask her. If not they'll have to stay in the van, not ideal with deliveries but we'll make it work. Can you watch Juniper? I won't be long." Gina has him swept up in her arms before I'm even out of the door.

"Hi, Fi," I say as I walk through the door, its little bell tinkering, letting her know she has company.

"Isabelle, lovely to see you, how are you?" she asks as she kisses my cheek. It's like we're old friends; something about her is very comforting.

"I'm great, thank you, just a flying visit. We have some floral stands we need to store for Friday, only five of them, but we don't have a huge amount of space. I don't suppose you have anywhere we can put them for now?" The smell of sandalwood fills the air; it's such a welcoming scent.

"I'm just finalising a sale," she says, nodding towards an older couple standing in front of one of the paintings of the lady dancing in the red dress, "Can you give me five minutes?"

I walk around taking in the beautiful artwork again. I don't think I'd ever get bored of looking at them. The beautiful peony picture catches my eye and I instantly spot the 'SOLD' sign on it. My heart sinks a little. I hadn't considered buying it but knowing it isn't a possibility saddens me a little. It's going to make a stunning addition to somebody's home.

"Sorry about that," says Fi as she approaches. "We do have some space out the back. Do you want to take a look and see if it's big enough?" I follow her to the back of the building and confirm that it's more than enough.

"Is it ok if we bring them across now? My colleague Dom can help me; it won't take long."

"Of course," she replies, "I, um, won't be able to help. I'm sorry, I'm not supposed to be lifting things at the moment. Erica will throttle me if I do and she finds out. I'm pregnant, you see, very early on but it's been a very long, often heart-breaking process…" she says sadly, "but we're very optimistic this time."

"How wonderful! Congratulations," I say hugging her, "Don't you even attempt to help. We can manage! I'll go and get Dom now and get started."

"Oh Isabelle," she calls as I'm about to leave, "we haven't told anyone yet, well, two people actually, we want to wait until the safety of 12 weeks arrives before we share our news, so mums the word," she says smiling broadly.

"Mums the word," I reply with a wink as I walk away with a spring in my step.

The rest of the afternoon is spent moving the stands to the gallery and keeping an eye on my new furry responsibility. I think it's safe to say he is very happy in his new home. Just as I'm about to close for the day, after I have sent everyone else home, Fi pops her head around the door, waving a mobile phone at me. "You left this at the gallery. Sorry, I've only just noticed it," she says, coming in to hand it to me.

"I hadn't even realised," I say, patting down my pockets as if to confirm mine isn't with me, "Thank you so much, I've been so busy today. What a ditz!" Juniper curls himself around her ankles, purring loudly.

"Ah, you must be the lucky cat I've been hearing all about," she says, bending down to stroke him. "Can I?" she asks, gesturing to pick him up.

"Oh please do, he loves people and cuddles, so you'll be his new best friend." I glance at my phone, a couple of messages in the group chat that can wait until later, and a missed call from a random number that definitely looks like a scam.

"He's adorable. I'll tell Erica that I've had the pleasure of meeting him and how well he's doing. She'll be delighted! Don't be surprised if she turns up at some point to see for herself," she laughs. "Right, I need to get going, lots still to do before Friday. I just wanted to make sure I got the phone to you before you left. We can't seem to be without them these days. I know I'd be lost without mine."

"I know what you mean, though mine is generally messages from my group of girlfriends and scam calls; nothing more interesting than that!"

"Well, you never know when you might get an unexpected message," she says with a wink.

We say our goodbyes. I put Juniper in his carrier, lock up and head home.

It soon becomes clear that he is as comfortable in my apartment as he is in the store. It doesn't take him long to get his bearings. Whilst he's running around and exploring his scratching post, I make myself dinner and pour a glass of wine. Before long, he is curled up on my lap fast asleep. His little purrs are adorable, but the excitement of his coming home day has taken its toll. I can't believe how utterly content I feel, sitting here with this little fluff ball asleep on my lap. I take a picture of him and send it to the girls with the message 'Meet Juniper.'

Jess: *'Gorgeous, I want one!'*

Rebecca: *'Look at that little face! I can't believe you actually got a cat!'*

Eve: *'Yeah ok, it's cute, but it's not a man! Any updates?'*

Me: *'Nothing to report. Over and out x'*

Despite feeling content with my new companion, I decide to pass the time whilst he's sleeping and have a little browse. The app informs me that I have 5 new messages. One catches my eye, James. Then I remember: he's my 'favourite'. Oh my god. I sit up straight and take a deep breath. I read his message a few times. I like it, it's sweet and polite. How can I not reply?!

'Hi James,

You had me at puppy clinic! Please tell me this involves cuddling and playing with little balls of fluffy cuteness. What a fantastic job! Was it a childhood dream to become a vet?

More about me? As you know I'm a florist, I own a little store that was left to me by my grandmother, it's my pride and joy. I spent many happy childhood years there helping her, she loved to teach me everything she knew about flowers, and I loved learning about them. I like to think she'd be proud of its success. We survived the pandemic so that in itself is an achievement.

Now to the important stuff. Pizza. I'll happily share, but what is your choice of topping?

I'm looking forward to your answer with anticipation because, let's be honest, this could be a deal breaker!

Isabelle x

PS You aren't as lame at this as you think ;)'

I spend the rest of the evening feeling happy and optimistic. Something feels different about this guy. I don't know what, but I can't stop smiling.

Chapter 22

James

I walk into the coffee room at the clinic to find Jim already there. I look at the clock, 7.45, and I thought I was in early. "Good morning, how was the rest of your Sunday?" I ask as I pour myself a coffee. "No more dramas, I hope?"

"Morning, James, it was actually very pleasant. I assisted with the delivery of five springer spaniel puppies up on the Clarences' farm. Millie got into a bit of trouble during labour, but with a little help they were all delivered safely. Mum and pups are all doing well." The Clarences own a huge farm on the edge of town; they provide all of the local produce and have done so for years.

"Great news," I say, patting him on the back, "I shall look forward to seeing them for their check-ups. Why are you in today anyway? You've been on call all weekend; today should be your day off."

"I need the distraction," he says, looking solemn, "It's the day my divorce gets finalised. It's for the best, but it's still a sad situation for us. So, if it's ok with you, I'll work through today."

"I'm sorry to hear that, Jim. It's not something I've experienced myself, but I have friends that have been through it. It's never nice for anyone involved. Am I right in thinking you don't have children?"

"No, we don't, it was always on the cards, something we both wanted but it never happened. Now looking back, maybe that was for the best." I can't help but notice how sombre he looks at the mention of children, or more the lack of them.

"Well, if you fancy a beer tonight, I'm more than happy to oblige. I have nothing planned; we could pop to Dan's place in town, have a few beers, and bite to eat. No pressure, have a think about it and let me know. I promise not to take it personally if you would prefer to be in your own company."

"Thank you, I really appreciate that. Can I let you know later? See how the day goes?"

"What am I missing?" asks Erica as she makes a dramatic entrance through the door. "I could hear you both chatting away, what's the gossip? And is there more coffee?" she asks, looking at my cup. I know that's my cue.

"Here you go," I say, handing her the steaming mug, "How was the weekend?"

"Busy. I've been helping Fi with the final plans for Friday. I'm not sure how many 'to do' lists one person can have! She really wants it to be a success for the artist she's helping; she knows how difficult it can be when you first start out. Trying to make a name for yourself isn't easy, but she has some good contacts, most of whom are coming, so fingers crossed for him." She takes a sip of her coffee. "That reminds me, James, you are definitely coming, aren't you? And you of course Jim, please do come along. It would mean a lot to us, well, Fi, but the bigger the success it is, the more peaceful my home life will be," she says with a cheeky wink.

Jim raises his hand. "I'd love to come. I don't know many people here yet, so I won't turn down any social invite!"

She looks towards me. "As if I'm not going to come; you'd both kill me. You know I'll be there."

"Even if you get a better offer?" she asks.

"If by any miracle, I was to get another offer," God help me if I say better offer, "my date with you would be my priority. Happy with that?" I say throwing my arm across her shoulders.

"Deal," she says, kissing me on the cheek. "Right, let's get some work done."

Later that day, Erica sticks her head around my clinic door. "Are you busy?"

"Not right this second. What do you need?"

"Not me, Fi, she needs help moving a few things. She doesn't like to ask, and I don't want her doing anything she shouldn't be. I thought seeing as we have Jim here unexpectedly today you might pop down and give her a hand?" she says, fluttering her eyelashes at me.

"Are you ok? Do you have something in your eye? Here, I could take a look for you," I say, picking up the little eye torch.

"Oh, sod off," she says with a grin, "I'll take that as a yes. I won't tell her you're coming so prepare yourself. Thank you, I really appreciate it."

"Give me ten minutes to finish up and I'll go down."

I find a parking space easily, which is usually a challenge in this town. It has a little history behind it. The buildings are stunning, and the churches always bring the tourists in, not to mention the canal path and little shops and cafes, all locally run. It's so nice to see that they all survived the pandemic and seem to be thriving again. I decide to pop into the little Italian Deli. I need a coffee, and I know Fi loves anything sweet. A little treat won't hurt; she is eating for two after all.

"Ciao, Sir," says a little voice from behind the counter, not what I was expecting at all. The little girl is wearing an apron that matches the older man's, whom I recognise to be the owner. "What can I get for you today?" Her English is superb. Her accent is strong, but she's clearly been raised speaking more than one language.

"Hello there, you must be new here. I haven't seen you before. Are you the new baker?" I ask, and she lets out a little giggle.

"This is my granddaughter Sofia. They're visiting for a while so she's helping her old grandad out," says the older man.

"My brother was here but he's gone fishing, so I'm helping Papa," she says proudly.

"It's lovely to meet you, Sofia. I have to say, that apron suits you perfectly!" She beams at this compliment.

"Thank you, Sir."

"Oh, please, my name is James. Now could I have an Americano to take away? I think we'd better let your Papa do that one," I say with a wink, "but I would like to take a cake for my friend, something very sweet with lots of sugar. Could you pick one for me?" She takes her time looking along the delicious looking pastries behind the counter. There's clearly a lot of thought going into this. The older man leans across and whispers something in her ear.

"A cannoli? That's my favourite thing to eat ever!" she says excitedly.

"Then a cannoli it is!" I watch as she very carefully takes the tongs her granddad passes to her and gently places the delicious treat in a brown paper bag.

"Thank you very much, Sofia," I say as I tap my card to pay, "I hope you enjoy the rest of your trip."

"Ah," says Fi as I walk into the gallery, the little bell tinkling. "I'm assuming you've been sent to help me? I told Erica it could wait. I'm sorry, James, you really didn't have to come down here," she says, kissing my cheek.

"It's no bother, it's a chance to get a decent coffee," I say, holding my cup up. "And a treat for you," I continue, passing her the bag.

"Oooh, what do we have here?" she says as she peers inside.

"I didn't know what drink to get you. I'm sure Erica said you're off caffeine, so I wasn't sure," I say taking a sip of mine. When I look up, she's already biting into the sweet treat. "Good choice then?" I ask with a laugh.

"Heavenly," she says, licking the cream from her fingers. "Don't judge, I'm eating for two."

"I'm here now, so what can I do to help?"

"The florist popped by not long ago with some stands for Friday. You've literally just missed her with the last of them; they're out the back but I forgot I need space to store the extra tables that are coming tomorrow. Any chance you could just jig a few things around back there and make a little room for them?"

"At your service," I reply with a comical salute. It doesn't take me long to rearrange a few boxes and stands to make the extra space she needs. I'm glad Fi asked me to come down, some of the boxes are heavier than they look. Just as I'm finishing up, I notice a mobile phone on the windowsill.

"Fi, is this yours?" I ask, heading back out into the main gallery.

"Nope," she says, taking it from me and looking it over. It's in a simple protective case, with a beautiful sunset beach scene as the wallpaper. "Where did you find it?"

"Out the back, it was on the windowsill."

"It must belong to the florist, or her assistant. He came with her earlier. I'll ring her number, see if it rings."

Within seconds, the phone is ringing, Fi's name flashing up on the screen. "Definitely hers, I'll drop it over to her. Thank goodness you found it, I rarely go out there," she says, nodding towards the back room.

"Do you want me to take it? I think I'm pretty much done here, and there's no point in going back to the clinic. They'll be closing up about now. I'll give them a quick call to see if they need me, but it won't take me five minutes to take the phone over."

"Very kind of you, love, but I can run it over. I might even treat myself to some flowers whilst I'm there. You get yourself off. Erica is on call tonight so You go and have a relaxing evening. I'm secretly hoping she gets called out early so I can watch my art shows in peace. Don't you ever tell her I said that!" she says, giving me a stern look.

I kiss her on the cheek and call the clinic on my way back to the car. Jim assures me everything is fine and takes me up on my offer of a beer and food. We arrange to meet at The Meeting Place in an hour, just enough time to get home, shower, and change.

"You can't stay away," says Dan as I take a seat at the bar. "Usual?" he asks as he takes an empty pint glass from the shelf above him.

"Please. I'm meeting Jim, the new locum at work. His divorce is finalised today, I'm not entirely sure if we're celebrating or commiserating, but either way, I thought he might appreciate some company."

"Not something either of us have had the pleasure of, thankfully," he says handing me my drink. He fills me in on how Dylan got on yesterday. "I think this will be really good for him, earning his own money, and he's great with the customers. I feel like he's really turning a corner, but we'll see. Teenagers can be very unpredictable. I'm choosing to stay optimistic, I have faith in him."

"I get the impression that's one of the many things he's been missing, someone to have just a little faith in him." I think back to my time with him. He really did seem like a different kid yesterday. I, like Dan, have faith that he can, and will, turn things around.

Jim arrives a few minutes later. We order our food and find a quiet table. "How are you doing?" I ask. I don't know him well enough to pry too much into why his marriage failed, and it's not really any of my business, but I want to offer him the chance to talk about it if he needs to.

"I'm ok, better than I thought I would be actually. I'm sure working today was the difference between being ok and feeling like a right miserable arse, so thanks for letting me work through." He takes a sip of his pint. "It feels like closure. We no longer have the need to have any communication, although most of it lately has been through solicitors. It's a strange feeling when somebody has been the biggest part of your life for so long, you make a very expensive promise to spend the rest of your lives together, then just like that, they're no longer there. Her family was my family, and likewise; it's a huge adjustment. That's why moving here was the best thing I could have done. A fresh start, new people, new experiences, and new friends," he says, raising his glass. I raise mine to tap his and we toast the moment.

After we've eaten, we sit at the bar chatting with Dan for a while. There's a really relaxed feeling in the air, people laughing, enjoying each other's company. They all look genuinely happy. I can't help but smile.

"I feel we're at that point in the evening where we have to talk about James's love life," Dan says to Jim as though I'm invisible. "Terrible state of affairs," he continues. "I mean if he had a face like the arse of a cow, no job, was living with his parents… You know, I'd get it. But let's face it, he's a handsome bugger, has a great job, owns his own place, drives a nice car, and even more annoyingly, is a really nice, genuine guy. I just don't get it."

"Can I just point out that we are all single! All three of us, sitting right here, are single, so why is the emphasis on me and my love life?"

"Fair point. Ok, Jim here," says Dan putting a hand on Jim's shoulder, "has literally just had his divorce finalised. Correct me if I'm wrong, but I'm guessing dating is the last thing on your mind, right?" he asks, looking at Jim.

"You are not wrong. I'm out of the dating game for a while yet," he replies.

"And me," Dan continues. "You know I'm not one for settling down. I get all the casual dates I need from this place," he says, spreading his arms wide. "That is why the emphasis is on you. You want to settle down, the wife, the house, the kids, and you deserve that. You come from a family of strong marriages. Look at your parents, rock solid and still madly in love. Your brother and his wife, rock solid, or so I assume from what you tell me and what I've seen over the years. Of course you want that. It's coming for you, I just know it, and I think it's closer than you realise."

We all sit in silence for a few moments, taking in Dan's words.

"So, who's gonna win the rugby on Saturday?" asks Jim, and we all laugh at his successful attempt at changing the subject. The rest of the evening passes without another mention of my love life.

As I lay in bed, I remember my message to Isabelle. I have been so busy all day, it hadn't occurred to me that she may have replied. I pick up my phone with a little trepidation. There may not be a reply. But that little nagging voice in my head kicks in, 'But what if there is?'

And there it is. She's replied. It's a lovely message. I feel a little flip of something in my chest, excitement? Nerves? Acid reflux? I stop myself from writing a quick, monotonous reply. I want to do this properly, get this right.

Hi Isabelle,

Thank you for your lovely response. I should probably address the most important question first, pizza! The minor ones about career choices can wait.

I'm afraid to say I'm a little dull on the pizza topping side, give me a good old plain cheese one, or pepperoni. In my very humble opinion, anything more than that just becomes too much, keep it simple I say. I am happy for you to correct me on this if you would like to take on the challenge, but I must warn you, I am stuck in my ways on this one!

As for being a vet, it's absolutely what I wanted to do, for as long as I can remember. Helping animals gives me a purpose. They can't tell us when they're in pain, or where it hurts, we have to figure that out for them. I hate to see an animal suffering, but I can't describe the happiness it brings to see them recovered and pain-free. They aren't just animals, they're family. I know that sounds cheesy, but it is so true, I see it every day. Puppy clinic is pretty much as you described it, just with a few injections and medications thrown in. It's not something I get to do as often as

I'd like, our nurses tend to run them, but I love to do them when I get the chance.

I loved reading about how you came to own your store, there's something really special about having something handed down to you that a loved one has put their heart and soul into. They're placing their trust in you, and that is an incredible thing. Isn't it wonderful when you find and are able to make a living from doing something you love? I feel so grateful every day that I have that.

When you aren't working, what do you like to do for fun? How do you relax after a long day?

I'm looking forward to hearing more about you.

Goodnight, or maybe good morning, depending on when you read this,

James x

I am so terrible at this messaging malarkey. Maybe I should just invite her for a drink? Or is it too soon? She seems down to earth, friendly; there is something honest and open about her message. I know that sounds silly, but something is telling me I need to pursue this. I guess I'll just have to wait and see if she replies. I try to ignore the little flipping still going on inside my chest as I attempt to sleep.

Chapter 23

Isabelle

This week has flown by. It's Thursday already. Preparations for the art show have kept us all busy at the store, plus Rebecca and Isaac's wedding is only three weeks away. Between organising flowers for the two events, meeting the girls to finalise plans for the big hen party, getting Juniper settled and trying to keep my sanity, I feel like my feet haven't touched the ground. One thing has kept me smiling through it all, well, two things actually. One being Juniper. Adopting him was one of the best decisions I have made. It's like he's always been here with us. He's fitted in at the store perfectly. He just roams around doing his own thing. He loves the fuss he gets from the customers, and Gina adores him. She keeps bringing him 'leftover' fish from home, I'm quite sure she buys it and cooks it for him, but it gives her so much pleasure, I don't question it, and Juniper certainly doesn't complain. He is living his best life.

The second is James. We have exchanged several messages over the last few days. I'm still being cautious, trying not to give too much away. I don't know exactly where in Wiltshire he is, and vice versa. I get the impression he's been stung whilst travelling the online dating path before. I like that we're just keeping our chats casual. I really look forward to his messages. Last night he asked if I would like to meet him for a drink. My heart backflipped when I read that. Yes, James, I would love to meet for a drink! We've agreed to wait until next week; it seems we both have a lot on over the next few days. He's on call over the weekend; he said he would rather wait until he can relax and not worry about getting called out whilst we're together. There's something very thoughtful, gentlemanly, that comes across in his messages. It's hard to explain. It's like I already feel safe with him. I know I probably sound a little crazy saying that but that is the only way I can describe it. I haven't told the girls yet, there is far too much excitement around the upcoming nuptials, and I quite like having this just for me. It's like I have my own little secret. Gina of course has picked up on something. I'm not sure she's buying the whole 'It's Juniper, he's such a sweetheart, and I'm so excited for the wedding' excuse, but for now, that's all she's getting. I just want to enjoy all the things I'm feeling without any interrogations.

"Good morning," I say as Gina walks into the store, "What a beautiful morning." I've been here for over an hour already. I had a lovely catch up with Mitch as we unloaded today's delivery. He's always a familiar, welcome reminder of grandmother. He still talks so fondly of her. "There's a selection of savouries on the counter from Luca's, help yourself. I'll make the coffee."

"Good morning to you," she says, leaning down to stroke Juniper. Of course she was talking to the cat and not me. She unwraps the little foil package that he is already very familiar with and instantly knows he's in for his breakfast treat.

"You spoil him," I say, smiling, "He's going to start wanting to go home with you rather than me at this rate."

"And he'd be very welcome," she says, patting his little head as he devours the fish in his bowl.

"How are we set for tomorrow?" she asks, taking a sip of her coffee, then silently cursing as it burns her lips.

"I've triple checked everything, so if anything does go wrong, it won't be down to human error, not on our part anyway. I'm going to pop over shortly, just to touch base. You know I like to keep in close contact with clients just before an event."

"Talking of events, how is the bride to be feeling? It's come around so quickly this wedding. Seems like only yesterday you were telling me she had a new fella."

"She astounds me. She is taking everything in her stride, she's not stressing about a thing. Her actual words to me were 'it doesn't matter what happens on the day, as long as I come away with Isaac as my husband, that's all that matters.' You should have seen Eve's face," I say, laughing at the memory.

"I'll be amazed if that one ever settles down," she says, referring to Eve, "and good for her. Too many women sacrifice their careers for love, babies, and marriage. Some of the stories I read in my magazines," she says, shaking her head, "She's got her head screwed on the right way, that one."

On any other day, I would ask her for a little more clarification on these magazine stories. I love our chats whilst we preen and prune away, but today we have a lot to do. Dom is out on deliveries most of the day; he'll be popping in and out to pick up the fresh bouquets as we make them, but it'll mainly be just the two of us, and Juniper of course.

Later in the morning, once we've caught up with the orders, I pop across to the gallery to see Fi.

"Hello," I call as the little bell tinkles, "It's only me, Isabelle."

"Hello," says a man I don't recognise from behind the counter. He's impeccably dressed in a three-piece suit, and that hair, not a strand out of place. "Fiona will be back in just a moment; she's gone to get lunch. I'm Alistair," he says, walking towards me, holding out his hand for me to shake. "I'm her new assistant." I can't help but notice how incredibly well-spoken he is.

"I'm Isabelle," I say, shaking his outreached hand, "I'm the florist doing the arrangements for tomorrow evening. I just wanted to check in and make sure everything was going to plan at this end." I feel hugely underdressed standing in front of him. I realise I'm still wearing my apron, and I have a little dirt under my nails.

"Ah, you are Isabelle. I've heard wonderful things about you. Please take a seat, she won't be long. Can I get you anything?"

"I'm fine, but thank you, I'll just wait here for her," I say, taking a seat on the plush grey sofa. As I look around, I notice a beautiful painting leaning against the counter, not on display like the others. It's a young girl sitting on the floor, dressed in a full length, pale pink ballerina dress. She's leaning down to tie her ballet shoe. Delicate white flowers sit in her blonde curls. She looks thoughtful, like she's concentrating on the task in hand, wanting to get it just right. It's sat in a distressed, white gilt frame. It looks like an oil painting, but as we have already established, I have no idea about art at all.

I hear the tinkle of the door. I wonder if I should get a bell for the store. I decide against it. I think it could get a little annoying.

"Isabelle, what a lovely surprise." Fi places the brown paper bags she's carrying on the counter and comes to take a seat next to me. "Alistair," she calls, "lunch is here. Why don't you take yourself off for a break, get some fresh air? It really is beautiful out there. Yours is the one on the right," she says, indicating to the bags. "My new assistant," she says when he's safely out of earshot. "Fresh out of uni and very eager to learn. With the baby coming, I thought it would be wise to get a little help around here, and Erica has been nagging me so…" she says with a warm smile.

"Makes sense, you need to prioritise yourself and the baby. He's very well presented. I felt so shoddy next to him!" I say with a glance down at my mucky apron.

"Oh darling, I shall be addressing that shortly, look at me," she says, stroking her purple velvet dress. "I'm not one for formal dressing around here. I think he's just keen to impress. Now, what brings you here?"

"I just wanted to check everything was going as planned for tomorrow, see if there is anything else I could do to help."

"It's all in hand, but you are an absolute diamond for asking. It's all going incredibly smoothly."

"I couldn't help but notice that beautiful ballerina painting over there. It's stunning. Did you paint it?"

"Ah, yes, isn't it just? Not one of mine, I'm afraid. A dear friend has been asking about a ballet picture for his little niece. I knew the right person to ask and here it is. I just hope it's what he's looking for. That reminds me," she says, standing from the sofa, "I have something for you."

I'm a little puzzled as she disappears off behind the counter. She returns with a package wrapped in brown paper.

"This is a little thank you from me. I know I'm paying for your services, but you have gone above and beyond to get this job done for me, and in such a short space of time," she says as she hands me the package.

I sit there looking at it for a few seconds. "For me?" I ask, feeling very confused, and a little overwhelmed.

"Go on," she says excitedly, "open it."

I can feel my hands shaking as I start to gently peel off the tape that's holding the paper together. And then I see it. The beautiful peony painting I fell in love with. I can feel the tears brimming. "Fi, I can't possibly…."

"Nonsense," she says, interrupting me, touching my shaking hand gently, "You absolutely can, and you will. You know, I was always told it's rude to turn down a gift," she says with a wink and a warm smile. "I knew you had to have it that day I saw you looking at it. It's meant for you. It can't possibly go to anyone else; it wouldn't feel right."

I can't stop the tears that spill over. I put the painting down and hug her. "This is the most thoughtful gift anyone has ever given me," I say as my tears roll down her shoulder. "Thank you, thank you, thank you!" I pull away to try and compose myself. "I hope nobody comes in now," I say as I wipe my eyes with my sleeve. "I can't see myself but I'm sure I'm ugly crying," I say, laughing through the tears that refuse to stop. "Are you sure you want to give this to me now?" I ask, "What if tomorrow goes horribly wrong?" I'm only half joking.

"Then I'll send you the invoice," she laughs. "I have every faith in you, Isabelle, I'm not worried about a thing."

"I can't tell you how much this means to me," I say as I look at the stunning piece of art in front of me.

"You don't need to tell me, I can see it," she says affectionately, "And it brings me absolute joy that I am able to do this."

"This is really going to put my framed posters to shame," I say, still sniffing from the crying, and we both laugh.

"I'll have Alistair re-wrap it when he gets back. Do you want to take it later today or tomorrow evening? I could get it delivered if that's easier?"

"Oh gosh no, please don't do that. I'll collect it tomorrow evening if that's ok. I have a few errands to run after work today and I'd be heartbroken if anything was to happen to it. I'll take it with me in a taxi rather than the battered old work van."

"It'll be ready and waiting for you tomorrow. I am so excited for this. I've done shows before of course, many of them, but there's something about this one. It feels like something magical is about to happen. I can't quite explain it. Sounds crazy I know, maybe it's the pregnancy hormones," she says, rubbing her belly.

"It doesn't sound crazy at all. I've had a few of those feelings myself the last few days," I say, staring down again at the beautiful ballerina picture.

"I'm intrigued. Tell me more, even if just to prove I'm not crazy, please," she says, laughing.

"Ok," I say, sitting a little taller, "I haven't even told my friends this, but I have been messaging a guy on an online dating app. Please don't judge," I add quickly, "I've had some horror stories, which I'll save for another time, but this time there's something different. He's polite, thoughtful, and gentlemanly. When it comes to love and romance, I am a realist. I don't do fluffy love stories, so these feelings are new, exciting." I can feel a little flutter of something in my tummy as I say it. "He's a vet, and I've just adopted Juniper, just little things really. He feels safe. OK, I just actually heard myself, now I think I'm the crazy one. James just seems different. One thing I have learnt, though, is that men can be anything they want to be online, so I'm trying to stay a little cautious, but my heart is definitely starting to rule my head on this one."

"Huh, James, you say," she says, shuffling in her seat. "And he's local?" she asks.

"All I know is he's somewhere in Wiltshire. We haven't talked specifics yet, maybe that's why I feel safe," I say with a little laugh, "Wiltshire is a big place." Something lights up In Fi's eyes. I can't quite tell what it is.

"And have you made plans to meet this handsome man yet? Something tells me he's as handsome as he is charming," she asks, sounding almost as excited as me. "Sorry, I'm just a sucker for a love story and a happy ending. Please tell me to mind my own business if I'm being too nosey."

"Not at all. We're hoping to arrange something next week, we both have a lot on over the next few days so it just makes sense to put it off until we can relax a little. And yes, he is incredibly handsome, almost too good to be true," I say. I have butterflies at the mere thought of seeing him. "I have taken up too much of your time. I'm sure you have lots to do, and I should get back to the store," I say, standing to leave, "thank you again for the most wonderful gift. Ok, Now I really have to go, or I'll cry again."

"So, I'll see you tomorrow then," says Fi, hugging me, "I know I'll see you throughout the day, but you promise you're going to come? In the evening, I mean?"

"I promise I will be here," I say as I turn to leave. As I walk away, something makes me look back through the window. Fi is standing there, gently toying with her necklace. She has the most glorious smile on her face; it's almost like she's relishing in sharing my secret with me. Before going back to work, I sit for a while on a little bench overlooking the river. I need a few minutes to take in what's just happened. Other than the store being left to me, the painting is the single most wonderful gift I have ever been given. Fi's generosity is overwhelming. I sit for a little while longer, listening to the birds, feeling the gentle breeze on my skin. Fi is right; it does feel like something magical could happen. And this is coming from the realist! I don't think I should share these thoughts with Eve. She'd have me carted off for therapy. Right, back to reality and the huge number of flowers waiting to be arranged.

"Blimey, love," says Gina as I walk into the store, Juniper already at my feet to welcome me. "You practically skipped through that door. What have you been up to?" she asks, eyeing me suspiciously.

"The most incredible thing just happened at the gallery." I go on to tell her about how I'd originally fallen in love with the painting and that Fi had given it to me, just like that.

"Well, I'll be blown, that's a very generous thing to do. Can I see it?"

"I don't actually have it with me now," I say, feeling like I'm stating the obvious. "I'm going to collect it tomorrow at the show. Honestly, Gina, it's one of the most beautiful things I have ever seen. I still can't quite believe it's mine," I say, clasping my hands together.

"What a week it's been, eh, love, what with this little one coming along," she says, gesturing to Juniper, who is now happily sitting on the counter, watching the world go by through the window, "and now this gift. They say it comes in threes," she says, giving me a wink, "I wonder what could be next."

"That is true, but even without a third, I am more than happy with my two. You're right though, it's been quite a week. Actually, I was looking over the books last night," I say thoughtfully. I have an accountant, but I like to look over them myself. It's a habit I picked up from my grandmother, plus I think it makes good business sense to know what's going on with the finances. "If things continue the way they're going, I think this is going to be our best financial month since I took over." I can't help but say it with pride.

"Really? Oh love, that's wonderful," she says, coming to hug me, "I know I say it all the time, but she would be so proud of you. There you go then, that might be the third."

"Let's not jinx it. We'll say no more on the matter until the end of month figures are finalised." Something tells me I'm going to be very happy with those figures. I think back to what Fi said about something magical and smile to myself as I carry on with the day.

Chapter 24

James

"Hello sunshine," says Erica as she pops her head around the door of my clinic room. She waves a brown paper bag at me. "I brought breakfast."

"Hmm," I say, eyeing the bag suspiciously. "You want something. Come on, out with it," I say as I take the bag from her. I missed breakfast this morning so it's a very welcome gift, or bribe. I think the latter is more likely.

"What makes you think I want something?" she asks, trying far too hard to look innocent, "Can't I bring my colleague and friend breakfast for no reason?"

"You can, but I know you better than that. Come on, what is it?" I hear my phone make its little beep to let me know I have a message; I pull it out of my pocket. Isabelle. I can't help but smile. I quickly put it away to read when Erica has left.

"Who's that?" she asks, leaning over the counter towards me. "Come to think of it, you have been mighty spritely these last few days, anything you want to share with me?" she asks, looking towards my pocket where the phone is safely tucked away.

"Nope," I say simply. "Now, what is it I can do for you?"

"I was hoping you would do my afternoon farm visits so I can go and help Fi get ready for tonight. I don't want her doing anything she shouldn't. If I'm there, I can keep an eye on her. I looked at the diary; your caseload is pretty light so maybe Jim could see your clients…."

"Of course I will, but I have already agreed to go and help her this afternoon, hence the easy caseload. You've both waited so long for this baby; she won't do anything to jeopardise hers or the baby's health, you know that. But if it'll make you feel better to be there, to keep an eye on things, then of course I'll do it. You didn't have to bribe me for this one," I say, kissing the top of her head. "I know you're both eagerly awaiting the 12 week mark. I am here to help ease your worries in any way I can."

"Have I told you lately that I love you?" she says, coming around the counter to give me a hug.

"Just forward me your booked visits and I'll take it from there. I'll speak to Jim and we'll jiggle a few things around."

"You're the best! By the way, Fi keeps asking if you'll definitely be there tonight; she must have asked me about ten times last night. Ok, slight exaggeration, but she asked a few times. I have assured her you will be. You wouldn't let your hot date down would you?" she asks, winking at me.

"You know I'll be there; would I dare stand you up? I'd fear for my life!" I say with a smile. "What's the dress code? I don't need a suit, do I?" I'm hoping the answer to this is no, for two reasons. One being I never feel comfortable wearing a suit, and two, mine needs dry cleaning.

"It's smart but no suit is needed. You always dress impeccably so you'll look devilishly handsome in whatever you wear."

"Stop the flattery," I say, laughing, "I've already agreed to help you out later, now will you sod off so I can get some work done, please? I believe I have a cockapoo with a bowel problem to attend to."

"Oh the glamour..." she says as she walks out of the door.

I pull out my phone again to read Isabelle's message. We've been in contact for several days now, and I can honestly say that I cannot wait to meet her. We both have busy schedules over the weekend, so we've decided to wait until next week to arrange a date. Usually I would be feeling nervous, anxious even, but there's just something about her. All I feel is excitement. I haven't told anyone about our messages or plans to meet up. It's nice not having the pressure of questions and expectations from others, all done purely with good intentions, but it does get a little draining, so this time, I'm telling no one.

A little later in the morning, I spot Mrs Richards in the waiting room. Rachael is sitting in the chair next to her chatting away, Dougie at her feet, clearly loving the fuss he's getting.

"Well," I say as I approach them, "somebody is looking better." I reach down to give the pooch a stroke.

"He's much better now, thank you, Doctor James; the medications have worked a treat. He's back to his old self again. I'm just waiting to see Doctor Jim."

"I have a few minutes before my next patient. I'm happy to give him a look over rather than have you waiting."

"That's very kind of you, but I'm happy to wait my turn. I'm having a lovely chat with Rachael, she's made me a cuppa. Anyway, it'll be nice to see Doctor Jim again. Why don't you get a cuppa yourself, love, make the most of the break you have," she says, taking a sip of her tea.

Out of the corner of my eye, I see Rachael give me a look of surprise, but I don't react. "Do you know what, Mrs Richardson, I think I might do that. It's been a busy morning." I say my goodbyes and head off in the direction of the coffee room. Well, there's a turn up for the books!

"How was Mrs Richards?" I ask later when I see Jim outside. The sun is shining. It seems we both had the same idea of sitting outside to eat our lunch.

"I think I have a new friend," he says with a chuckle. "I hear she turned down your offer to see Dougie. I wasn't expecting that," he says, taking a bite of his sandwich.

"You and I both. Maybe she's softening in her old age. All set for tonight?" I ask, changing the subject.

"I'm looking forward to it. Art show at a gallery feels very sophisticated. I best dig out something to wear. Do I need a suit?" he asks, looking worried. "I don't really do suits."

"I'm with you there, but Erica has assured me it's smart but not suit-worthy."

"Marvellous, I'm sure I can throw something together. I'm yet to meet her wife, sure she won't mind me coming?"

"Fi is a sweetheart, you'll love her. I've known them a long time. I adore them both; they're like family. I don't know what I would do without them," I say with a smile.

"Must be quite a woman to keep up with Erica. She's a force, that one."

I can't help but laugh. "She is indeed. I best get on with her farm visits or I'll be feeling the full force, and that is not something I want to experience. I doubt I'll see you before tonight. Do you know where it is?"

"I checked it out last night, but thanks. 6 pm, right?"

"6 pm," I confirm, "Thanks again for helping out this afternoon, see you later."

My farm visits pass without drama. One unexpected, very heavy rain downpour that we weren't expecting had me silently cursing Erica. Luckily I always keep a raincoat and wellington boots in the car for such situations. It didn't last long; the clouds soon parted and the sun reappeared to give us another beautiful afternoon. Just as I'm leaving my last visit, I get a text from Fi.

'Just checking you'll be here tonight, 6 pm sharp, don't be late! Xx'

'I will see you at 6 pm x'

I can only assume her persistence is down to her eagerness to make it a success for the artist, or pregnancy hormones, or both. I check the clock and see that it's nearly 5 pm already. Traffic please be kind.

As it turns out, the traffic was kind. I made it home quickly, leaving me ample time to get ready. I start to look through my wardrobe. I know the shirt I want to wear but I have a feeling it's in the dry-cleaning pile. Yes, it's gotten to the point where it is now a pile. I make a mental note to rectify that next week. It would seem the universe is working in my favour today. The shirt I'm looking for is hanging right in front of me, clean and crease-free.

I arrive at exactly 6.01pm. I'm barely in the door before Erica approaches me. "There you are. Don't you look dapper," she says, eyeing my outfit.

"You don't look too bad yourself. You look beautiful," I say, kissing her cheek. She's opted for a cream linen dress that is very flattering on her. It's a far cry from the old jeans and t-shirts she wears to work. I hold my arm out for her to take. "Drink, my lady?" I ask. She slips her arm through mine, and we head towards the makeshift bar to get a glass of something bubbly. The gallery looks stunning. The tables are placed superbly. They give enough space for people to move around freely but allow for small gatherings around them. The lighting enhances the artwork to perfection, and the simple flower arrangements give it an air of sophistication. Classical music is playing quietly in the background. I can see Fi chatting away vibrantly to somebody who Erica informs me is the artist.

"I hope more people are coming than this," I say, looking around. There must only be seven or eight people here.

"It's early, the doors have only just opened. People like to be fashionably late these days, and the invites say 'from 6 pm'. The place will fill shortly. Come on, let's take a look at this guy's work."

We walk around looking at the pieces on display. It's clear he's very talented. His art is a little too modern for my taste but I can see why some people would like it, and it's a world away from anything I could paint so I'm in no position to judge.

"Here you both are," says Jim as he approaches us, glass already in hand. "Lovely place this, you must be very proud, Erica. Where is this wonderful wife of yours I've heard so much about?"

"Busy hobnobbing at the moment but as soon as she's free, I'll introduce you. That's her over there in the red dress," she says, indicating to where Fi is standing with a nod of her head.

As we continue to wander around, the place starts to fill, and the atmosphere amplifies.

"You're all here, wonderful," says Fi as she joins us in front of a very interesting piece of art. I say interesting because I have no clue what it is, or what it's meant to be. After a brief introduction to Jim, Fi turns to me. "James, can I borrow you for a second, I have something for you," she says, almost in a whisper. "It's just out the back; it won't take long."

I follow her to the back room, more than a little intrigued. Standing there on an old easel is one of the most beautiful oil paintings I have ever seen. It's of a young ballerina.

"Is this for me?" I ask, completely dumbfounded.

"Well, I was thinking more for Ella," she replies with a chuckle. "Is it ok? Do you like it? I got a great deal on it from an old friend. The invoice is attached to the back. If it's more than you were hoping to pay, please just let me know. I'm sure I could sell it here and find you something more suitable. I wasn't sure if you'd think it was a bit too 'grown up'," she says apprehensively.

"Fi, I love it! I'm not sure what I was expecting to be honest, but this, it's just perfect, thank you," I say, hugging her. "Ella will love it." I walk over and take the piece of paper that is attached to the back of the painting in a brown envelope. Although it doesn't really matter, I already know Ella needs to have this painting. "Really?" I ask after briefly looking it over. "This is all they want for it?"

"Like I said, he's an old friend, one who owes me many favours," she says with a grin. "Can I assume you'll take it?"

"Yes! Absolutely! Thank you, a million times," I say, gazing again at the beautiful artwork in front of me.

"Perfect. I'll get it wrapped and you can collect it over the weekend. Something else…." she says with a brief pause, "before you leave tonight, there is somebody I really want to introduce you to. Promise you won't go anywhere until I've had a chance to do that. They aren't here yet but as soon as they arrive, I'll come and find you." I give her a perplexed look. "I must get back to my guests," she says as she disappears out of the door. I don't even get a chance to reply.

I re-join Erica and Jim and tell them about the stunning painting for Ella. "She does have a way of connecting people to art; it's a gift," says Erica.

"Talking of connecting, she's asked me to stick around so she can introduce me to somebody, any idea who?" I ask curiously.

"Nope, not a clue, sorry," she says with a gentle shrug, "Now, why are we standing here with empty glasses?"

"I'll go. You two stay here and save this spot. It's starting to fill up in here," I say as I take their glasses to be refilled.

As I'm standing at the bar waiting to be served, Fi almost pounces on me. "James, here you are," she says excitedly, "There's somebody I'd like you to meet." As I turn to look at her, I catch sight of the person standing beside her and my heart skips a beat.

No. It can't be.

"This is Isabelle," says Fi, her face beaming.

It's her. It's Isabelle, the florist from Wiltshire.

And suddenly it all falls into place. Fi knew. I don't know how, but she knew.

Chapter 25

Isabelle

"James?" I ask, "I can't believe it." The surprise must be evident on my face.

"I'm going to leave you to get acquainted," says Fi with a knowing smile as she heads off into the growing crowd.

Then it dawns on me. She knew. She figured it out yesterday when I was telling her about him. She's orchestrated this.

The background noise fades. It feels like we're the only two people in the room. My heart is racing. We both stand there for a second, not knowing what to say. It all just feels very surreal. Then, I don't know why, but I laugh. I just burst out laughing. He must think I'm mad, but I can't help it because it suddenly becomes very clear that we have met before, and more than once. Seeing him in person has brought it all back. I realise he's laughing with me.

"This isn't the first time we've met, is it?" The same realisation has dawned on him.

"I don't believe it is," I say with a smile, having composed myself.

"Shall we get out of here?" he asks, not taking his eyes from mine.

I look across to Fi. I'm eager to be alone with him, away from this busy room, but I feel obligated to stay.

"I don't think Fi will mind," he continues, clearly picking up on my apprehension, "In fact, I think she'd encourage it."

I glance across to Fi again. Her eyes meet mine, and she gives me a subtle nod laced with a warm smile.

"Let's go," I say as I put my glass down on the bar. He takes my hand and leads me out into the warm early evening sunshine. It feels like the most natural thing in the world, like he's been holding my hand my whole life.

"Where would you like to go?" he asks, looking down at me. I raise my hand to shield my eyes from the sun. Gosh, he's handsome. My heart is doing cartwheels.

"How about The Meeting Place?" I ask, "we have already been there before, just not together," I say with a smile.

A grin spreads across his face. "Ok, disclaimer. My best friend Dan owns it; that's why I was working there that night, and several other nights. I help him out when he's short staffed. He'll be there tonight so maybe you'd like to change your mind?" he asks, "Go somewhere else?"

"Why would I want to do that?" I ask, aware that I'm sounding a little mischievous. I'm not sure if it's intentional or not but the look on his face tells me he approves.

Still holding my hand, he leads me across the cobbled streets towards the bar. I stop outside Luca's deli. "Do you remember when we met here?" I ask, looking through the window, seeing the memory in my mind like it was yesterday.

"I was on my way back from an early morning run. I stopped in to pick up some water. I remember thinking what a lovely smile you had."

I refrain from telling him I remember thinking what a lovely backside he had.

"Ready?" he asks as he holds the door open for me to The Meeting Place.

"I think you're more worried than I am," I say with a wink. Where is this flirty Isabelle coming from? Where has she been hiding? I like her.

I'm glad to see it's not too busy. It was here or the little wine bar up the road, but that feels a little too intimate for our impromptu meeting. This is perfect.

The man behind the bar looks up as we walk in. Judging by the way he's looking at us, 'pleasantly puzzled' is the only phrase that fits, he is Dan.

"James, nice surprise!" he says as we approach the bar.

"Slight change to tonight's plans," he replies. "Dan, I'd like to introduce you to Isabelle. Isabelle, meet Dan."

Dan leans across the bar to shake my hand. "Pleasure to meet you, Isabelle," he says warmly.

"You too," I say, returning his smile.

"Now, what can I get you both to drink?" he asks, throwing a cloth over his shoulder.

James looks at me, encouraging me to answer first. Such a gentleman.

"I'll take a Sauvignon Blanc, please."

"Same for me please," says James, looking around. I can tell he's looking for a quiet table, somewhere we can be away from the other customers.

"Those people over there have just paid their bill," says Dan, indicating a little table in the corner. "Give me a few minutes to clear it and it's all yours."

I feel like he's read both our minds. I excuse myself to go to the bathroom. I need a few minutes to take in everything that's happening, and if Dan is anything like my friends, he'll be wanting the full run down on the evening's events.

As I stand at the bathroom mirror, applying a little gloss to my lips, I can't stop smiling. All of this tonight, us meeting, would have happened regardless of the dating app. Fi would have introduced us. We would have realised how our paths had crossed before, the deli, here in this bar, my store, and Juniper, sweet, sweet Juniper. They all played a part in making this moment happen. In bringing us together. Fi's words about something magical happening pass through my mind. This definitely feels magical.

I head back out to the bar to find James sitting at the table, a bottle of wine in a cooler and two glasses in front of him.

"Dan insisted," he says as he pours us both a glass.

"I like Dan," I say with a grin.

We sit there looking at each other, both of us just grinning like idiots.

"I'm sorry I was so forward in asking if you wanted to leave the gallery," he says, his finger running down the side of his glass, "but as soon as I saw you there I just wanted to be away from the crowds, and the prying eyes," he says with a smile.

"If you hadn't suggested it, I'm sure I would have. I've been looking forward to our first meeting so much," I say. I can feel a blush creeping up my cheeks.

"I'm curious to know how Fi knew we'd been messaging. I knew she was up to something tonight. I just didn't know what. I thought it was just because she wanted to give me a painting for my niece, but clearly she had something bigger in mind," he says, taking a sip of his wine.

I lean my chin on my hand, my elbow on the table. "I can help solve that mystery. I popped by yesterday and we got chatting. I hadn't told any of my friends about us, but something about her just makes you want to open up, to share your secrets. She must have put two and two together."

"Ah, that explains it," he says, "whatever the reason, I am just happy she introduced us this evening. The thought of waiting until next week to meet you was driving me crazy." The way he looks at me when he says it makes my cheeks flush again. Please kiss me, James. Right here, across this table. I don't care if the whole room looks at us. I clear my throat gently in an attempt to vacate that thought from my head.

"I believe I have you to thank for saving my new furry companion," I say, referring to Juniper.

"I think you'll find that was you; you're the one who brought him to us. I think it's lovely that you've taken him in. You've given him a second chance," he says, looking at me intently. "That's a really special thing to do, Isabelle." I love the way my name sounds when he says it. I'm desperate to minimise the distance between us across the table, to be closer to him. As if reading my mind, he brings his chair closer to mine. "Do you know how many times our paths have crossed?" he asks, taking my hand in his, slowly trailing his fingers over mine.

My pulse quickens. The scent of his aftershave fills my senses. I tilt my head slightly. Every part of me is begging him to kiss me. He reaches up and gently pushes a few stray hairs from my cheek as he brings his lips to meet mine. The kiss is slow and tender. His hand cups my cheek, sending a little shock through me. As our lips part, he leans his head towards mine, and we sit for a second, just like that, our heads together, not wanting the tender moment to end.

"Part of me wants to apologise for that, but I'm not sorry. It's all I've been thinking about since Fi introduced us. Maybe not the most romantic setting for our first kiss," he says with a little glance around, but it's obvious that nobody is paying us any attention.

"I happen to think it's the perfect place for our first kiss," I say, putting my hand gently on his neck, pulling him back to me.

Epilogue

Three weeks later...

James

As I watch her laughing with her friends over glasses of champagne, smiling for the photographer, my heart swells. Her green satin dress makes her look radiant. Actually, that's not true. She emits radiance. The dress makes her look simply stunning. Isabelle lights up the room. She has the kindest heart; she has no idea how much she touches people. I see the way she talks to customers in the store, strangers on the street. She has a playfulness that is endearing. I feel like the luckiest man in the world. The last three weeks have been incredible. I can't even remember what my life was like before she came along. We're already planning a trip to France in a few weeks to visit my parents. They are extremely keen to meet her, and the feeling is mutual. I think Dan has a new best friend; he adores her as much as I do. Fi is of course taking all the credit for us meeting. 'The stars aligned, and I gave them a little nudge' is what she says. Who or what is responsible, it doesn't really matter to me. What matters is that I did find her. I found the one who feels like home.

Isabelle

It's been a whirlwind three weeks. The most incredible whirlwind. I can't believe I'm sitting here at Rebecca and Isaac's wedding reception with James. James, the vet from Wiltshire. This man has just come along and turned my world upside down in the most wonderful way. His thoughtfulness knows no limits, the little things he does, not just for me but for everyone around him. The way he can make you feel like the most important person in the room when he's talking to you. He's a true gentleman, chivalrous and polite. I look across to where he's sat, deep in conversation with Eve on the other side of the table, and I just smile. I'm grinning like the cat that's got the cream. I know it sounds cheesy, but I know we were meant to be together. There were just too many synchronicities for it to be a coincidence. If Fi hadn't introduced us that night, we would have met the following week as arranged. Even for me, the realist, I have to give the universe a little credit here.

Just as the band is striking up their next song, he stands up from where he's sitting and walks around the table to me. "May I have this dance?" he asks, holding out his hand, that handsome smile I've come to love and know so well spread across his face.

I put my champagne glass down on the table and take his hand. "You may," I say as he takes me into his arms and sweeps me onto the dancefloor.

Acknowledgements

It's so hard to know where to start with this. Firstly, I have to thank Fin, for your unwavering support and encouragement, and of course your technical skill.

Thank you to Wayne for not only introducing me to the world of self-publishing, but for your patience and guidance through the process (and introducing me to the wonderful programme that is Canva!) Your knowledge has been invaluable.

To my Mum, for reading the chapters as I wrote them and telling me they were brilliant, but let's be honest, you were never going to tell me they were terrible!

To Rikke, my unofficial proof-reader. Your little notes and suggestions, no matter how small or subtle, have helped make this book what it is.

To my girlfriends, for just being you.

This book has been over three years in the making. I chose not to tell a huge amount of people I was writing it, choosing to focus on my children's books instead, but to those who did know and have supported and encouraged me, I thank you all from the bottom of my heart.

And finally, to you, the reader. Thank you for buying this book, and for making my dream of becoming a published author a reality. I will be forever grateful to each and every one of you.

Printed in Great Britain
by Amazon